ACQUA

CALDA

D0833116

ACQUA

CALDA

Keith McDermott

CARROLL & GRAF PUBLISHERS
NEW YORK

ACQUA CALDA

Carroll & Graf Publishers
An Imprint of Avalon Publishing Group Inc.
245 West 17th Street
New York, NY 10011

AVALON
publishing group incorporated

First Carroll & Graf edition 2005

Chapter Eight appeared under the title "Acqua Calda," in somewhat different form, in the Summer/Fall 2004 issue of *The James White Review* and in *Fresh Men*.

Library of Congress Cataloging-in-Publication Data is available.

ISBN: 978-0-7867-1765-1

Printed in the United States of America
Interior design by Maria Elias
Distributed by Publishers Group West

For Eric Amouyal,
the best thing that ever happened to me

ACKNOWLEDGMENTS

My deep thanks to Edmund White, whose generosity to writers is as legendary as his prose; to Patrick Merla, who has guided me through two careers; and to my writing mentor and friend, Martha Hughes. I am forever grateful to my editor, Don Weise, for his insight and unflagging enthusiasm for my book. I thank Encke King, Mina Foster, and Lisa Wohl (the best writers make the best readers). For the last five years I have had a magical place to work, and I am eternally grateful to Craig Lucas and John McDermott for generously sharing their upstate home—a writer's and reader's paradise; and also to Andrew Dillman, for my New York "office." Thank you, David Rogers, for your healing kindness. Thank you, James Murphy and Douglas Stewart, for your selfless service to me and so many others: *namaste*. Finally, I give my heartfelt thanks (and my heart) to Eric Amouyal for his wisdom, unwavering love, and total support.

PROLOGUE

Gerald was as well prepared for death as anyone could be. Over the winter, after the last of his three hospital stays and in an interval of relative health, he'd made a last will and testament, a living will, assigned a health care proxy, and arranged his own cremation. He'd thrown out hundreds of eight-by-ten photos accrued over his twenty-five years as an actor, a tattered porno collection, and all his journals. He'd acquired a hefty collection of barbiturates in case things got too "icky." His parents were dead, so they weren't a concern, and he'd stopped returning calls from well-meaning friends. He'd shut out everyone really, except Barbara, who faithfully checked in on him or called every few days; if something happened, he didn't want to get left until the neighbors noticed a bad smell. Gerald was as ready to go as the dinner guest in coat and gloves standing at the open door.

"Unbreak my heart . . ." The electronic purr of a white-noise machine failed to annul the noisy jukebox in the Irish bar downstairs. But it had been worse earlier, when the drunken bar patrons were having their three A.M. sing-along. That's when Gerald turned the machine on. At this hour, only the bar-tender remained, tallying up the evening's take.

Gerald lay on his bed without hope of falling back to sleep. What was today? He'd had a doctor's appointment on Wednesday, was that yesterday? Oh. Today he had to go to one of those government places where poor people with jobs decide if poor people without jobs are eligible for assistance—food stamps, disability. He'd been putting it off. He had enough money to live—and nothing else—for a few months, but he'd be penniless by December if he didn't arrange some kind of cash flow. Another winter, with or without penury, was an ominous thought. In icy weather, he was more vulnerable to colds and flu which might, like last winter, turn into pneumonia and send him to the hospital.

Was today Friday? He could look on his bedside table at his pill arranger, the one area of his life in which he was diligent. He didn't even believe the pills—part of a trial study by a pharmaceutical company—did anything. In fact, the study had a placebo arm, so his religious adherence to a three-times-a-day schedule might just be adding a daily tablespoon of sugar to his diet. And if he *were* getting the actual drugs? Friends who'd taken AZT, or the massive doses of penicillin some quack in Brooklyn had prescribed, had just shifted from slow decline to downhill plummet. If it's a placebo I'll die, Gerald reasoned, and if it's the real stuff, I'll die quicker.

"So why do you take them if you don't think they're doing any good, Mr. Negative?" Barbara asked.

"Because I want to be part of the effort to find a cure, even if it kills me," Gerald said.

"That's so noble, sweetie."

Gerald wanted to kill her. Barbara was a petite ingenue with a bright soprano range and a show biz dream when they'd met in college. Now she was an obese legal secretary, who still worked out weekly with a vocal coach, didn't audition, and insisted that under Gerald's grim expectations, he clung to a fairy-tale hope that the pills just might work.

Thursday's compartments in the weekly pill arranger were empty, so today must be Friday. The bartender had gone home and the jukebox was quiet. Gerald turned the white-noise machine off with his foot and sat at the folding card table he used as a—dining room table was too euphemistic—flat elevated surface to eat off. Among the unopened mail and dirty dishes was a recently excavated note left by the previous tenant that read, "If the garbage downstairs starts to smell too bad, sprinkle perfume on the lamp bulb." Gerald must have kept the note because, at the time, he thought it grimly funny.

Gerald only intended to sublet the place for a few months. Now, eight years later, he knew he'd never leave the charmless Midtown studio, unless it was to go into one of those renovated SROs turned AIDS homes—hospices really, considering the turnover. Friends told him he was crazy to live on Eighth Avenue, a block from Times Square. "It's dangerous. You should be in the Village—or Chelsea! That's the new hot spot. Where you live is so *seedy*." And *sexy*. Those same friends who disparaged his neighborhood gorged themselves on his tales of tourist trysts: the Ohio husband who spent a steamy half hour in Gerald's apartment while his wife and children waited at the Marriott, the Harvard undergrad in town for a Dukakis convention, the pimply eighteen-year-old sailor, here for fleet week, who'd seen four Broadway musicals in three days. Sightseers, foreigners, conventioneers. In those days, Times Square meant sex, and the out-of-towner lingering outside Show World, or the businessman glancing nervously at his watch on Forty-second Street, were looking to get laid.

But that was then. Now that Disney and the Hard Rock Café were gelding Forty-second Street, Times Square was about as sexy as EPCOT Center.

Gerald crumpled the note and pitched it in a wastebasket full of used Kleenex by his bed. He scooped up the pile of unopened mail and threw it in, too. The dirty dishes could wait—for Barbara—but he better hide the candy dish that housed his barbiturate collection. Just the sight of the pretty pills—purple and black, green and yellow, brown and green capsules, pink tablets—infuriated Barbara. She'd threatened to throw them out, and Gerald had no doubt she eventually would ("I did it for *your* sake, sweetie!). He picked up a handful of pills and let them run through his fingers back into the bowl. For when things get too "icky," he reminded himself. By which he meant *physically* icky: crippling neuropathy, blindness from CMV retinitis, lymphoma, or the deep purple lesions of Kaposi's sarcoma. But was so visceral a symptom necessary for icky? What about hopelessness, or just over-it-all-ness?

Before Gerald left the hospital, a social worker wearing a small gold cross on her neck was sent to his room, and after she'd advised him on services for which his disease would make him eligible, they'd had a let's-get-real talk about death.

"Gerald, if you were to pass next week—and I'm not saying you're likely to—what regrets would you have?"

Did she imagine he hadn't spent bedbound hours dwelling on those regrets? He was ready with the short answer.

"I never traveled—not outside the United States. I never

had a lover, not a long-term lover, and never one I lived with. And I won't be here for the two thousand millennium."

Gerald sensed the social worker's hand gravitating toward his, and he folded his arms.

"And why can't you be here for the millennium?" she asked.

"It's in five years," Gerald replied flatly.

The social worker looked down at her hands, twirled her wedding ring, and looked up brightly.

"You might manage a shortish trip, you know. Toronto is lovely."

Gerald didn't answer.

"Oh, Gerald," the social worker said, reaching out to grasp his folded arm with both her hands and gazing at him with a dreamy *Mists of Avalon* smile. "The possibility of love is always there—for all of us."

For most of his adult life, "the possibility of love" got Gerald out of bed, fueled his busy day, and kept him up too late at night. He was a promiscuous romantic—"I fall in love with everyone I have sex with," he admitted, "*everyone!*"—and his congenial good looks and compact muscularity gave him sexual confidence and insured him better-than-average success in meeting men. But Gerald never let his ardor fan the spark of a brief encounter into a lasting, romantic flame, and he didn't know why. Career perhaps; for many years he was a member of a collective of actors, dancers, and other artists, an insular family committed to the vision of a gurulike director. Gerald had only quit the group three years ago (just as the company was beginning to garner attention in the international art world), and he wondered if its hold over him had precluded a serious relationship. Or maybe the glib explanation he gave to friends was more accurate: "I'm too big a slut to settle down." At any rate, since his interview in the hospital with the social worker, he'd amended his "serious lover" regret to include "casual lay," because that hope was over, too.

The telephone rang. Who was it at five in the morning? Either a wrong number or an emergency. Gerald picked up the receiver.

"Hello?"

"Gerald? It's Bill."

"Bill! Where are you?"

"Berlin. What time is it in New York?"

"Five A.M. , but it's okay, I was up."

"Listen, I'm doing the premiere for a very, very, very prestigious arts festival in Sicily. Everyone—I mean everyone in the European art world—will be there. I probably shouldn't even be doing it, I have so many other things going on. Did you hear about the opera we just opened in Berlin? It's an enormous hit. Anyway, the piece in Sicily is called *Rivers, Saints, Space* and I think you should be in it."

While Bill described the play—"The earth cracks open, the stars fall from the sky, we see a procession of saints—I may fly all the actors, if I can get the rigging . . ."—Gerald thought about the shock of the telephone ring. It seemed weeks since someone had called him. How could he have thought it was an emergency? I'm the emergency, he realized. If it had been an emergency, we'd be talking about me. And why did Bill call? They hadn't spoken in three years. Was it the letter?

In a nostalgic and drugged moment, Gerald had written to Bill from the hospital. A final-goodbye sort of letter, but understated—or so he hoped. He confessed that his years acting in Bill's company had been the best of his life and hinted that leaving the company had been a terrible mistake.

In a later, lucid moment and days after the letter had been sent, Gerald cringed over the death-bed sentiment. After all, five of the fifteen years he'd worked for Bill were about trying to get out of the company.

"I want to be in regular plays again, have regular hours, pay my Actors Equity dues," he'd told Barbara, who'd become a William Weiss groupie, saw every show, and begged him not to quit. The letter had apparently reminded Bill of Gerald's existence, but had Bill understood what it *really* said (in an understated way), that Gerald was dying?

"The Berlin critics have been amazing—in Paris, too, and Salzburg. The British press is another story, they never get my work. And really, I'm almost glad," Bill continued.

He's just the same, Gerald thought, he hasn't even asked me how I am.

Outside, on Eighth Avenue, a driver laid on his horn for several seconds: a prelude to the early rush-hour traffic. Gerald flipped the white-noise machine on with his foot. Italy. He could check off the travel item on his list of regrets. Though given a choice, he'd have preferred to have the lover or greet the millennium.

CHAPTER ONE

O verhead bins flew open. Coats and bags tumbled out.
Gerald's headset flew off as his neighbor in the window
seat, a young man wearing a sleep mask, blindly grabbed his
arm with both hands.

"Holy shit!" said the young man, ripping the mask off.
"What the fuck was that?" His eyes were green and wide with
incomprehension, like a child awakened from a nightmare.

"We 'ave n-countered n-ah air-ah pocket and experienced
a drop n-ah altitude. No need for ah-larm," the Air Italia pilot
explained over the intercom then repeated, with the same
unreasonable calm, in Italian.

The only flight attendant on this small plane from Rome
to Palermo rushed down the aisle with a first-aid kit. "Sit!" she
spat at a passenger reaching toward a fallen carton of cigarettes. An old woman across the aisle from Gerald hiccuped
sobs into a handkerchief, and an infant in back wailed like an
emergency siren.

Apart from a brief acknowledgment when he took his seat,
Gerald had avoided contact with the sloppy kid in camouflage
cutoffs and a T-shirt sitting next to the window. Privileged,

he'd guessed, partying in Europe before the fall semester. Another college kid with the stink of potential.

The young man's handsome face was creased and puffy from sleep, his fair skin shaded by an incongruously hearty two-day growth of beard. He cleared his throat and freed a long strand of reddish-blond hair from the corner of his mouth. "I woke up thinking . . . we're gonna crash."

"You had reason to," Gerald said, glancing at the complimentary airline slippers on the young man's feet.

The attendant, now wearing plastic gloves and carrying a trash bag, paused to respond to a passenger in the row ahead.

"The pilot says four meters," she confided, stooping to pick a piece of Brie from the carpet. "But closer to six, I think."

"What did she say?" asked the young man.

"We dropped six meters in altitude."

"How many feet is that?"

"Twenty." Gerald spoke firmly, hoping his guess would go unquestioned.

"We fell twenty fucking feet?" The plane shuddered, the seat belt sign flashed with an electronic ping, and the passengers gasped in unison.

"Oh, fuck, no!"

The boy—and that's really what he was, under the attitude and whatever drug he took to sleep—clenched the armrests and pushed himself into the seat back. Blank dread glazed his unlined face.

The rough ride lasted a minute at most, but left the passengers traumatized, silent.

"Mild turbulence," announced the unflappable pilot. "No cause-ah for alarm."

"What a fucking trip," the boy said.

"Like being on a Mexican tour bus," Gerald said.

Something about the boy—the way his sleep-swollen lips remained slightly parted, his lightly freckled complexion and dirty-blond hair—reminded Gerald of a childhood friend, and memories—his family's ranch-style home in Florida, rolled sod stacked into a pyramid on a wheelbarrow, the palmetto grove at the end of the block where the Show Your Butt Club met—flashed through his mind like pages in a flip-book.

"Have you been to Italy before?"

"No," Gerald said, giving the word a curious twist to imply, *odd isn't it, after all the other European countries I've visited.*

"Second time in Italy, first in Sicily," the boy said.

Gerald glanced down the aisle, hoping a second beverage might be offered after the terrible air scare.

"I'm going for work," the boy continued, gazing at the seat back in front of him.

"Oh, yes?" said Gerald, waiting for further explanation.

The boy's brow furrowed.

"Did you think we were gonna, you know . . . ?" he asked, still staring ahead.

"Crash? I thought the wings would snap and the plane would spiral down in flames," Gerald replied.

"Oh, come on!" the boy said, his cheeks flushing with color.

"I *did* think we'd crash—just for a moment—and I was terrified."

Hearing the faint lament of violins, Gerald picked up the fallen headset from his lap and pressed one of the foam pads against his ear. The lush strains of Barber's Adagio for Strings wrapped him in its sentimental tentacles. Nobody had

3

screamed. Just polite gasps, like the reaction to a balloon burst at a children's party. We fear embarrassment more than death. He looked at the boy. Was that glassy-eyed stare due to shock or chemicals?

"So what kind of work are you doing in Sicily?" Gerald asked.

"I've got this gig."

"Are you a musician?" Gerald foresaw the conversation dead-ending with the name of an unfamiliar rock band.

"No, *acting* gig, I'm doing a play."

"You're an actor?"

"Yeah," said Ian, with the humble grin of a minor celebrity recognized by a fan.

"And you're doing a play in Sicily?"

"Yeah. There's this festival, I'm doing a play by this director—William Weiss—I don't know if you've ever heard of him?"

Gerald's heart sank. He wanted to savor his first impressions of Italy alone, not *connect* with a cast member. But it wouldn't do to lie.

"Heard of him? I'm in the cult."

"Cult?" The boy looked at him with suspicion.

"I'm working for Bill, too—in *Saints, Rivers, Space*—I'm Gerald Barnett."

"Wow," said the boy, then closed his mouth to contain a burp. "'Scuse me. Wow. I'm Ian." He studied Gerald as if they might have met before. "You know, I think they told me there was an older actor—I mean, older than me—gonna be on the flight."

"Did they?"

The Italian producer had said nothing to Gerald about flying with another actor when he had phoned to bargain down Gerald's already measly salary, citing the in-season airfare. Was this Ian making more money? Gerald felt a tiny seed of pain above his right eye and squeezed the bridge of his nose between his thumb and forefinger.

"Have you worked for William Weiss for a long time?" Ian asked.

"You mean because of my advanced age?" Ian probably *would* consider forty-five an advanced age, but Gerald regretted his comment, remembering how distasteful—or incomprehensible—age references are to the young. "I was twenty-four when I joined the School for Life—that's what we called the troupe in the old days—I was in the company for about fifteen years. But I left the company a few years ago."

"What were you in?"

"A lot of the early stuff. Let's see, *Fourteen White Boxes, Come Down From That Mountain/T.V., People of the World Relax.*"

"Wow, I've seen pictures of *Relax*, it was like ten hours, right?"

"Twelve."

"And *Fourteen White Boxes* was fucking brilliant."

"But that was in seventy-eight, you must have been—"

Ian pushed his hair away from his face and sat up in his seat. His cheeks were flushed and he'd lost his glazed look.

"I saw all the early stuff on video. Last year I took this course, Masters of the Avant-Garde, at Wesleyan—did my term paper on William Weiss. What did you do in *Boxes*?"

"White monkey in the first act—you won't remember me,

there were eleven of us. In the second act, I was the Enfant
d'Albinio. You might recall the entrance, which I made
through the ceiling, hanging on a—"

"Chain! Cool! That's right, you were spinning."

"Yes."

Gerald leaned back against his seat. He always felt more
relaxed with someone who'd seen him perform; there was less
social positioning, less to explain about himself. And he was
pleased Ian had seen him as the Enfant, when he was athletic,
in his twenties, practically naked and covered in chalky white.
Now especially, after the weight loss of the last year, his face had
grown gaunt and his hair was graying. He hadn't been to a gym
or a dance class in over a year and missed the tight musculature
he once had (though in positive moments he found his look
Beckettian).

"I remember you did this weird vocal stuff and went
through all these physical contortions."

"We took master classes with Grotowski."

"And your head was shaved and you were all white."

"Bill's *bhuto* phase, he'd just come back from Japan. Have
you worked with Bill before?" Gerald asked.

"No, this is our first collaboration."

Collaboration? When Gerald was in the company, Bill's do-
this-do-that style of direction was about as collaborative as boot
camp. Was this arrogant boy really under the assumption he was
collaborating with William Weiss?

"How did you meet Bill?"

"He gave this really cool lecture at my school. I talked to
him at the reception afterward. Said he was doing this play in
Sicily and asked if I'd like to work on it."

"Just like that?"

"Well, we left the reception and he came to this campus bar with a bunch of us. It was a pretty incredible evening. We talked about everything."

As Ian talked about "everything," Gerald's mind wandered back to the first William Weiss work he'd seen. A friend, who'd heard the play was long and boring, offered him a ticket. At the time, Gerald's aspirations as a young actor were commercial. Avant-garde meant the early plays of Edward Albee, which he'd read in college, or perhaps *Hair*, already an institution when he arrived in New York. Although Gerald was an avid theatergoer, everything about that evening was different. The play started before the houselights went down. A boy and a girl, dressed in ordinary clothes, were on either side of the stage, slowly turning in place. Their simple, hypnotic movements never suggested "performance." They were dressed in khaki pants and sneakers, and the only hint of theatricality came near the end of their "dance" as the houselights began to lower. Almost imperceptibly, their revolutions increased in speed, and as their hands rose from their sides, he saw their palms were dyed an orange hue as if pressed in turmeric.

The play itself unfolded in a series of scenes, unconnected by narrative or plot, but fantastic in design, exquisitely lit, and often extraordinarily slow. The piece was not naturalistic, yet it contained performances so "real" (Timothy, a sixteen-year-old black deaf boy, sang "He's Got the Whole World in His Hands" with utter conviction and completely off-key) that, at times, the accepted distance between actor and audience vanished completely.

People left in droves, sometimes muttering insults over

their shoulder as they stormed down the aisles, but this only increased Gerald's pleasure in the work. Every play he'd seen or been in suddenly seemed old-fashioned, corny, the style of theater he'd been trained for, all false noses and British accents. He was confused and elated at the same time. How could these scenes with no story produce in him so much emotion? At intermission a woman shouted hysterically about "child abuse," referring to the ebullient Timothy. Part of the audience stayed through the curtain call, only to jeer and boo at the actors. But Gerald, along with most of the remaining spectators, rose to his feet and applauded and cheered for call after call. When the houselights came up, releasing him back into the city night, he felt as if he'd fallen in love.

Gerald sniffed at the air. Urine. A heavyset man, who'd boarded the plane in a wheelchair, was heaving past him, using seat backs for support. A stain darkened the leg of his gray sweatpants.

". . . and when somebody asked Mr. Weiss what he thought of Ionesco," Ian was saying, "he said 'Who's Ionesco?' It was so cool, he's so *not* academic."

"Did he draw on a napkin?" Gerald asked.

"What? Oh, yeah, he drew scenes from the play on some bar napkins."

"Did he complain about funding?"

"Yeah, some."

"Boulevard drama?"

"Well, we both hate Broadway."

"Did he do the great German actress plucking the rose, pricking her finger, and looking in the mirror one last time before she dies?"

"No."

"He will—it takes about half an hour to forty-five minutes, depending on how much he's had to . . ." Gerald stopped.

He was already gossiping about Bill. Just as he had, months after he'd left the company, when he continued to drop by the studio to gossip with the actors about Bill's eccentric demands, a financial coup Bill had engineered to keep them from repossessing the sets and costumes, or to defend the director's early twelve-hour plays. Finally, he had to make a clean break from the Lifers, as company members referred to themselves. He ended the visits, stopped talking about Bill, he even managed to stop thinking about him. He skipped the last New York productions and begged out of fund-raising events for the company. Until the phone call a few weeks ago, it was only in dreams Bill returned, unbidden, into his life.

"Sounds like you know him pretty well," Ian said.

"We met in seventy-two."

Ian looked thoughtful. "That's when I was born."

"Done much acting, Ian?"

"Not much. My major was philosophy. But acting's cool. I'll do this gig and see how I like it."

"Medicine's cool, too, why don't you try a little surgery?"

"What's that supposed to mean?"

"Just joking—everybody thinks they can . . . But I mean, you're right, Bill's work is a more inclusive sort of discipline."

"I studied indigenous dance—Balinesian, Native American, Near Eastern—that's what interested Bill."

"Yes, he's a real cultural gleaner."

Ian yawned. "How long before we land?"

Gerald looked at his watch. "A half hour, I think."

"Okay." He took the sleep mask out of the seat pocket. "This turbulence stuff's got me wiped out. Mind if I . . . ?"

"No, go ahead. Should I wake you if they bring a snack?"

"Don't bother," Ian said. "Ciao." He pulled the mask over his eyes and wedged the little pillow between his head and the wall.

Gerald adjusted his seat to the reclining position, but knew he wouldn't sleep. He glanced around the cabin and noticed the other passengers were also awake, vigilant, braced for the next midair jolt. The old woman had stopped her sobbing, but now her lips trembled in silent prayer. Gerald imagined slapping her the way one slaps a hysteric. His friend Sherman, before he died, jokingly admitted a desire to "pick off" old people at the grocery store. "I hate them because they've had long lives and I won't," he said.

The seed of pain in Gerald's head had sprouted into a discomforting throb. I've no business taking a trip like this. I've just gotten over pneumonia, a staph infection, and a zillion other complications. Why, he asked himself, when I'd finally reached a sort of, well, not peace but *acceptance*, why did I say yes to Bill? Was it really for the chance to travel or did I say yes because, as an actor, my hand is always out, so when a job is offered without my supplication, I'm too flattered not to accept?

"I need someone who understands my esthetic—not intellectually, but someone who's *breathed* it," Bill had said. Gerald, who was always powerless in the face of the director's flattering enthusiasm, convinced himself that Bill's offer was also a chance to escape New York after years on the deathwatch. If fact, there had been silly "Barbara" moments when Italy seemed to offer an escape from death itself. Though he also suspected the trip might kill him, and he'd almost convinced himself to cancel when he received the letter from his friend Ariela. "Hooray!" she wrote. "I knew you'd come. Timothy will be there, too." He was glad, now, he'd told her about his illness. With his precarious health, he'd need a confidante.

Gerald reached down to his knapsack and removed the travel brochure he'd received from the Italian producer, along with his contract and plane ticket. He'd opened and refolded the brochure so many times it had begun to tear along the creases. He spread it out carefully on his lap.

In the center was a simple map of Sicily dotted with little iconic drawings of tourist spots—Roman baths, temple ruins, a dormant volcano—and picturesque photos were inset around the edge of the brochure. One photo showed a town built on the side of a steep, craggy hill above a blue-green Mediterranean. Simple, whitewashed buildings dotted the hillside, and tiny streets ran like capillaries down to the sea. One building had been circled with a ballpoint pen and beside it, in tiny letters, was written "actor's lodgings."

The captain's voice came over the loudspeaker. He announced that the plane would soon descend into the Palermo airport, spoke of clear skies, gave the temperature in Fahrenheit and Celsius and apologized for the "little bump-ah" earlier in the flight. During the same speech, repeated more fluidly in Italian, Gerald let his head fall forward to release the tension in his neck. He refolded the brochure, replaced it in his knapsack, and closed his eyes. He imagined a small whitewashed room with one window covered by a blue curtain, and he pulled the curtain aside to let the sun and sea air flood in.

CHAPTER TWO

The Palermo airport was sweltering. Passengers awaiting their bags gazed stupidly toward the rubber flaps at the end of the conveyor belt. Ian, still wearing the airline slippers, stood with one foot on the edge of the motionless luggage carousel. Gerald stood behind him. Half an hour and still no sign of their luggage.

"Worst fucking flight of my life," Ian muttered.

Gerald plucked his damp shirt away from the small of his back.

The carousel started up with a jarring mechanical whir and luggage began to emerge through the flaps. When an army-green duffel bag came round, Ian grabbed it, hefted it onto his shoulders, and stood with his feet apart supporting the bag like Atlas holding up the world.

"Where's yours?" he asked.

"I don't know," Gerald said. "Coming, I suppose."

Since their meeting on the plane, Ian seemed to assume they should leave the plane together, wait together at the luggage carousel, go through customs together, and find their ride to the festival together. The trip had been tiring for Gerald, and the additional social burden seemed a gargantuan and cruel imposition. A reminder to pace myself in the future, he thought. I'll spend a lot of time in my room, maintain a meditative state of silence, and save myself for rehearsals.

"What's it look like?" Ian asked.

"White," said Gerald, staring down the carousel.

He wished now he'd bought a new suitcase, but he was afraid to spend the little money he had for the trip. It was one thing being broke in New York, but being broke on foreign soil? The thought terrified him. He'd kept himself on a penurious budget and used his old suitcase—his grandmother's old suitcase, really.

"A *white* suitcase?"

"Yes, white leather."

Grandma Love had died on a visit to his family's home in Florida, the week before he began his freshman year in college. The night before he was to leave home, he discovered her suitcase lying open on his bed like a big ugly clam. His mother came in with a stack of his clothes, washed, ironed, newly labeled, and arranged them neatly inside the case.

"I'm not taking *that*," he said.

She slapped a new three-pair pack of Jockey briefs into the case.

He pointed to the initials, *L.L.L.* (for Loretta Langly Love), embossed on the flap.

"Those aren't my initials," he said.

His mother pulled out a sock-filled dresser drawer and dumped its contents into the case.

"And it's not even real leather."

"Gerald," said his mother—she'd been unable to sleep since her mother's death, and she stared at him with her flat, exhausted gaze, the empty drawer hanging at her side. "There's nothin' worse than a poor snob."

He'd held on to the case because it was Grandma Love's, or because even though his mother was dead, too, he still needed to prove he wasn't a snob. Over the last twenty years the case had sat at the back of his closet as a storage container for out-of-season clothes.

"That one?" asked Ian impatiently.

"I told you, mine's white."

"Ya know, someone from the festival is supposed to be picking us up—the flight was late and we've already been down here—"

"What do you want me to do? Leave without my suitcase?"

"I just meant, if it takes much longer . . ."

"Go on ahead, then."

A white suitcase, cocooned in plastic wrap, slid through the rubber flaps onto the carousel.

"That it?" Ian asked.

"Maybe," Gerald said softly.

He'd noticed some rotting in the fabric along the zipper when he packed but thought it would hold.

"Musta come open," Ian said.

He stepped back to give Gerald room to grab his bag, but Gerald was immobilized as the conveyor belt carried the case past.

"Why didn't you pick it up?"

Ian dropped his duffel bag and chased around the carousel. He set Gerald's suitcase down in front of him and gave him a look.

"It would have come round again," Gerald said, staring

down at Grandma Love's old suitcase in its tacky new plastic makeover.

The handle was buried under several layers of plastic, so Gerald was forced to cradle it awkwardly in both arms. The last passengers from their flight were already out of sight as he trudged after Ian.

Ian stopped. Heaving the duffel bag off his shoulders onto the floor with a soft thud that made Gerald picture neat piles of Laundromat-folded clothes, he reached for Gerald's case. "Give it to me," he said.

"No! Leave me alone! I'm fine! I can carry my own goddamn suitcase!" Gerald shouted, clutching the case to his chest.

"I was gonna cut the tape on top so you could at least hold it by the handle."

Gerald's lips froze in the trumpet shape of an O. In fact he wanted to say, "Oh," but the effect of adrenaline shooting through him was so visceral, he could have sooner puffed up like a toad or changed his coloring than uttered the tiny "oh" of understanding.

"D'ya think I was gonna steal it?" Ian asked.

Gerald set his case on the floor. His arms ached.

"All of a sudden we seem to be traveling companions, and I didn't anticipate having one."

"Oh, no problem, man, I'm outa here," Ian said, hoisting the duffel bag back on his shoulders and striding down the corridor after the retreating passengers.

The adrenaline wave ebbed as quickly as it had flowed and left Gerald feeling empty. His headache was back. He lifted the suitcase off the floor and carried it to a row of chairs along the wall, sat and dropped the case at his feet. He took out his New

York apartment keys from the pocket of his knapsack and, with the jagged edge of a Medeco key, began to cut the tape from around the suitcase handle.

No festival emissary waited for them on the other side of customs. Ian stood in the middle of the terminal lobby with his hands on his hips, his duffel bag at his feet, scanning the crowd that awaited the international travelers.

"I'll be right back," Gerald said on his way past, not waiting to hear Ian's reply.

In the airport men's room Gerald leaned over the rusted metal sink. Gathering cold water in cupped hands, he rinsed his face, then ran his wet hands carefully over his gelled hair. The Manhattan barbershop he'd chosen the day before had offered cheap cuts by apprentice barbers. "Leave some length on top," he'd instructed the gum-snapping boy who cut his hair without ever appearing to look at his head. The result, close-cropped sides and spiky top, made him look like a middle-aged rocker. His only recourse, until his hair grew out, was to flatten it back like Fred Astaire and go for a sort of old-fashioned elegance.

A convex dent ran down the middle of the metal mirror, and its surface was pitted and stained. In fact, Gerald had mistaken tarnished metal for soot on his face and tried to rub it off, leaving a red mark on his pale skin. As a youth, he'd hated his Gaelic complexion, which turned pink and freckled after a few minutes in the Florida sun. As a young man, his skin suggested the window-to-the-soul quality usually attributed to the eyes. The slightest embarrassment or self-consciousness produced deep blushes. The area under and around his eyes telegraphed mood or lack of sleep as it took on the blues, greens, and pale pinks of an opal. During and after sex, his face, neck, and torso blossomed with ruddy patches.

"You'd do great in Italy," suggested a trick whose words, but not his face, Gerald could still remember.

"What do you mean?"

"Oh, you know," said the man, tracing a finger across the faint raspberry clouds cumulating across Gerald's belly. "You can make out in Scandinavia if you're dark, fair in the South, and have a hairy chest in Japan."

Gerald laughed at the man's ideas about sexual tourism, but for years after, he fantasized about sex with swarthy lovers in foreign places: carnival in Rio, the back of a shop in Istanbul, on a mossy carpet in an Italian olive grove. If only he'd traveled then, when his fair coloring counted as currency. But the "Lifers" had only begun to tour after he'd left the company, and then . . . well, there had never been enough money, or time to travel, or, in later years, he always seemed to be attending some dying friend. People with my coloring age badly, he thought, staring into the mirror as he recalled his redheaded father who'd faded to the color of dried straw by the time he was fifty.

A man came in the bathroom with a small boy. Just as he freed a drawstring on the boy's shorts and let them fall to his ankles, a yellow stream shot out of his little uncircumcised penis and splashed across the bathroom tiles. The man hoisted him up to the urinal, looked over at Gerald, laughed, and said something in Italian. Gerald nodded, laughed back, and with a final glance into the dented mirror, ran a hand over his skulltight hair.

The main terminal of the Palermo airport was a semicircle

of ticket counters on one side, kiosks and a coffee bar on the other. Ian sat at the coffee bar, so apparently their ride had not arrived.

On his way to get aspirin, Gerald passed through a crowd waiting for arriving passengers. A young Italian dressed like a B-movie star—dark glasses, coat thrown over his shoulder, black hair slicked back—came through the turnstile. The man scanned the waiting crowd. A child shouted sweetly, "Antonio! Antonio!," and six or seven people converged upon the handsome man. He lifted the happily screaming child into the air, threw shadow punches at what appeared to be a younger brother, spun a laughing teenage girl (his sister?) in a circle, kissed an old man passionately on both cheeks then embraced a squat older woman dressed in black who dabbed at her eyes with a Kleenex.

The reunion scene immobilized Gerald. Since his illness, he'd been horrified to discover that familial moments filled him with sudden emotion. Watching a television commercial, in which a college student surprised his father at work with a long distance call, caused Gerald to weep, and after witnessing a mother kiss the scraped knee of her wailing toddler, he'd cut his errands short and returned home.

Gerald's own parents were not undemonstrative in their affections, but in an emotional crisis they favored stoicism. He didn't learn of his mother's mastectomy until after her death, and at the memorial brunch held in lieu of a funeral, his father announced to the guests there would be no "sentimental gee-haw—we're here to *celebrate* Gladys's life." Two years later, Gerald was in a show when his father was found dead of a heart attack in his assisted-living condo. Gerald flew to Florida after the Sunday matinee, took care of business on Monday, and was back in time for the performance on Tuesday.

The child pulled at the hand of the handsome Italian man to regain his attention. When the teenage girl tried to gather the little boy in her arms, he screamed again, "Antonio! Antonio!" Gerald felt the boy's anguish like a fist in his chest and had to open his mouth to breathe.

"Auntie, who are you cruising?"

Gerald spun around. "Ariela!"

He threw his arms around her, but she held the handle of a compact case on wheels and returned his embrace awkwardly, with one arm.

"Sorry," he said.

"What for?" Ariela asked. She had a dancer's posture and, like a dancer, her hair was tightly pulled back into a long braid that hung down her back.

"Because I went for you like a drowning man goes for a life preserver," he said.

"Are you drowning, Gerald? Shall I rescue you?"

"Ariela, my plane hit an air pocket and dropped fifty feet."

"Really?"

He stepped back to look at her.

"Are you taller?"

"No." She glanced with a guilty smile at her ankle-high suede boots with high heels.

"Look at your shoes, you've become a prostitute."

"Do you think Bill will hate them?"

"And you're wearing a dress, I don't think I've ever seen you in a dress."

Ariela was eighteen and just off a kibbutz when she first

arrived at the Weiss School for Life. An American patron of the arts had seen her dance and sponsored her apprenticeship in New York. The young Israeli immediately impressed everyone in the company with her self-possessed manner and her beauty. Her parents were Sephardic Jews from Yemen, but she looked Egyptian with a Cleopatra nose that started high between the feathered ends of graceful, naturally tapered eyebrows and descended between closely spaced, almond-shaped eyes. She spoke little at first, her small mouth pressed into the kiss of self-control dancers learn to wear on stage, or sometimes tightly drawn into a novitiate's vow-of-silence dash. Even Gerald had been a little awed by her until, during a particularly dull rehearsal, she gave him a goofy grin that suddenly made him aware of her enormous ears. Over rehearsal chitchat they discovered they both shared a randy nature, a high regard for silliness, and a love of gossip, the chief skill, Ariela claimed, one mastered at a kibbutz.

"When did you get here?" Gerald asked.

"Oh, hours ago. I came with Timothy."

"Timothy's here?"

"We've all been on tour. Didn't you get my letter?"

Gerald glanced back at the Italian family. They were still fussing over their handsome hero, who laughed as the little boy tried to wrest a suitcase from him. Suddenly, the man looked up from his struggle with the boy and spotted Ariela.

"Oh, no," said Ariela, turning away.

The man, ignoring his family, grinned broadly.

"Another bus and truck Don Juan," Gerald said.

Gerald was used to seeing men reduced to a state of idiocy in Ariela's presence. She had the curves of a pinup, rather than

21

the anemic thinness of a ballerina. Cab drivers braked in midstream traffic to gawk. Spanish teenagers assumed ridiculously cocky postures, or muttered vulgar invitations. Fathers pushing baby strollers stopped and turned casually as if they were searching for a lost binky to stare with sad resignation as Ariela walked past.

Gerald found the straight men's attraction to Ariela sexy. All the same, he was bothered that his presence had little effect on her admirers. Did they just assume he was her *gay friend*?

The Italian still cast backward glances at Ariela as his family ushered him away.

"How are things between you and Daryl," Gerald asked, "still married?"

"We don't speak, he hates me," said Ariela.

"Well, you're an icy cold bitch."

"You know it was a marriage of convenience. He married me for my green card, and because Bill told him to."

"But you knew he *was* a little in love with you."

"He says I led him down the path of the garden. And he's drinking. He's so awful when he drinks."

"Where is he?" Gerald asked.

"I left him with Timothy and a guy with long hair who said he sat next to you on the plane."

"I bet he said he sat next to an *older* actor, didn't he?"

Ariela laughed. "Yes, he did say that. Is he nice?"

Gerald shrugged. He felt the little wave of panic return, a reminder that he was doing too much. How many hours had he been up? In New York, he'd become a nap addict, but now it felt as if he hadn't slept in several days.

"I can't wait to get to the home," he said, and was about

to amend "home" to "hotel," when Ariela, who hadn't noticed his slip, spoke.

"He told me he admired my work. He's seen videos. I thought he was *very* nice."

"He's not. Where the fuck is our ride?"

"I think they're waiting until we all get here."

"What do you mean? Who's 'we'?"

Ariela smiled. "Timothy and me, you and this Ian . . . and the Germans. They're coming from Berlin, and their flight gets in later."

"What Germans?"

"Well, there's Holgar—and two others I haven't met."

Ariela's head pivoted gracefully away from Gerald's questioning look, gazing serenely off to some distant spot as if she were watching the sun sink below the horizon, until she broke into her silly, big-eared grin.

"So, you've already bagged a man for this gig? I might have known," Gerald said. He drummed his fingers mindlessly against his thigh. With a boyfriend around, would Ariela have time for him?

"I just spent four weeks with Holgar in Munich, two in Stockholm and four in Barcelona," Ariela said. "Yes, we're . . . doing it." She began to laugh. "But I'm sick of him! How do I dump him, Auntie?"

"Will you stop calling me that. We haven't seen each other for two years, and two seconds after we meet, you call me that."

"I'm sorry, Gerald," she said, "I'll never call you Auntie again—in public."

Her mouth, now a thin line of contrition, fought the tug of a smile. She was Archie to his Miss Grundy, the penitent novice to his mother superior. He felt both grateful for and repelled by the familiarity of their comedic roles.

"Is this Holgar an actor?"

"Lighting technician, but he was too pretty to waste, so Bill put him in the show. Come on, Gerald, we have lots of time—let's have an espresso. And Timothy is dying to see you." She looked down. "Gerald, what has happened to your suitcase?"

"Nothing, it just came apart, and the airline wrapped it in plastic. Better than giving me my stuff in a garbage bag, I suppose. Oh, shit!"

"What?"

"All my pills were in this case, I hope they didn't confiscate them or lose anything."

"Have something good?"

"Poison, most likely."

"Well, at least you have a positive attitude."

"By the way," Gerald said, as he lifted his case, "Ian doesn't really admire your work. He told me he thought your dancing was insipid."

"He's right. Especially now. I just go through the motions."

"I don't believe that. Listen, would you carry my suitcase and let me pull yours?"

"Just put yours on top of mine—look, the handle extends—and I can pull them both."

Gerald balanced his suitcase on top of Ariela's compact case.

"I'll take it," he said.

"No, let me, Gerald, I'm stronger."

Ariela laughed as she started off, easily pulling both cases behind her.

The white Formica tabletops in the coffee bar looked like tall mushrooms. There were a few stools, all taken.

Timothy stood with his back to them, a hand on either side of the tabletop, holding it like a big steering wheel and swaying rhythmically to some inner beat. When he was in his thirties, reviewers still referred to him as "the hearing-impaired *boy*." Now, he was nearly forty, and despite Madras shorts, checkered sneakers, two different-colored socks, and a Coca-Cola T-shirt, he looked his age. He'd also put on a good deal of weight, which made him appear less bouncy and frenetic.

"Jrrr-all, Jrrr-all, Jrrr-all," Timothy said, when he saw them.

It was useless to ask Timothy to speak quietly in public. He only responded with his version of a whisper: just as loud as before and two octaves higher.

"Hi, Timothy," Gerald said. "What are you drinking?"

"Fun-ta."

"He loves Fanta," Ariela said, "and Gerald, you don't have to shout too."

"I know, I know. I forgot how good you are at lipreading, Timothy."

"Wha?" Timothy yelled.

"I said, I forgot how good you were at reading lips."

"Wha?"

"Timothy, stop shouting," said Ariela, putting a finger to her lips.

"Wha?" Timothy yelled in a falsetto.

"Oh, I see, you're making a joke," Ariela said.

25

Timothy's laugh sounded like the screech of a large tropical bird, and Gerald was aware of the other people in the coffee bar staring. But then, Timothy was the only black man in the airport.

They stood at the mushroom table with their espressos, Timothy with his orange Fanta. People around them periodically glanced toward Gerald's table. What a charismatic trio we are, he thought. Perfectly poised and centered Ariela; the ever-swaying Timothy, humming like a happy machine; and me, "clean favored and imperially slim." He remembered the descriptive phrase from "Richard Cory," a poem he'd learned in high school. At the end of the poem, the rich, admired Richard Cory "goes home and puts a bullet through his head." As a teen, he'd identified with the eponymous hero. But now, instead of dying, Gerald thought, I'm in Italy with friends and a job. He felt an annoying sentimentality well up and lowered his head.

"Awww," Timothy said, patting Gerald's forearm.

"What, Tim?" Gerald asked, looking up with a smile.

"He knows you were sick, and he's glad you're better," Ariela said.

"Thank you, Tim," said Gerald, touching his own breast. Then turning his head slightly so Timothy could not see his lips, he asked Ariela, "Does he know what I was sick with?"

"Wha?" Timothy said.

"I didn't want to scare him—I told him you had cancer," Ariela said.

"Oh, thanks."

"Wha?"

"Nothing, Timothy," said Ariela. "Do you want to look around the airport?"

Timothy got off his stool tapping his chest, pointing, shaking his head.

"I'll watch your bag and no, we won't leave without you."

"You understand everything he doesn't say," said Gerald when Timothy had left.

"We're like lovers," Ariela said, groaning and burying her face in her hands. Then quickly, changing her posture, she sat up straight. "No, I don't mind. I really *do* love Timothy, but as you know, he can be high maintenance."

"You're a saint."

"No I'm not! I'm terrible. I tell him to shut up all the time. Or I just send him off on his own."

"Well, you're not paid to be his babysitter."

"I know. And he doesn't need a babysitter. It's just we're all so used to taking care of little Timothy."

"Not so little anymore."

Ariela laughed. "I know. I say to him all the time, 'Timothy, you've gotten so fat.' Or I go like this." She pushed her slim stomach out and patted it. "He gets very mad at me. I see him try to hold in his belly in the dressing room around the girls—but he never stops eating."

Gerald noticed a man preparing to leave his seat. "Oh, thank God," he said, walking casually but quickly toward the stool. He arrived before the man had left. "Thanks," he said, picking the stool up by the seat.

"*Prego*," the man said.

Gerald sighed as he sat down.

"Tired, Auntie? I mean Gerald?"

"You better show a little respect. A few months ago I almost croaked, you know."

She gave him a disapproving look. "May I remind you I offered to come and you said no," she said. "But you didn't croak, Gerald. And you look good."

"I do not. I look like the poster boy for memento mori."

"What's that mean?"

"'Remember death.' Didn't they educate you on that kibbutz?" Gerald touched the gelled shell of his hair. "Do I really look all right?"

"What did you do to your hair? You look like Fred Astaire."

Gerald heard Ariela through the dull ache in his head. He'd forgotten his mission to buy aspirins.

"I was so glad Terry couldn't come and you could, Gerald," Ariela continued. "We're going to have a great time."

"Terry?"

"Oh, you remember him—very tall with dreadlocks? His wife is having a baby, and he couldn't come to Sicily. That's why you're here."

"So I'm a replacement? Did you get Bill to ask me? Is this a charity job because I got sick?"

Ariela laughed. "Bill? Charitable? Hadn't you sent a letter or something? It was on his desk when he got the news about Terry. He just looked down and said, 'Let's get Gerald.' That was it."

Ariela held her neck long and her head tilted down. She dipped a biscotti into her coffee.

"Gerald, I know I'm being selfish, but I don't care how it happened. You're back. That's all that matters."

Gerald stared into his empty espresso cup. He shouldn't have been drinking coffee at all with his unpredictable digestion, but since he was, he should have had a cappuccino, which might have at least lasted longer than two sips.

"Here comes Daryl. He drank so many vodkas on the plane, I hope he won't be too obnoxious, and he's with your new friend Ian."

Daryl and Ian, similar in size and shape, looked, at a glance, like best college buddies as they walked side by side. But Ian's sloppiness was more studied, more self-conscious, as he gazed curiously around the terminal, following Daryl toward the coffee bar with the self-centered preoccupation of a character in an Ayn Rand novel. Daryl, on the other hand, *was* sloppy. His thongs were ringed with dirt in the vague shape of his foot. His legs were spotted with what looked like scratched mosquito bites. He gave Gerald a crushing bear hug, engulfing him in an aura of perspiration and liquor.

"Hey, it's been like a thousand fucking years, man," Daryl said. He was still young enough to be counted on the bright side of seedy, though when he stepped back, Gerald noticed a new puffiness in his face, red irises, and a receding hairline.

Gerald and Daryl had had an affection for each other, enhanced by their mutual interest in Ariela. But while Gerald had kept up with Ariela, he had not stayed in touch with Daryl.

"Uh-oh, the dangerous duo is back together," Daryl said.

Ariela ignored him.

"Ian, have you met my ex-wife?" Daryl said. "Oh, excuse me, my ex-*green card* wife."

Ariela stared coldly ahead.

"Sorry, Ariela, I didn't want Ian to imagine we were legitimate. Have you met Ian? He's going to be in the show. Ian, this is . . . what's your name again?"

"I see you found the airport bar, Daryl," Ariela said.

"So?"

She turned to face him and spoke quietly. "Keep it up. Maybe you'll do us all a favor and get sent home."

Daryl looked as if he might reply, but instead he veered around and stumbled his way across the terminal lobby.

"He's been like this the whole tour, but I know that's no excuse for being so mean," Ariela said quietly, staring into her empty cup.

"It's a great excuse. What a bad drunk. Maybe I can talk to him later." Gerald raised an eyebrow. "He used to revere me, you know."

"He has reverence for nothing anymore, so good luck."

Ian gave Gerald a smug smile, before turning away to follow Daryl across the terminal.

"You know what's so amazing," Gerald said to Ariela, "is that people play out the most soap operaish aspects of their lives just like they do in soap operas. You know—confrontations, recriminations."

"He's drunk. Usually I can frighten him off—and Bill's warned him to stay away from me, but it isn't easy when you're touring together."

Gerald pinched the bridge of his nose between his thumb and forefinger. "Will you watch my bag while I go buy some aspirin?"

"Oh, don't leave me." Ariela tilted her head in Ian's direction.

"I'll be right back."

The woman at the kiosk did not understand Gerald's request for aspirin until he mimed "headache" by placing his hands on either side of his head and moaning. "And one of those," he said, pointing to a ten-pack of cigarettes half the size of an American pack. He hadn't smoked for over a year and he felt as if he were having an out-of-body experience, as he slipped the perfect half-pack in his shirt pocket and handed the woman one of the brightly colored bills he'd exchanged in New York for American currency.

Gerald held little hope that the aspirins would relieve his pain this late into a headache, but he took three with a sip of metallic-tasting water from a fountain and sat down on a bench to let fatigue wash over him. A voice crackled over an anti-quated speaker system, announcing the arrival of a flight from Berlin.

Passengers stood in line at the ticket counters fanning themselves. Two young men, both with black curly hair, saun-tered arm in arm across the terminal, stopping under the screen listing flight arrivals and departures. They looked like party guests admiring a host's art collection. Gerald had always heard men in Italy, especially young men, walked that way, touching one another. *That doesn't mean they're gay.* He was sure he'd heard that too.

Arriving passengers pushed through the old wooden turn-stiles under the watchful eyes of *poliziotti* wearing white gloves (in this heat!). A blond giant appeared, dwarfing all mortals around him. He came through the stiles, put his case down, and looked around the airport with his hands on his hips, an Olympic champion approved by Leni Riefenstahl. Has to be Holgar, thought Gerald. No wonder Ariela is still fucking him even though she claims he bores her. A young man and woman joined the blond giant, huddling behind him like children in the shadow of a parent. When the blond man spotted Gerald he waved him over.

"Hi, how did you know who I was?" Gerald said.

"Hello, I am Holgar Kuntz."

He was older—more thirties than twenties—than Gerald had at first thought. The fine lines cutting across his forehead and around his eyes gave him a cruel look. "I would like to make an exchange of money before we leave the airport," Holgar said in his clipped German-accented English. "Do you understand English?"

"What? Oh. Yes," Gerald said, realizing Holgar's mistake. "But I'm not the driver, I'm an actor in the company." Gerald smiled at the young couple behind Holgar to show them he was not offended by their friend's little faux pas. They looked up at Holgar. "I'm Gerald," he said, extending his hand.

"Oh!" Holgar said, pointing down at Gerald, making him feel tiny. "You are Ariela's friend. She talks much about you." He gave Gerald's hand a firm shake. "Is she arrived yet?"

"She's over there, at the coffee bar." Gerald smiled again at the boy and girl standing patiently behind the towering German. "Hi, I'm Gerald."

"These are Zuzie and Otto," explained Holgar. "We arrived together from Berlin."

"I am so pleased," said Zuzie, an attractive, carefully made-up girl, whose sudden, ingenuous smile Gerald found too intimate for a first meeting.

"Gerald worked with William Weiss many years ago," said Holgar, gazing over his head.

"Well, not that many," Gerald said, "it was after the war."

"Oh, I admire the work of William Weiss more than any

other director. In Germany, he is considered a god. I am very fortunate to be cast in his play," gushed Zuzie, with a touch of posh British in her accent. "I am an actress," she added, needlessly.

"So am I," Gerald said.

"I am from *East* Berlin," announced Otto in a loud voice. He'd set his case down to light a pipe. The big handlebar mustache under his small boyish nose appeared fake, pasted on.

"Berlin is Berlin, now," Holgar snapped. "Daryl is here too?"

"Yes," Gerald said.

"*Scheiss!* " Holgar hissed.

"And Timothy and an another American named Ian. We've been hanging around this airport for two hours. The people from the festival probably waited until your flight arrived, so they'd only have to make one trip. I suppose, now that you're here—"

Holgar abruptly started for the coffee bar while Gerald was in mid-sentence.

"I am very pleased to meet you, and I look forward to a long conversation regarding your experience with the director, William Weiss," Zuzie said, bestowing upon Gerald another twinkling smile, as she followed after Holgar.

Otto shrugged his shoulders. A permanent blush marking the boy's cheeks spread across the rest of his face. He picked up the case, inserted the pipe between his teeth, and gave a sharp little nod of farewell before hurrying off to join his two countrymen.

Soon after the Germans had arrived, a serious young man in wire-rimmed glasses with a sign that read "Festival dell'Arte" appeared and led the actors out to an ancient van. Gerald was sure the vehicle was too old to be air-conditioned, and the back windows were the sort that only pushed out an inch or two at the bottom. The midday heat, as the pilot had warned, was ferocious and the aspirins had done nothing to quell his headache. He felt he must sit in the front passenger seat or die. As the actors filed through the sliding door into the back seats, Gerald hovered near the front door lest anyone else try for his spot. When Otto, the young German with the mustache, and the driver finished stowing Otto's duffel bag in the boot, Gerald made his move, but found the door locked. He stuck his head into the back, reached round and pulled up the button, just as Otto opened the front door and climbed in.

"The back of an auto makes me ill," he said, climbing in, closing the door, and lowering the front window.

In the end, Gerald had to wedge himself between Ian and Zuzie in the back seat. During the long ride, he gave up hope of distracting himself with the scenery and instead stared two rows ahead at the back of Otto's head as he imagined looping a thin wire round the boy's throat and executing him, Mafia style.

"How far is Taormina?" Gerald shouted at the driver over the roar of the motor. The driver didn't answer.

"Taormina?" Zuzie said with a tinkling laugh.

"Yes, Taormina, to our hotel."

"We don't stay in Taormina," Zuzie said, twisting herself around to face Gerald.

"Yes we do. I have a brochure," Gerald shouted impatiently.

"No, you are mistaken, we stay in *Bellina*. That is where the festival is located," she said.

"Bellina? Is it on the sea?" Gerald asked.

"On the sea?" Zuzie cocked her head to the side and smiled generously. "No, not at all. Bellina is inland."

Gerald leaned back in his seat and closed his eyes. It must be by the sea. They had circled Taormina on the map and written "actors' lodgings." I shouldn't have come, he thought, I was never happy when I worked with Bill, and I won't be now. He rubbed his forehead with the flat of his hand, as if he were clearing a blackboard with an eraser.

CHAPTER THREE

G erald stared in horror at the cheap brick façade of the
Centro Sociale, built around a courtyard of dried earth
in which a few lonely palm trees had somehow managed to sur-
vive. The ugly motel was located beside a highway on the out-
skirts of the unremarkable inland town of Bellina—everything
opposite to the hotel he had imagined where every room offered
a view of the turquoise sea.

Surely there were other accommodations that might have
been considered, he wondered indignantly. Until those options
were explored, he'd need to take immediate inventory, since
rooms might be offered on a first-come-first-served basis. But
that, too, had been decided for them. Rooms and roommates,
he found, had already been assigned. The women and members
of the technical crew had been given singles, the men had been
doubled, or in his case, tripled up. His name, along with
Daryl's and Timothy's, was on a white card pushpinned to slats
on a louvered door. Inside, the charmless room was furnished
with three scant mattresses on the floor, shrouded under faded
paisley-print sheets, and a plywood wardrobe housing a single
coat hanger.

"Not acceptable," Gerald muttered to himself, throwing his bag on what he judged to be the least undesirable of the mattresses because it was slightly separated in an open alcove off the bathroom. No one should have to room with the miserable Daryl. And Timothy might be sweet and savant and all that, but as Ariela noted, he was certainly high maintenance. Gerald stormed across the courtyard past Ian, who was scanning doors for his name. And besides, it didn't matter who the roommates were, just *that* they were. Didn't Bill make anyone aware of his seniority, not to mention his medical condition?

"May I speak to the manager?" Gerald attempted a polite smile. Four Italian men, just finishing their lunches at a communal table, were being served coffee by a young girl and a middle-aged woman. All the men were dark and had short, curly, almost Negroid hair. A family business, thought Gerald. "Is one of you the manager? I want to change rooms." He pointed in the direction of the room to which he had been assigned, then pressed on a few inches of air between both hands: "Too small for three people." One of the men said something in Italian to the women, who began to clear dishes as the men got up from the table. "Never mind then, I'll talk to someone from the Festival," Gerald said. Turning to leave, he saw Ian, leaning against a post with a smirk on his face.

"What's the matter, *Ger*, didn't they didn't give you the star's suite?"

Ignore him, thought Gerald, until he noticed Zuzie and Otto standing nearby, under the shade of an awning. Ian's sarcastic remark must be responded to in front of the newcomers.

"If they assigned rooms according to artistic merit, *Eee*,

you'd be sleeping in the latrine." Gerald tried to feel vindicated, but worried the reply made him appear brittle and bitchy to the Germans.

"Is not lunchtime *well* past serving?" asked Otto, oblivious to their exchange.

A stiff silence hung over the table as the eight newly arrived guests were served eight thin gray slices of veal, each looking lonely on its mismatched plate. Gerald, unfamiliar with the common practice of primo and secondo courses, had wolfed down the skimpy pasta course. Though he was no longer hungry, he ate, fearing the additional entrée was an introductory luxury that might never come again.

"Where'd ya learn Italian, Sash?" Daryl asked Zuzie. He gave the question a leering quality as if he were a rogue in a nineteenth-century melodrama.

"I am also fluent in French, Spanish, and Portuguese," she explained, including the rest of the table in her answer. "My father is an actor with the Talia Theater, but he performs in movies also. I often went with him on—how do you say this in English? On location—and picked up the language."

"Zat right? Mus'a been fun," Daryl said.

"Yes, although I must admit," she added, "much of my Italian and all of my Portuguese I learned in the Berlitz-bedroom manner."

"Huh?" he asked, in openmouthed stupefaction.

"You know," she said, smiling coquettishly. "If you wish to learn a language, make love with the natives."

Daryl gave her a leering smile. "Wanna learn American?"

"Oh, you're a master of the innuendo, Daryl," Gerald said.

"Thanks," he muttered, looking pleased with himself. "How's your German coming, Ariela?"

"Another Fanta, Timothy?" asked Ariela, ignoring Daryl.

"Yes, please."

Timothy sat up very straight in his chair, cutting his veal in a stiff, robotic manner. In addition to his deafness, Timothy's autism—a diagnosis Bill called meaningless—gave him a savant's mastery of dates and numbers, but a child's grasp of social skills. For behavioral cues, he cast constant sidelong glances at his neighbors and his manners were a formal, inexact copy.

"*Grazie tante*, " Zuzie purred, as the waiter took her plate. Gerald, sensing the usefulness of the Italian phrase, repeated it to himself.

"Grass is . . . *green*!" Timothy barked with furtive glances left and right. The waiter withdrew his hand quickly, as if the bizarre young man might bite it.

"Bravo, Timothy," Daryl said.

"Does anyone realize where veal actually comes from?" Ian asked. His long hair was still disheveled from his travel nap, and he slumped deeply in his chair at the head of the table, one leg dangling over the arm. The complimentary airline slippers were still on his feet.

"Little cows!" Otto shouted, like a *Jeopardy* contestant. "We have in the East this meat!" He volleyed the revelation with a hard jut of his chin and nervously twirled the end of his mustache.

"Yeah, from calves. And they get penned up in their own shit for their whole lives. They never move, so that—"

"Stop," Zuzie begged.

"It's true," Ian said.

"So don't eat it," Gerald snapped, "but veal is commonly served here, so stop talking like a stupid American tourist,"

"Maybe I am a stupid American," Ian said.

"No argument there," Gerald said.

He hated himself for engaging with Ian and glanced across the table at Ariela, who sat posture-perfect in front of a plate of untouched food, eyes downcast like a geisha. Next to her, Holgar, her Aryan poster boy, heartily chewed his last bite of meat, then speared Ariela's veal with his fork, bringing it to his plate with a thud. Daryl gave a belligerent grunt.

"Oh, did anyone else want this meat of Ariela's?" asked Holgar with a smile, displaying a perfect set of white teeth.

"Perhaps you might offer Daryl a little piece," Gerald suggested, feeling a desperate need for Ariela's attention. "He looks like he could use some."

"I've had enough to last a lifetime," sneered Daryl, with a sour drunken laugh, echoed in a bizarre, staccato rendition by Timothy.

Ariela rose so effortlessly from her chair it appeared her body was lifted by strings. Her unsmiling eyes brushed up to meet Gerald's, then lowered before she turned and left the room. Holgar, dropping his fork with a clatter, followed.

"Oh. Oh. Oh," Timothy called out.

"Follow them," Daryl shouted. "Don't let them out of your sight for a minute."

"Oh. Oh. Oh," Timothy repeated, squirming in his seat, anxious to follow Ariela, but fearful of missing another serving of food.

"Stay with us, Timothy," Gerald said, holding his hand up. "Would you like the veal that Holgar didn't finish?"

Timothy nodded vigorously, softly settling back into his seat. He had never, in Gerald's memory, rejected an offer of more food.

Gerald noticed Zuzie staring desolately around the table. What a waste to be the only woman left with this crowd, he thought. There's deaf, autistic Timothy, Cold War Otto, drunken Daryl, unkempt Ian, and homosexual me. His gaze met Ian's, and for a moment, Gerald feared he'd actually voiced his ungenerous appraisals. Ian placed a large olive loosely between his lips and began rotating it with his tongue. Is that behavior for my benefit? Gerald wondered.

"Have you worked with Bill before, Susie?" Gerald asked, in an effort to ignore Ian. She, too, had been watching Ian roll the olive between his lips, and could barely pull her attention away to respond to Gerald.

"It's pronounced with zed, like so, *Zuzie*. But, no"—she glanced back at Ian—"I have not, though of course I am very much in love with the works of William Weiss."

Gerald wondered how on earth this one got her job and then remembered Bill mentioning the daughter of one of Germany's greatest actors in his phone call. But Gerald had taken little notice, because Bill had always gone on, during Gerald's stint as a Lifer, about the greatest actor in Germany, or France, or Austria—safe territory since none of them knew famous foreign actors who hadn't appeared in a Hollywood movie or on the Broadway stage.

"And you, Otto?" Gerald wanted to rip the silly mustache off the boy's face. "Where did you meet Bill?"

"I vas in de production of *Der something, something, something,*" Otto said, naming one of umpteen plays Bill had directed in Germany in the last few years.

"Oh, yes," purred Zuzie, "I heard it was very beautiful."

And dull, dull, dull, thought Gerald. From all accounts the piece was an unsuccessful collaboration with an American intellectual who had written a stultifying libretto.

Silence returned to the table as the remaining diners sipped Nescafé, picked cookies from a tin, or finished off glasses of wine. Gerald looked out the window. Someone had once built a fire in the awful courtyard, in winter perhaps, and the burned wood remained. Now the sun seemed to scorch everything—the soil, the charred logs, the palm trees—to the same bland hue. Ian let an olive pit drop from his mouth to the plate, but Gerald refused to look over. I hate him, he thought, I hate all these young people. I never should have answered Bill's phone call. He only gave me this job because he felt sorry for me—but not sorry enough to give me my own room.

After lunch, Gerald had to get away from the Sociale. Not yet knowing what lay beyond these rooms surrounding this impoverished courtyard suffocated him, made him feel jailed. But he had no idea if the streets were safe. He thought of the murder of Pasolini by young Italian thugs and wondered if his clothes—T-shirt, shorts, and sandals—marked him as gay, or a tourist, or both and therefore an obvious mark. He passed Ariela's room and longed to knock, to persuade her to accompany him. But, of course, she was with Holgar; the louvered door was shut. He hurried across the barren courtyard and through the gates of the motel.

The town of "New" Bellina was new because "Old" Bellina, a once-charming, hillside village some twenty miles to the north, had been destroyed by an earthquake in the late sixties.

The local government, hoping to attract tourism to the reconstructed city, had elected to sponsor an annual arts festival. Contemporary Italian artists were commissioned to create sculptural environments, a ruse to give the town "avant-garde" appeal. The result was a cityscape of block after block of cheaply constructed stucco homes reflecting the ugly architecture of the period, interrupted by designed "spaces." A square was dotted with three-story stacks of newspapers sculpted in concrete, a corrugated steel "Madonna" undulated through a vacant lot, or, in the center of town, a bar was built in the shape of a toppled figure eight. The odd esthetic was confusing, but more confusing was the fact that the streets were completely empty.

At three in the afternoon, homes were shuttered and stores locked tight. In one store, behind a window display of clocks, Gerald spotted an elderly woman stooped over a counter. She appeared to be sleeping. The old woman—scarf on her head, apron tied round her squat figure—was the prototype of an Italian granny.

Thinking to buy the travel alarm he'd forgotten to pack, Gerald tapped on the glass. In this nowhere town a sale must be welcome at any time of day. The woman looked up sharply and made an unmistakable gesture with her index and little finger extended. Gerald backed away from the shop as if he had been slapped and hurried down the street, hardly daring to believe the old woman had meant to communicate to him, a friendly American visitor, such a vulgarity.

Hot and exhausted, he returned to his room at the Commune Sociale, but was unable to nap while Daryl and Timothy snored away on neighboring mattresses. He'd tried to refresh himself in the primitive shower until he noticed water flooding the bathroom, seeping under the door to the room where his roommates still slept. He ran outside in his flip-flops, towel, and a wet T-shirt to confront, once again, the "staff." The two women sat smoking in the kitchen and did not understand his dilemma until he pointed to his room and mimed the Australian crawl. Giggling behind her hand, the younger woman handed him a mop.

After mopping the floor, Gerald dragged the room's only chair into the baked courtyard to drape his soaked shorts and T-shirt over the back and seat.

The late afternoon was still hot, but one side of the building was now shaded from the boiling sun. Gerald sat on the surprisingly cool cement and leaned against the outside wall of his room. He was pleasantly surprised to see cigarettes in his pocket, then remembered buying them. He ripped the cellophane off the minipack, took one out and lit it from one of the stick matches he'd also purchased.

The motel appeared to be as empty as the street. The actors were either out exploring the barren town or resting in their rooms.

The worker ladies reappeared without their aprons. One of them carried a paper shopping bag and he wondered if it contained the leftover veal and pasta from lunch. They spotted Gerald and began to laugh. The older woman "swam" toward the front gate, as the younger woman shrieked with laughter, and they both disappeared onto the street.

Chapter Four

Gerald was unable to join the others for dinner at a local restaurant for which they'd been given vouchers. Instead he took a pill from Ariela which drew him into a drowsy sleep. Voices and laughter punctuated the evening as the others returned from dinner. Later, as his new roommates prepared for bed, their noisy interruptions became a vague soundscape in an unremembered dream.

Gerald awoke early the next morning with the calm emptiness that often followed a bad headache, as if pain acted as a thought purgative.

Timothy snored. Daryl, sprawling off the mattress, looked like an adult in a child's bed. Gerald got dressed quietly and tip-toed over the clothes left strewn across the linoleum floor.

All the louvered doors surrounding the earthen courtyard were shut. The palm tree cast a long shadow in the early morning sun. Wasn't that his T-shirt and shorts draped over the chair under the tree. Oh, yes, the shower, the flood, and like a sleepwalker he drifted through the double doors of the motel entrance, retracing yesterday's route back toward the town.

A hint of night's moisture still softened the air. Two old

women holding identical net shopping bags chatted in front of the obelisks of concrete newspaper. The shop woman's vulgar gesture, was it only yesterday? He bowed his head and hurried past the women.

There were other people on the street, shops were open. Gerald stopped in a coffee bar. The three men standing at the counter reading newspapers looked up when Gerald entered. They watched him proffer a handful of change to the counterman, who named the value of each coin as he removed it from Gerald's palm.

"*Grazie tante,* " said Gerald, wondering if he'd been cheated. He finished the espresso in a gulp and fled the shop, nodding and smiling on his way out.

In a little *farmacia,*—he looked up the word in a pocket Italian/English dictionary—Gerald bought familiar toiletries whose brand names, written in a foreign language, seemed more intriguing than anything he could get at home. He bought yogurt, a bun, and cheese in a *negozio di alimentare* and fruit from a *fruitivendola*. Still unable to discern the unfamiliar coins, he paid for each purchase with bills, and on the way back to the motel, his pockets were bulging with change.

The tenants of the Sociale were up, and many of their doors were ajar, exposing opened luggage and unmade beds, but Ariela's door remained closed. As Gerald walked into the courtyard to retrieve his clothes from the back of the chair, he heard voices in the dining hall. Part of him wanted to join the actors at the breakfast table, to get a rehash of the missing evening, but he imagined his postheadache calm bursting like a fragile bubble against the ragged edges of their chatter, so he decided not to.

"Morn, Jrrr-ow." Timothy followed his greeting with noises

and gestures which Gerald was able to interpret as "where have you been?"

"Town, Timothy."

"Oh."

"What's on your toast?" Gerald asked, pointing to the triangle of toast Timothy gingerly held between two fingers.

"Nu'nella."

"What? Oh, Nutella." Gerald gathered his clothes from the chair. He pointed at his watch. "Timothy, when is rehearsal?"

Timothy was the expert on matters of time and brought his watch close to one eye. "Four-three," he said.

"Four-thirty?" Timothy shifted his weight from one foot to another, his action for frustration. "Oh, in forty-three minutes we have to be at the theater." Timothy nodded. "Where is the theater?"

Timothy kept his eyes focused to his extreme left, while he extended the hand holding the toast up, to the right, past Gerald's head. Gerald turned to face a steep hill rising beyond the motel. Near the top of the hill he noticed a fortresslike structure, gleaming white under the rapidly rising sun. He'd heard they were to perform the play in a renovated palazzo and was amazed he hadn't noticed the building until now. "I'm going to walk, Timothy. Wanna come?"

"No! Darah drive de vah," Timothy said, rocking from side to side.

"Don't worry. You stay here and ride in the van with Daryl. But will you tell him." Here, Gerald pointed to the hill behind. "Tell him I walked, don't wait?"

Timothy nodded vigorously.

49

Gerald started off in the direction of the theater, following the highway in back of the motel until it curved around at the base of the hill. A cast-iron grapevine, its tendrils looping and curling at the top to form the name "Palazzo dell'Arte," arched over a newly paved road exiting off the highway. The road continued to wind up the steep hill, up to the castlelike building at the top. But forking off the road, a gravel path zigzagged less circuitously up the slope through the vineyards and, farther up, into an olive grove of precisely spaced trees. Gerald chose this steeper, unpaved route for his journey.

Along the way, he stopped to shake stones from his sandals. The sun was pleasantly warm on his bare arms and legs, and he felt the working of muscles in his thighs and calves as he climbed. Imagine the strength he could build walking (eventually even running) every day, up this hill. He pulled his shirt off over his head and tucked it into the back of his shorts. The warmth of sun against his bare shoulders and chest was both familiar and foreign. Growing up in Florida, he and his friends were shirtless as often as not. Even as an adult in New York, he was the first to take his shirt off on a warm day in the park or on a humid dance floor. He heard a grinding of gears behind him and turned to see an old flatbed truck winding slowly up the road. Field workers stood in the open back of the truck. Now, not having exposed this much of his body to anyone but doctors for months, he felt self-conscious. He recalled "white as a fish's belly," a phrase his father used to describe Northerners on the beach during the Christmas holidays. He pulled his shirt from his shorts, but putting it back on under the scrutiny of the field workers felt more awkward still. As the truck passed he squared his shoulders, stared into the ground, and slapped at his back with the shirt as if he were swatting off flies.

The path led up to a gravel parking lot adjoining the Palazzo dell'Arte. The two buildings, separated by a stone courtyard with a fountain, were connected on the parking-lot side by a long, arched breezeway. Gerald had read in a festival brochure that the palazzo was once home to a wealthy vineyard owner, and the town at the foot of the hill, now New Bellina, had consisted of a handful of dwellings erected for his field workers. The palazzo was built in gleaming white marble. The front building was used as an arts complex with second-story apartments for the visiting artists. In back, on the other side of the stone courtyard, the vineyard owner had built a chapel for his wife and workers, and it was in this domed rotunda, in its new incarnation as a performance space, where the actors would perform in the premiere production of William Weiss's *Saints, Rivers, Space.*

Gerald, thinking to explore the theater later, climbed the stone steps leading to the breezeway, which led to a paved porch framed by a low stone wall and running the length of the arts complex. The porch overlooked the hill: the grape arbors, olive groves, all the way to the town below. Much had been made in the brochure of the architectural and landscaping integrity, which honored the natural rise of the hill. An archway, cut through the center of the complex, covered steps leading up to the stone courtyard and the chapel beyond. On one side of the archway, the costume shop was housed. Behind the glass front of the shop, dressmaker's dummies stood like sentries on long fabric-wrapped tables. At the far end of the patio Gerald discovered the Café dell'Arte, with tables under umbrellas in front, and inside, a café. The counterwoman was still setting up, but she smiled warmly when Gerald came in, as if he'd been expected.

I was smart to come up here before the others, Gerald thought, as he went up to the counter, bought *un caffè latte*, and took the cup outside, to a table on the porch. The air smelled sweeter up here and the morning sun warmed and relaxed him. He adjusted his chair for a view down the hill. The field workers were trimming tree branches in an olive grove below. Honeybees swarmed round the residue of sugared coffee staining his cup.

Gerald still felt fatigued from yesterday's journey, but also pleased that he had hiked to the palazzo, earning him this moment of relaxed solitude. The problem still gnawing at him was the indignity of his housing situation. So far, he'd avoided his roommates, but his precarious health depended on sleep, and moments spent alone, refueling. Besides, the producers had told him he'd have a single room and he would hold them to their word.

I'll talk to Bill, he thought. The director, whose schedule never left a free minute, was due to arrive just in time for rehearsal. That meant he should be on his way from the airport now, if he wasn't already here, in one of the artist's apartments above. Gerald looked up. All the windows had closed curtains. He heard a car and saw the van coming up the winding road, toward the palazzo. His solitude was over.

Otto appeared at the end of the patio wearing a broad-brimmed hat, walking shorts, and thick sandals with socks pulled up to his knees. He saw Gerald, and in a flash, was standing before him.

"The theater is locked. You have seen any persons from the production staff?"

"Good morning," Gerald said, squinting up at him.

"Excuse me, but the call was for ten. Our van did not leave until twenty after this, and now it is ten and thirty-five. I am telling the proper person that I am not responsible for lateness because the van did not leave on schedule." Otto's lips were drawn tight, and his mustache glistened golden red in the sunlight.

"Otto, we won't start until Bill arrives and Bill is always late. Would you like a cigarette?"

"Thank you, no."

Otto strode back across the patio to Ariela and Holgar, who had just arrived. As Otto babbled furiously in German to the towering Holgar, Ariela, ignored by the men, walked away.

"Well?" Gerald said, as she reached the table.

"Well what?" asked Ariela, smiling.

"What went on last night? Anything?"

"Oh, buy me a coffee and I'll tell you everything."

Gerald rushed to the counter in the little canteen, excited by the prospect of a gossip with Ariela after his solitary morning. He returned, placed the tiny cup of espresso on the table, and sat beside her.

"Well, I'm the only one sleeping with anyone so far, if that's what you want to know."

"That's hardly news."

"But only half a time."

"Half a time?"

"I don't want to be anybody's *girlfriend*."

"So what was the half?"

Ariela laughed. "Oh, you know. The disappointment

would have killed him, so I let him—a little—while I napped."
She laughed again.

"And what happened at dinner? Anything?"

"Do you mean did I let him . . . ?"

"No! What was the restaurant like? Did anyone hook up? I saw Zuzie and Ian eyeing each other at lunch."

"Oh, that one."

"Who, Ian?"

"Well, him, too, in those stupid airline slippers, but I meant *Zu*-zie." Ariela offered Gerald a grotesque imitation of the girl's smile. "'I am so pleased to have been asked to perform in the company of the great William Weiss.' Bill's going to hate her. Have you seen him? Is he here yet?"

"No, not yet. What was the restaurant like?"

"You'll like it, Gerald. Old waiters, very slow, but it's got an outdoor garden and they bring lots of wine to the table. Everyone got very drunk."

"Ian, too?"

"Of course. He asked where you were."

"What did you say?"

"I told him you weren't feeling well."

"What did he say?" Ariela giggled and covered her mouth with her hand. "*What* did he say?" Gerald repeated, trying to keep the annoyance out of his voice.

"He asked, were you taking a geriatric nap."

For a moment Gerald was silent.

"Talentless baggage. How on earth did he get cast in this show?"

"He's just young. He was probably trying to get back at you for putting him down at lunch."

"You noticed that?"

"I notice everything." Ariela sighed and, with eyes closed, tilted her face up to the sun.

The company waited at the Palazzo dell'Arte full of anxiety and anticipation. The first rehearsal of any play always held uncertainties—unfamiliar faces, the director's concept for the play, the first displays of "talent"—but a William Weiss production carried even more unknowns. There were, as yet, no scripts with which the performers could have familiarized themselves. Due to the abstract nature of the work, the roles the actors played or danced, even the lines, developed as the piece developed.

Some preliminary work had been done. In the winter, Bill had flown to Sicily to conduct workshops with local actors from Palermo. A title, a concept, a cast size had been roughed out. There were rumors of special effects: helicopters; explosions; angels; George Washington crossing the Delaware; Cerberus, dog from hell. But Gerald knew any original concepts or designs were subject to change. In fact, he suspected Bill's real efforts only began under the pressure of an opening and the preliminaries were smoke screens sent up to assuage the money people.

By one o'clock, the rehearsal had still not begun. The actors sat around the small tables in front of the canteen, huddled under the shade of umbrellas, waiting to be told—anything. Hot, hungry, hungover, and jet-lagged, most remained silent and sat motionless. Even Timothy, who worried a great deal about unscheduled time, sat utterly still at the table with Ariela and Gerald, his hands folded in his lap, a faraway expression on his face.

At two-thirty, as the actors, on the brink of mutiny, talked of returning to the motel, three small cars and a minivan were spotted, slowly winding up the road toward the palazzo. Voices and laughter echoed up the hill.

"Hardly Bill's traveling style," Gerald muttered to Ariela.

The vehicles disappeared around the side of the building. Car doors could be heard opening and closing, and soon groups of young Italians began arriving on the patio until about twenty-five or thirty people clustered at the far end. They remained there, glancing over without making real contact, as if they feared they might be asked to leave. A less spontaneous chatter, the studied way they placed their bags along the wall, readjusted their clothing, suggested they knew they were being observed.

The heat inspired a variety of sensual gestures: shoes were removed, buttons undone, skirts fanned, and long hair held off the neck. The women took out mirrors, applied lipstick, and brushed their hair.

"There are so many of them," Ariela whispered. "They must have really been crammed into those little cars."

"And they must be dancers," Gerald said, "or actors. I can tell from the bags; they've brought their warm-up clothes."

"I bet they're the actors from Palermo that Bill used in the winter workshop."

"They're gorgeous," Gerald said in a reverent tone.

The Sociale group scattered around the little tables stared silently.

A handsome young man with a shirt open to the waist posed shamelessly with one leg up on the stone wall. Finally, another man with a shaved head, wearing a black silk T-shirt and a gold loop in his ear, ventured toward the seated group and addressed them in Italian. Though Gerald could not understand what was actually said, Zuzie's answer, also in Italian, sounded full of innuendo. But when she pointed to the canteen, he realized she'd simply told the man where to buy coffee.

The man seemed pleased and shouted something back to his fellows, who responded with expressions of relief and headed toward the canteen.

Gerald, unable to take his eyes off the Italians, noticed Ariela watching him.

"See something you like, Auntie?"

"See something, Jrr-al?" Timothy repeated.

"No, Timothy," said Gerald, pulling his attention away, "your friend Ariela is just being a bitch."

"No she not," said Timothy, anxiously pulling on his hands. "Ariela's not. She's not, Jrr-al."

"Yes I am, Timothy," Ariela said, laughing.

A tiny fellow approached their table. Though small, he was not at all boyish. His stubble-shadowed jaw, craggy features, and short hair made him look like a convict in miniature, and his velvet vest and animal-patterned shirt suggested "boutique." Staring at the cigarette Gerald had just lit, the man waved two little fingers of his tiny priest's hands in front of his lips. After he got his cigarette, he pointed at Gerald.

"Wheel-yam Whys?" he asked.

"Pardon?" Gerald said.

"Wheel-yam Whys?" he repeated, smiling to expose a gold front tooth.

"No, I am not William Weiss," Gerald said.

The tiny man continued to stare.

"I said, I am *not* William Weiss." Gerald glanced up at some of the Italians who were filtering back from the canteen armed with coffees and sodas.

"He want to know if you *work* for William Weiss," explained a woman standing nearby. She was older than the others, about Gerald's age. Her arresting features were accented by bright splashes of color. Above her small almond-shaped eyes, the brows had been plucked and redrawn in auburn arches, her lips were dark red, her nose was broad and pierced through the nostril, and her hair, straight and parted in the middle, was hennaed an unnatural magenta. She muttered something to the little man, whose name was Ernesto, then dismissed him with a wave of her hand.

"Holgar's pouting; I've got to go," Ariela said abruptly. She cast a disapproving glance at the woman as she got up. Timothy followed her.

"Hello, I'm Gerald," he said, "would you like to sit down?"

"I am Mima," said the woman, accepting an abandoned chair. She pulled a cigarette from her bag. As Gerald extended a lit match, he noticed a large mosquito feeding on his forearm. Before he could react, the woman squashed the thing with a little slap.

"Shit," he said, rubbing the spot where a welt was already beginning to rise.

"Oh, you have another on your leg. Let me," Mima said. She removed a tube from her bag and began to rub ointment on a red bump above his knee.

How Italian, he thought (though he'd known few Italians), this complete stranger is massaging unguent into my thigh without the slightest hesitation. He noticed Ian watching.

A young woman, bursting with intention, appeared on the bright patio and began to count heads. It was impossible not to watch her. Her small sharp features and tiny eyes were upstaged by a pair of huge designer-frame glasses that gave her face an impoverished look and she nervously fingered the whistle hanging around her neck.

"I'm Bonnie, the stage manager for *Rivers, Saints, Space*," she announced in a clipped schoolmarm tone. "Actors, you are to report immediately to the theater where you will be given a three-by-five index card. You will print your name and contact number on the card, which you will return to me. I will then take a Polaroid of each of you. We will do this quickly before William Weiss arrives for the auditions."

The mention of the director's name sent the Italians into a flurry of animated conversation. Panic joined the stew of tension already governing the young woman's face as she realized half her audience didn't speak English. She began again. "Eh—Io—vene . . ." Mima came to her rescue with a translation, and the people on the porch began to gather their belongings.

"We will talk again later, yes," Mima said to Gerald.

"Yes, sure," Gerald said, forcing a smile.

At the stage manager's mention of an audition, his blood had turned to ice. He found himself more anxious than when his plane dropped twenty feet in midair.

Though Gerald knew it unlikely he would not be cast after being flown to Sicily, the thought of auditioning in front of everyone—even auditioning for a part he already had—filled him with terror. Gerald was never the type of actor at home as the center of attention. As a youngster, he never showed a precocity for mimicry or broad physical humor, was never an extrovert or a person you noticed at a party, the guy with the "bigger than life" personality. Gerald was the type of actor for whom acting is overcoming: the stutterer who sings, the diminutive fellow who becomes an action hero, the painfully shy teenager who stars in his class play. Gerald was all those things. Small (in his junior year he shot up to five seven), he stuttered on b's and p's and surprised everyone by appearing in plays.

To some extent acting *did* help overcome his challenges. Through dance training and fencing his posture improved and he seemed taller, and his stutter disappeared completely. And though the terror of being in front of an audience never left him, he grew facile at hiding his fear. In fact, he sometimes felt the extraordinary effort needed to overcome fear gave his performance an edge that raised him above the mundane.

Gerald entered the theater through the big wooden door where the stage manager stood sentry, trying to hurry the actors. The change in light, from the relentlessly sunny courtyard into the dark cathedrallike space, made him light-headed. An oval saucer of light shimmered on the marble floor, its source a mystery until Gerald was able to focus on the yellow, mote-filled rays of sunlight slanting down from a domed skylight high above.

Voices instinctively dropped to whispers as the actors explored the big open space. At one end of the room, a pair of floor fans had been set up on either side of a sawhorse table. Techies—members of the technical crew—organized papers and put out glasses and pitchers of water.

Despite the fans, the heat inside was stifling until two garage-sized doors at the rear were pushed open, letting in more air and light and revealing a back patio of flattened dirt. Beyond the patio the hill continued up another fifty feet.

"Ladies and gentlemen, signori and signore, please take an index card," Bonnie the stage manager said. "Mister Weiss will be here soon—*pronto.*

The Italians began to change into rehearsal clothes. Gerald was used to a lack of modesty among actors, but marveled that this group of newcomers—both the men and the women—was so unselfconscious. Tights were pulled on, underwear taken off and replaced with dance belts. Actors prepared. Ian and Zuzie were locked in a concentrated stare while doing a mirror exercise. A group of Italians had formed a circle and were on all fours, going through the contractions and releases of the Graham technique. The man who had posed with his foot on the wall, in spandex shorts, used a pillar to perform barre exercises. His movements had an undertone of sexual intent.

The sight of so many beautiful bodies made Gerald feel physically ill, or as if he'd been punched in the stomach, and he busied himself in his knapsack. Gerald noticed Mima watching him from across the room and avoided her gaze.

Bonnie handed out index cards.

"I'll fill out a card, but I won't be auditioning," Gerald told her, holding the card like a soiled Kleenex between two fingertips.

"Why not?" she asked.

"I've already been cast in the show. You're an American. Did they bring you over and ask you to *try out* for your stage manager job?" Gerald said, with false calm.

"Mr. Weiss wishes *everyone* to participate in the selection process," she said.

"We'll see," he said, returning her glare with a smile.

He'd worked for Bill for fifteen years and never knew what the man wanted, how dare this woman presume to know. But still, he worried he'd overstepped himself. In the School for Life, displays of ego (other than Bill's) were not tolerated. Even the brightest lights dimmed in the glare of the director's genius.

Bill had lured one Scandinavian actress, a Great Legend, back to the stage with daily bouquets of white roses and blatant flattery. In performance, he bathed her in lights of every conceivable hue, from every direction, gave her miraculous costume changes aided by an army of dressers, harnessed her, flew her twenty feet in the air for a final speech delivered amid a sea of floating stars, and yet the reviews only gave her brief mention after the lights, the costumes, the set, and of course, the direction. Only one famous opera diva had held her own. And she was so enormous that not only could she not be flown, it was a cruelty to ask her to walk. She could stand, and she could sing, and neither mammoth sets, nor brilliantly constructed clothes, hid her great size or distracted from the heavenly sound of her voice; she was directorproof.

Of course, he just needs to see us all together, it's not really an audition, Gerald reasoned. He stared at his index card. His mouth felt dry and metallic. What can he have us do, for God's sake? There are no scripts.

But Gerald was familiar with Bill's working methods. They would each be asked to perform some ordinary movement in an absurdly specific time: "tie your shoe in three minutes and ten seconds," "scratch your ear for two minutes and thirty seconds," "do nothing for six minutes." He discouraged *acting*, by which he meant anything presentational. "Just walk," or "just sit," he often admonished.

The prospect of acting or *not* acting in front of the others filled Gerald with dread. Nowadays, he felt less capable in nearly every aspect of his life and worried his long association with Bill placed him under particular scrutiny from the rest of the company. Besides, his stomach felt awful. Tales of toilet trauma and public humiliations due to incontinence were accepted lore within the HIV community. Why had he put himself in this dreadful situation when he could have stayed at home, in his own apartment, near his own toilet?

So far Gerald had found only one public men's room in the palazzo. There must be another, more private facility and he was leaving the theater to look for it when Bonnie stopped him.

"You must get your picture taken," she said, directing Gerald to stand behind a line of white tape. Don't smile, he told himself. The girl stapled the undeveloped picture to his card and returned it, but Gerald didn't even glance at the Polaroid. He was in no mood to see himself looking pale, gaunt, and lipless with frightening red eyes. He was nearly at the door, when William Weiss walked in.

Gerald moved behind a marble pillar. He had forgotten how imposing the director was. At six feet four, William Weiss was not only the tallest person in the room, but he carried with him an air of urgency—in the manner of the continually late—that demanded attention. His hair had thinned and he was heavier, but freshly shaved and in a double-breasted sports coat worn over jeans, he looked even more handsome and well groomed than Gerald remembered. As he passed by the pillar, Gerald caught the familiar scent of expensive cologne.

Four men and a woman trailed behind Bill like ducklings. Though Gerald had not met the designers and the production staff, he'd always made a point of learning the names of those important people before he began a show, and now, he could guess who was who. The balding, rather handsome middle-aged man in the expensive linen suit, who beamed generously around the room, must be Fernando Arcuri, the producer. The woman next to him with hair dyed blue-black, pierced nostrils, and armored with silver jewelry was probably Annalisa, the assistant producer; Gerald had spoken to her over the phone in New York. A crumpled professorial type carrying books must be Martin Lustinger, the dramaturg, and Gerald guessed the pale nervous man with white-blond hair was Lars Einder, the agoraphobic Swedish artist Bill had lured over to build set pieces (Ariela said he was a genius, and that he lived with his mother). By elimination, the heavyset man with the wild look in his eyes had to be the costume designer, Jean Donnett, who had a reputation for being brilliant and difficult.

The actors stopped their warm-ups. The sharp clip of Bill's stride could be heard on the marble floor. When he stopped suddenly, those following were caught in comic near-collisions. All movement ceased; the sole sound in the room was the low whir of the electric fans. Only Bill, glancing about casually, acted normal. In an ill-judged move, Bonnie approached.

"Mr. Weiss, I've collected Polaroids of all the actors."

Bill made a sharp half-turn away from her and spoke softly. "These tables are in the wrong place."

A buzz arose among the production team. Orders were given in harsh whispers. Assistants lifted the long plywood tops and sawhorse supports and waited as Bill walked slowly to the center of the room, stopped, executed a military turn, and began a measured pace. Turning again, he surveyed the space and gave a single nod. The production assistants hurriedly placed the table in its new position.

Other adjustments were made. A choice was made for silence over comfort, so the fans were turned off and an ashtray found so Bill could smoke (though Bonnie shook her finger at one of the Italians who started to light up).

The well-dressed producer sat on one side of Bill and the dramaturg on the other. All faces turned toward Bill.

Gerald continued to watch from the shadow of the pillar. He had witnessed the fuss, the manufactured tension, and the kowtowing subordinates many times before, and as a School for Life actor, he'd felt a guilty thrill to be part of it. But after he'd attended the deathbeds of so many friends, the offstage drama began to seem unreal, even repellent.

The other actors, even Ariela, stared at Bill with reverent attention. As Gerald watched from the shadow of the pillar, he felt only tired and detached. Sitting at the center of the anxious production staff, Bill looked like Christ in an artist's rendering of the Last Supper.

And only one apostle is missing, Gerald thought. It is I, Judas Iscariot.

Bill nodded to the producer, and Fernando Arcuri rose and introduced himself. He had a neatly clipped beard, a steady smile.

"You have come from Germany, America, Sweden, France, and from our own Palermo, and I welcome you," he said. Gerald glanced around, wondering who among them was French, and remembered Jean, the costume designer. "I am so

very flattered, to have so many fine performers auditioning—
and it is my deep regret that not everyone can be in the play."

The Italians turned to each other with quizzical looks.
When a translation of the producer's words was given in Italian,
they seemed even more uncertain, and a brave man with curly
salt-and-pepper hair spoke up.

"We have understood, Signore Arcuri, that for those of us
who rehearsed with Mr. Weiss in December, the roles were
guaranteed," he said.

The producer answered the man in Italian, and though Gerald
couldn't understand the words, he understood the content: "I'm
so sorry for the misunderstanding. If it were only up to me I
would hire each and every one of you, et cetera, et cetera."

The Italian actors looked at each other as if one of them
might have a remedy for this inequity. How had this misunderstanding occurred? Gerald knew Bill handed out roles like party
favors, and he'd obviously been doing the same thing since the
roles were guaranteed to Italian actors in December. But the
cast for the festival production was limited by budget consider-
ations, and for each German or American invited to Sicily, an
Italian actor would lose a job.

"Five minutes," Bonnie announced.

As Gerald walked past Mima, she shook her hennaed head.

"Terrible, terrible," she said.

"I know," Gerald said, feeling the inadequacy of his reply
as he hurried off to find his bathroom.

Bill didn't bother to lower his voice when he forgot an actor's
name. "What's that one's name, again?" he asked Bonnie. She
referred to a Polaroid.

"Ginger," she said.

"Ginger, get on all fours and bark like a dog?"

Annalisa, the assistant producer, had taken over as translator. When she repeated Bill's direction, Ginger, a short, stocky redhead, shrugged her shoulders, got down on all fours and began to bark convincingly.

"Thank you," Bill said, interrupting her.

The girl got up and rejoined the actors.

Those who hadn't been called looked anxiously at the table where Bonnie drew another Polaroid and handed it to Bill.

"Antonio Tambella?"

"Yes, here."

A thin young man with a ponytail walked into the middle of the room and stood facing the table.

"Do you speak English, Antonio?"

"Yes, Mr. Weiss, a little," he said, seriously.

"Good. Can you walk in a circle?"

Antonio walked deliberately, carefully placing one foot in front of the other.

"A bigger circle," called Bill, "now skip."

The young man, unfamiliar with the word "skip," looked at Annalisa who repeated the command in Italian.

His skip was slow and methodical, and his arms flew out as he lurched from side to side.

"Skip bigger," Bill shouted, "cover more space."

Antonio grew more serious in his attempt to skip and more awkward until he looked as if he would lose his balance and fall to the floor.

"Thank you, Tony," Bill said, writing something on the back of the man's Polaroid, as he glumly joined the others.

Bonnie handed Bill the next Polaroid. He stared at it for a moment, then smiled. He looked over the actors sitting in a semicircle. "Hi, Gerald. Here's one for your scrapbook."

"That flattering, huh?" Gerald said.

"Would you like to see?" Bill asked.

"No, thanks."

Bill looked at the picture again and laughed. "I could hold this for blackmail."

"I think I still have the one of you from the *White Box* cast party."

"No!" Bill screamed. "No! Don't you dare!" He turned to the surprised stage manager. "What did I tell you, Bonnie? Gerald Barnett is the nastiest person on earth!"

During his years at the School for Life, Gerald's exchanges with Bill had taken on the character of a vaudeville routine or a spat between an old married couple.

Gerald was proudly aware of the other actors studying him. Who was this man who could joke with William Weiss?

"How was your trip?" Bill asked, leaning back in his chair.

"Long," said Gerald, walking onto the playing area as he labored to calm himself.

"Okay, Gerald, I know you know how to do this. I want you to come out of a house, pick a rose, and smell it," Bill said, "in three and a half minutes."

Gerald knew his hands were shaking and his breathing was shallow, but experience had taught him that an audience rarely sees the nerves beneath an actor's studied calm. He walked away from the table, turned and began the actions, careful to keep his movement simple, avoid anything sentimental.

"Do it again, that was too fast," Bill said.

Gerald stood with his back to Bill for a moment to catch his breath and let the tension drain from his muscles. As he turned to repeat the movement, the School for Life performance style seemed to take over his body. He reached for the rose in a slow, meditative movement, brought it up to his nose in a count of thirty.

"Okay," Bill said quietly, "good. Three minutes and twenty seconds."

The actors were quiet as Gerald returned to his seat. He tried to remember what he'd just done. But it's all so ridiculous, he thought, I could do the same thing tomorrow and Bill will hate it.

After the auditions, they were given a ten-minute break. Bill was gone when they were called back. Bonnie read the cast names of *Rivers, Saints, Space.* It was no surprise that all the actors staying at the Sociale were in the play. An Italian actress not called cried on Mima's shoulder. Others gathered their things in a defeated silence. Daryl announced that the van back to the Sociale was leaving. Gerald, shaking with fatigue, gathered his things and followed Holgar and Ariela out of the theater.

CHAPTER FIVE

The following day, Bill came into the theater with Martin Lustinger and Lars Einder. The three men sat at the long table, and Bill began to "sketch" out the play for the company, drawing each scene on individual sheets of paper. An overhead projector cast a reflection of his hand working across the page, lit and magnified, upon a darkened wall. With amazing speed and virtuosity, shadows were built by smears of graphite, or a scene peopled with quick swipes of a kneaded eraser. The presentation was, in itself, a performance, a wordless summation of the play.

Nearly wordless. The title of each scene was announce— "The Prophesy," "Cupid and Psyche," "Armageddon," "Hell of a Party"—by Martin, who offered an approximation of the action.

"Here, you see, Satan mingles with the guests at a fin de siècle Hell of a Party . . ."

Some of the listeners, especially the Italians, were confused by the narration, and glanced questioningly at each other, wondering if they'd missed a crucial detail. The actors more familiar with Bill's work, expecting nothing so dismal as a plot, stared at the screen as he sketched.

Daryl, looking more like a bodyguard than a personal assistant, stood behind Bill. He wore white cotton gloves, disposable "art handlers," to protect the drawings from the natural oil of the skin, as he removed them from the projector and placed them in labeled folders. All Bill's artwork, letters, and notes had market value and not even the most casual doodle was thrown away where it might be retrieved by someone hoping to own or sell a drawing, a scribble, or a relic from the hand of William Weiss.

"The moon falls, the earth opens, and the sky is drenched with blood," Martin explained.

"I think the actors should all come crawling out like giant toddlers, in this scene," Bill said to Lars.

The Swede smiled, and his face turned bright red. "Yes? Like babies?"

"Like babies with big heads," Bill said, "*enormous* heads."

"How many heads?" Lars asked.

"One for each actor."

"I could make a prototype in clay and you could look at it," said Lars, clasping his hands, pushing them into his lap and looking like a happy baby himself. "I go now to order the clay." He got up and hurried out of the theater.

When the drawing for the last scene was complete, Bill's hand withdrew from the projected square, and he placed the pencil on the table. Martin, unaware of the finality of this gesture, unwisely continued. "Psyche implores Venus, mother of Cupid—"

"Shhhh!" Bill hissed.

"—to permit her to couple—marry—with her son—Venus's son—Psyche."

"Shhhhhhhh!"

The room was quiet. For several seconds, the actors sitting on the marble floor and the production staff seated at the table stared at the completed drawing, as much to avoid looking at the fuming dramaturg as to view the sketch. The penciled images appeared kinetic, as if the deft hand of the artist continued to mold and form the setting, backdrop, and characters in the scene. The moment was broken when Annalisa approached the table, handed Bill a fax, and he rose to his feet and left the theater, the sound of his shoes clipping sharply on the marble floor.

Bill did not return for the rest of the morning, leaving the actors in a state of limbo. Bonnie chided them not to venture too far off, since rehearsal "might resume in the very near future." Gerald sat against the wall and opened his travel book, *The Ambassadors* by Henry James, but the circumlocutious sentences had a narcotic effect that made his eyes heavy and his chin fall toward his chest, until finally, the book fell to his lap, and he dropped off to sleep. At one P.M., with no sign of the director's return, Bonnie released the actors for lunch, reminding them to be back at two sharp, when "Mr. Weiss will stage the Prologue."

True to her word, Bill was waiting when Eunice ran out to alert the smokers and strays in the courtyard. "He's here! He's here!"

Martin Lustinger was waiting, too, and anxious to begin his explanation of the Prologue, in which the destruction of the world, or of Sicily, or of society—it wasn't clear which—was prophesied. As he spoke, Bill picked up the microphone that had arrived during the break and tapped it ominously with his fingernail. The dramaturg, alerted by the electronic click, glanced over, but once again, he had warmed to his subject and continued speaking.

"You see, the predictions in the Prologue echo the final scene of the play in which 'things fall apart, the center can not hold, mere anarchy is loosed upon the world,' and we have, as in the Yeats poem, a second coming, but in this case, the Christ figure is a hermaphrodite, not 'a shape with lion body, and . . .'"

Bill studied the microphone in his hand as if he'd never seen one before. He turned it upside down, then pointed it at the actors, sitting in a semicircle around the table, as if he were hosing them down. Slowly, as if he were executing one of his own exercises—*in seventy seconds!*—he raised it to his lips.

"Martin," he said softly but, with the amplification, to great effect.

Martin Lustinger paused, reached for his pack of cigarettes, found it empty and crushed it in his hand.

"This, you see, was the very first recorded case," he went on, refusing to look at Bill, "predating, of course, the Bible, of the foretelling of destruction on such a level, an Armageddon, if you will—"

"Martin! Fewer words."

Bill's second amplified command was followed by a long silence during which the dramaturg took a last drag on a dangerously short cigarette before angrily stubbing it.

"The seers predict the fucking end of everything—how is that?" he shouted into the tabletop.

"Seers?" Bill repeated. Martin looked up.

"The prophets, I explained all this to you when—"

"Men prophets or women prophets?"

"Men in this case, because—"

"Can I see all the men up here, please."

Gerald felt his heart racing as he joined the line of actors. It hardly matters if I'm chosen, he told himself. But his entire career had been based on being chosen, holding on as others were eliminated.

. "How many prophets are there in the scene?" Bill asked.

"Five," Martin snapped.

"Seven is better," Bill said.

Gerald needn't have worried. After eliminating the actors who were in the following scene and therefore not able to make the quick costume change, he was one of only six available men. Bill turned to Bonnie and pointed toward a woman standing off to the side.

"Who is that one in the blue tights?" His amplified voice echoed through the cavernous room.

"Eunice," the woman in tights responded cheerfully.

"Eunice, can you be a prophet?"

"Ooh, I can't see why not, Mr. Weiss," she replied.

Gerald recognized her Midlands accent from a college dialect class he'd taken twenty-five years ago. She must be the British wife of Vito, he'd heard the couple ran a ballet/mime school in Palermo.

"Good," Bill said, "so we have seven prophets." He pulled a clean sheet from a stack of paper and began to draw.

"Mr. Weiss? Shall I release the others?" Bonnie asked.

"They should each be sitting on the side of a mountain," Bill muttered, still drawing.

"Seven mountains?" asked Martin, incredulously.

"Yes," Bill said.

"Mr. Weiss, you understand we have to clear the Prologue set for the next scene?" Bonnie asked.

When Bill stood, the microphone fell to the marble floor with a loud electronic bang that made the room gasp in unison.

"Well, they won't be real mountains—it's a play! Daryl, note to Lars: Seven mountains." Bill gathered up a pile of recent faxes, handed them to Daryl, still in his white art-handlers, and asked, "What do these say?" as he left the room.

"Take five!" Bonnie announced.

As the other actors went to their bags to get drinks and snacks, or went outside to smoke, Gerald wandered over to the table and picked up the drawing. In the middle of the page was a small conical mountain, so perfectly rendered it looked the archetype of a mountain. A long graphite shadow was smudged along the bottom. On the side of—and nearly as big as—the mountain, sat a figure defined by a few firm lines. The play would open with seven onstage mountains, and he, Gerald, would be sitting on top of one of them.

"Have I shown you my mosquito bites, Ariela?" Gerald asked.

Bill had not returned to the theater in the afternoon, and the actors were dismissed for an early dinner. Gerald sat with Ariela and Holgar at the Arco Bellina, at a small table in an outdoor dining area under a trellis of plastic grapevines and dusty grapes.

The restaurant was one of two in Bellina that accepted the food vouchers given to the actors as part of their per diem. The other restaurant was in many ways nicer, and the food better, but Bill and the producers ate there, and the company, in unspoken accord, chose to eat at the Arco Bellina.

"Yes, Gerald, you've shown me your bites—twice," Ariela said.

"But you seem so underwhelmed. Holgar, what do you think of these?" Gerald asked, turning in his chair to lift his shirt to expose a patch of bright pink spots.

"Ach," Holgar replied.

"I knew you'd be impressed." Gerald turned back to grin at Ariela.

His cavalier manner hid real concern. No one else seemed to suffer quite as much from the mosquitoes, while his torso was a patchwork of red welts. Was he being a baby? He worried over any mark, any discomfort—a lingering cold, a skin discoloration—anything that might signal one of the ugly infections visited upon a compromised immune system. He hoped Ariela would tease him out of this hypochondria, tell him to stop being silly, these were only mosquito bites. They *were* only mosquito bites, weren't they?

Ariela offered neither scorn nor sympathy. She was in a somber, asocial mood. Small wonder, thought Gerald, watching Holgar stare toward the kitchen in anticipation of the next course.

Zuzie, Otto, Ian, and Timothy, the only other diners on the restaurant patio, sat a few tables away, and Zuzie's tinkling laugh floated over.

"I *hate* that woman," Ariela said, setting her fork down with finality, a sound which alerted Holgar to transfer his gaze from the kitchen door to her unfinished pasta.

Gerald glanced over. Zuzie was encouraging Timothy to taste the wine. Timothy preferred his orange Fanta, but had difficulty denying any request, especially one from a pretty girl.

All afternoon, Zuzie and Timothy had played Gotcha on the patio of the palazzo, Zuzie tiptoeing up to surprise him with a tickle and a "gotcha," sending Timothy racing down the patio, flapping his hands and squealing with laughter. Moments later, he'd return, pretending not to notice her, until she repeated the "surprise," and he repeated his run with renewed terror and pleasure.

The game, especially Timothy's enthusiasm, so undiminished by repetition, made everyone laugh. It also lent Zuzie status as the odd Timothy's playmate and provided her an opportunity to show off, in the blameless scenario of a child's game, her skills as a coquette.

Ian looked over—had he sneered?—and looked away. Gerald heard voices and turned to see the Italian actors enter the restaurant, filling the little outdoor patio with the melody of their voices. When the waiter came out of the kitchen, Eunice's husband, Vito, the enthusiastic man with curly salt-and-pepper hair who had spoken out at the auditions, stepped forward, and the group quieted.

Vito carried on an intense but civilized conversation with the waiter. How clichéd the expressive hand gestures would appear executed by actors playing Italians, Gerald thought. The waiter's reply was accompanied by similar gestures.

"This is not good," Ariela whispered.

"What's going on?" Gerald asked.

"The producers haven't given them vouchers to eat, like they've given us, and they're saying that since they will need to come here every night after rehearsal, they want the restaurant to give them a discount."

"Why didn't they get vouchers?"

"Fernando says, since they live in Palermo, they can eat at home."

"But Palermo is an hour and a half drive from here."

"I know," Ariela agreed, "and because of that they've had to rent an apartment in Bellina—which I'm sure must be crowded and uncomfortable."

The waiter, apparently unmoved by their plight, returned to the kitchen. Vito turned back to the group. He raised his hands in a gesture of defeat. The Italians wore the same grim expressions they'd had at the "audition."

"Wait," Ariela said, "I've got plenty of vouchers."

"But those must last us till the end of our time here," Holgar objected.

Ariela picked up her wallet and went to where the Italians still stood near the entrance. She took out a handful of vouchers and presented them to Vito.

"Here, these will cover your meals for tonight."

"No, it is not possible, we cannot take them," Vito said.

Gerald was standing next to Ariela holding out his vouchers. Zuzie, after explaining the situation to her table, came over, followed by Ian, Otto, and Timothy. The Italians would only take enough vouchers for the evening's meal.

"We will all go to Fernando tomorrow and you will get your vouchers."

Only Holgar remained seated, polishing off Ariela's pasta.

CHAPTER SIX

G erald lay awake on his thin mattress and arched his back
to reach a mosquito bite between his shoulder blades.
After five days in Sicily, his arms, legs, and torso were a calendar
of bites. The most recent puffed up into symmetrical pink hills
on the landscape of his flesh. Earlier ones oozed miniscule
amounts of . . . *something,* which formed crusty motes he periodically removed with a fingernail.

A soft dawn light filtered through the pebbled glass of the
bathroom window—the only window—and through the
wooden slats of the door. It was still too early to get up, and he lay
on the paisley print sheet stewing over his situation. Around two
A.M., Daryl had staggered into the room giggling and swearing as
he knocked over a chair and tripped over a suitcase on his way to
bed. No sooner had Gerald fallen back to sleep, than Timothy's
trumpetlike snores roused him again, and he'd dragged himself
up off his thin mattress to tug at Timothy's shoulder. Timothy
rolled to his side, and the snoring softened to a nasal rumble, but
by that time Gerald could not get back to sleep.

He'd been unable to have his talk with Bill about getting
his own room. He only saw the director at the theater and

always surrounded by other people. And Bill never appeared to see him. Bill had put off working on the Prologue and began instead with Holgar and Ariela as Cupid and Psyche. Gerald tried to watch the excruciatingly slow rehearsals, but Bill's microdirection of the scene and his frequent absences finally drove him away and most of his days were spent on the porch in front of the Café dell'Arte.

If the other actors were curious about Gerald after his casual repartee with the director, they seemed to lose interest when he chose to sit alone with his nose in a book. And in the evening at the Arco Bellina, when Otto, Zuzie, Ian, Jean the costume designer, Daryl, and the Italians pushed tables together and shared carafes of red wine, rehearsal gossip, and laughter, Gerald, Ariela, and Holgar sat at a table by themselves. Gerald would have preferred to sit alone with Henry James as his only company, but that was too reminiscent of lonely lunches in high school canteenterias. But Gerald left his dinner companions as soon as he was able. He liked the solitary walk back to the Sociale. He also liked to get back to the room before Timothy arrived (Daryl never came home until he was ready to pass out). Back at the empty motel, he could wash with no one waiting for the bathroom and divide up the following day's medication into the plastic compartments of his pill arranger.

Gerald reached under his T-shirt, and let his fingertips glide over the Braille of bumps and sores on his back. They felt worse than yesterday. Might as well get up, take a shower, and check the damage.

Knowing how quickly the temperature turned tepid, he turned on only the hot and stood under the wan dribble of water, wincing as it trickled down his back. After the shower, studying his red, mottled skin in the mirror, he recalled pictures from a medical textbook of skin diseases he'd seen as a child. Beyond a usual childhood fascination with the bizarre, Gerald had wondered about the patients in those photos. Who were they? Poor people? Had they been coerced into posing? Were they told they were helping science? And why had they and not the doctors been struck with such disfigurement? To calm his disquiet he forced himself to imagine after photos in which the woman covered in sores from Hansen's disease was shown clean-skinned and cured, gaily waving at the camera.

He twisted to see as much of the worried flesh as he was able. The raised, angry blotches were an unmistakable sign all was not right with him. At the same time, he felt a seed of relief: with so *actual* a symptom, no one could blame him, or rather he could not blame himself, for seeking the advice of a doctor just for silly mosquito bites. Of course, he was in a part of the world where his disease was probably thought of as divine retribution, but hopefully doctors were not so narrow-minded. Besides, the raised blotches were hideous, and even if he were taken to a quack who applied heated glass suction bulbs and leeches, something had to be done.

When Gerald was dressed, he tiptoed over to Daryl.

"Daryl! Daryl!" he said, shaking his arm. "I need to go up the hill."

"But I'm taking everybody up at eleven, can't you wait?" pleaded Daryl, one hand shielding his eyes from the early daylight.

Gerald, crouching beside the mattress, leaned back to avoid Daryl's breath.

"No. I'm sorry, I have to go up the hill now to talk to someone from the production office."

If Daryl had asked why Gerald needed to talk to someone, Gerald would have gladly shown him the bumps. He was already beginning to doubt his decision and would have welcomed another witness to the gravity of his skin condition. But Daryl, steeped in miserable unrequited love for Ariela, hungover and half-asleep, was the least likely candidate to offer sympathy.

"Okay, okay. I'll meet you by the van," Daryl moaned into the pillow.

On the way up the hill, sprinklers threw off sheets of water as they crept over the vineyards on long metal legs like enormous spiders. The Palazzo dell'Arte appeared empty. The canteen had not yet opened and the theater building was locked, but Annalisa's car was in the parking lot. The overworked producer's assistant always arrived early, before the second-floor suite used as a production office began to hum with incoming faxes and the soft click of computer keys. Gerald got out and thanked Daryl, who nodded briefly before swerving the van round to drive back down the hill.

"Gerald," Annalisa said, when he walked into the production office, "you are up very early, no?"

Petite and in her early thirties, Annalisa had a modest, kindly manner at odds with her appearance. Her tongue, nostrils (on both sides), and the hard cartilage of her ears were studded with silver grommets, and her long straight hair was dyed a harsh blue-black. She had acquired tattoos from her ankles up (a work in progress, she admitted), and she wore silver bracelets, wide silver rings on each finger (including the thumbs), and a silver necklace so heavy it looked more collar than necklace. This aggressive accessorizing, more suited to a rebellious teen, pointed up Annalisa's smallness and emphasized her modesty, directing the eye past the silver chain mail, tattoos, and black helmet of hair to a rather shy, very pretty, and superefficient young woman. Like the kindly wife of the sadistic professor in *Tea and Sympathy*, she was someone to trust while her boss, Fernando Arcuri, was someone to avoid.

"Annalisa, I need to see a doctor."

Before she could respond, Gerald was twisting his back toward her and had pulled his shirt up.

"Poor thing, what do you think is the cause of this?" she asked.

"I don't know. I thought at first it was mosquito bites, but no one else seems to be suffering from them and, well, there are so many." Gerald feared he might begin to cry. "I haven't been sleeping," he said, clearing his throat.

"No, this looks more serious than insect bites." Annalisa rose from behind her desk, came around, and touched him lightly on the side.

Relieved, Gerald sat in a chair while Annalisa called a doctor.

"The line is busy, but his office is in the town and he opens early. Let us just go there now."

During the ride down the hill, they spoke little, but Annalisa cast several sympathetic glances at Gerald and, once, patted his hand. Gerald was flattered by her concern and wondered if the time were right to bring up his need for a single room. No, he thought, but vowed to ask later, when the request could stand alone.

The doctor's waiting room was filled with elderly people who stared at Annalisa and Gerald with frank curiosity. Gerald expected to sit and wait until someone—a nurse probably—came into the room. But Annalisa surprised him by walking directly to the door between the waiting room and the doctor's office and knocking forcefully.

A nurse did appear and frowned, obviously annoyed at the interruption. When Annalisa spoke to her in Italian and gestured toward Gerald, the nurse pointed to the other people in the waiting room. Annalisa turned to the room and spoke in a surprisingly authoritative manner. The old people—cowed or awed by this tattooed Saint Joan—didn't object as Gerald and Annalisa were led into an examining room.

The doctor was as old as his patients. After conferring with Annalisa in Italian, he motioned to Gerald to remove his shirt. Gerald felt perspiration running down his sides, and pressed his arms against the shirt material to absorb the moisture before pulling it off over his head. The doctor, lifting Gerald's elbow, bent close to study the side of his torso where the welts were most prominent.

"*Lui è allergico?*" the doctor asked.

"Penicillin," Gerald replied, but he had to look to Annalisa for a translation of the next question.

"He asks 'Are you taking any medicines?'" she explained.

Another bead of perspiration rolled down Gerald's side. Annalisa, appeared to be studying something in the parking lot just outside the window. He supposed she had removed her attention from the room to give him privacy or, perhaps, to avoid his eyes.

Does she know? he wondered. He remembered an actor friend who worked well into his own sickness being described in a *New York Times* review as "disturbingly gaunt." Does everyone know? Gerald's brain sifted through casual comments of the last days: "How ya doin,' Ger?," "Feelin' okay?," "Sleep well?," "You didn't finish your lunch!" The communal sympathy, if that's what it was, made him feel like a person with a skin disease duped into posing in a medical textbook.

Gerald forgot for a moment that he was shirtless, as he squared his shoulders and looked into the eyes of the elderly doctor whose pen was poised above a manila folder.

"Acyclovir, oral ganciclovir, fluconazole, Bactrim, and a bunch of other pills—and vitamin supplements," he added, to show he took care of himself.

"*Bac-a-trim?*"

"Bactrim," Gerald repeated.

"*Perché?*" the doctor asked.

"For Pneumocystis—"

"*Lui dottore americano,*" Annalisa said before Gerald could finish.

When the doctor answered Annalisa he sounded angry.

"What did he say?" Gerald asked.

"He says if you take this drug and go in the sun, you will have an allergic reaction; he says stop taking the drug."

"He didn't say anything about . . . ?"

"No. Do you need to ask him anything else? And remember, Gerald, you are in a small town of unsophisticated and, often, very superstitious people."

"No," Gerald said, looking at the floor, "nothing else." The doctor prescribed a cortisone cream before they left.

Photosensitive. On the way out, he remembered reading the word on the bottle of Bactrim. Each day he'd been walking up the hill in the early sun. The worse the "bites" had become, the longer he lingered, shirtless, hoping to disguise his ruined skin under a light tan.

Gerald refused Annalisa's offer of a ride back to the Centro Sociale; he didn't want to be alone with her in the car. He didn't mind that she knew of his illness, but she would feel obligated to sympathize, or worse, they would sit in an embarrassed silence.

The Sociale was close by and he stopped at his room to rub himself with the cortisone cream he'd picked up at the *farmacia* and to change into a long-sleeved shirt and long pants. He borrowed a baseball hat from Timothy and left the motel without speaking to anyone.

As he walked up the hill, exhausted from his long morning, the truck carrying field workers passed, but Gerald didn't look up. He felt just as he had when he was in the hospital, like a person from another planet.

Last winter he'd watched, with detachment, as nurses and doctors bristled about with efficiency, and friends—the ones still alive—kissed him on the forehead or cheek, searched for a jar for the flowers they'd bought at the Korean market, or rushed about to get him ice water, lip balm, and another Tylenol (people from *his* planet appeared to live on Tylenol). He was amazed at their energy as they came and went with promises to return and bestowed more kisses and intimate little final waves at the door. His planet, the planet AIDS, was no bigger than the space between his hospital bed and the toilet. He nodded or smiled at the energetic aliens, though he could barely understand them through the atmospheric layers of nausea, inertia, weakness, and the mind-numbing boredom which made up the breathing matter of his world.

Amazingly, he began to get better. Soon, he could hardly remember being ill. Disease became an abstraction, something grave and terminal, something just around the corner, but invisible—for which he took a lot of pills.

Gerald shoved his hands deep in his pockets, shielding them from the poisonous sun.

CHAPTER SEVEN

As soon as Gerald quit taking his drugs, the itching began to abate. In a few days, the angry red welts covering his torso had waned to aspirin-sized moons of harmless pink. In all probability, only one drug had caused the severe skin reaction, but in a liberating gesture, he pushed all the pill bottles to the bottom of a laundry bag, out of sight and, he hoped, out of mind. The flood of guilt he had anticipated after stopping a habitual, possibly life-saving (though he didn't really believe that, did he?), routine never followed. And after a few days, he felt nothing but relief, even a sort of giddy fatalism, which raised his spirits and made him feel more sociable.

Gerald was not, by nature, an asocial person. He wondered now if all his excuses—too exhausting, the age difference, the language thing—boiled down to one: he was vain. Since he'd lost weight, he didn't like the way he looked, and when his skin was bad, he had resisted friendly overtures from the other actors and avoided joining the big group of Italians who ate together at lunch and dinner breaks. Now, he admitted that many of them were attractive, and a couple of them—a couple of the dancers definitely—were gay. Not that anyone's sexual orientation mattered, since he no longer even considered making the leap from attraction to action; those days were over.

To Gerald, the loss of his sexual confidence was, in some ways, more disturbing than the loss of his career—though the two were never mutually exclusive. Acting, especially when he was a young man, was always a form of seduction, from winning the role to "seducing" an audience. And though Gerald had always had sexual relationships with men, he always escorted women to public or business events. He wasn't ashamed of his homosexuality, but he reasoned that a visibly gay man could only attract other gay men, whereas a handsome man with a beautiful woman on his arm, even if his sexuality were in question, might potentially attract women, gays, and even straight men (envy being another form of attraction). And to attract was to succeed in his business. No wonder acting, which required being many things to so many people, was the most closeted of the arts.

When Gerald was in a play—"visible" as he put it—he guarded his reputation by staying away from gay bars (other gay men were the worst gossips) and kept himself free of the emotional entanglements which might require public association with a lover. Celibacy was out of the question, his continual need to prove himself attractive, on or off stage, precluded that sacrifice. Instead, he went out prowling late at night, when fewer people presented less possibility of recognition, cycling across town to cruise along a badly lit stretch of river walk at three A.M. , or following a stranger behind a parked truck in the meatpacking area at dawn. On the few occasions he did go home with someone, he did so only after assuring himself the man couldn't possibly be an agent or casting director, or worse, a fan, and then he gave false, monosyllabic names: Pete, Bo, Hank. If someone asked to see him again, he constructed a biography: "I'm only visiting my uncle," "It's back to Atlanta for me—tomorrow," "Nope. Can't. Live in New Jersey with my wife, but you can give me *your* number." Eventually, as role-playing continued beyond the life of a play and became an erotic end in itself, sex became theater.

It was a relief to be over all that, but lately, in this foreign land, around these young people, he'd felt the familiar ache of physical longing that had been such a driving factor in his life for so many years. He didn't intend to act on his feelings, his marketable years were over, but people seemed to like him. The Italians were always smiling at him, mispronouncing his name, patting him affectionately. Perhaps he'd try on a new role: the older actor, experienced, observant, and unattached to sex. And he'd drink more. He'd been abstemious for too long, and for what? Health? More likely as a self-inflicted punishment for getting ill.

The first thing Gerald needed to do was drop his dinner partners. Holgar and Ariela had become tedious. The couple was not getting on well. Holgar maintained a sturdy stupidity, and Ariela's posture at the table had become even more erect, severe. Gerald, consciously or unconsciously, aped her by pulling himself up in his seat, making his spine rigid, as if he were sitting in the formal dining room of a wealthy grandmother. Since discovering the sun was his enemy, he even dressed the part, covering his mottled skin, even in the Sicilian summer heat, with long pants and long-sleeved shirts buttoned to the neck. If his eye wandered to another table to watch the animated chatter of a Giovanni or a Letizia, it did not stray long. A head of brilliant black hair gelled back after the day's rehearsal, dark chest hair peeking out from under an open shirt, or the wine-glow of an olive complexion had the unsettling effect of a sucker punch.

Gerald thought of all this while he and Ariela sat with their coffee in the courtyard of the Sociale, under the warm rays of the morning sun. They were always the first ones up, and Gerald did relish this peaceful time of day, along with the strong coffee and reassuring gossip. Maybe he didn't have to break off all ties with his friend, but tonight he would join the Italians at the long table.

"No! No! No! Not a sound! Not one sound!"

It was nearly three and the actors were starving. Bill sat behind the long table with his arms folded. The stage manager sat beside him, bent over her production book. As Bill placed the pencil with which he'd been idly drawing on the table, she snatched it up and stuck it into an electric sharpener.

"Shhhhhh!" hissed Bill. "Do that outside!"

The entire cast was assembled for Hell of a Party, the scene described by Martin as a fin de siècle party attended by a dark angel. The women were to be dressed in evening gowns with feathered headdresses, the men in black tie. For the rehearsal, the actors borrowed approximations of their costumes from wardrobe. Zuzie had fashioned a headband from a scarf and stuck in it a peacock feather. Ariela pulled her rehearsal skirt up to chest level so it resembled an empire-waist tunic. Gerald wore a tuxedo jacket over his T-shirt. Bill blocked under the watchful eye of a video camera.

"Ginger, turn to Otto. Zuzie, throw a drink in Holgar's face, Timothy, sing 'Somewhere Over the Rainbow.' "

Timothy, the dark angel, wore a black graduation gown. His black wings were being assembled, feather by feather, in wardrobe. He began with off-key passion, "Some . . . *where*." The "where," two octaves above the "some," came out in a weird screech.

"Timothy," Bill said, raising his hand to stop the song, "sing very quietly, like there are a lot of people around and you're talking to yourself, but you don't want them to hear you."

"Huh?" Timothy said, cocking his head like the RCA dog in front of the gramophone.

Bill walked onto the playing area and stood beside him. He began the song in a voice so low it could barely be heard. "Now you try it," he said.

Timothy had understood what Bill wanted from watching him. He began to sing in the same passionate manner, but quietly, as if he were whispering. The tempo was quick, the tune surreal, and when he asked in the final line of the song, "If happy little bluebirds fly beyond the rainbow why, oh why, can't I?" the effect was eerily heartbreaking.

When Timothy finished, Bill said, "Letizia. Scream!"

She uttered a polite shriek.

"Louder!" Bill commanded. "More!"

She shrieked out a bloodcurdling, horror-film scream. The actors responded with nervous giggles. Gerald understood Bill's method. Timothy had sung with touching conviction and Letizia's scream put an effective period on the emotional effect. Sentimentality was a color Bill never let dominate his canvas.

"Gerald! Laugh!" Bill commanded.

"Do what?" Gerald asked.

As Satan in a church play, he'd been required to throw his head back and laugh demonically in God's face and the experience had left him laughterphobic—on the stage, anyway. Despite years of practice, diaphragmatically pumping out ha's, he's, and ho's, his stage laugh still sounded, to his ears, grossly inauthentic.

"Laugh!" Bill repeated, "Now!"

Gerald bellowed out a stagy baritone stutter of "ha-ha"s, and felt humiliated.

"Awful! Just laugh," Bill said, turning his attention to another player. "Enzo! Jump on the table. Say, 'I am.'"

Enzo had a large nose, thick lips, and a low prominent forehead, which gave him a brooding or, to be less kind, Cro-Magnon look. He was one of the sun worshippers on the palazzo patio, and over the last couple of weeks his coloring had gone from olive to aubergine, his skin becoming nearly as dark as his curly, close-cropped hair.

He was a large man, but his upper torso appeared frail or fragile compared to the thick muscularity of his lower body—a dancer's build, but undancerly in his ponderous, anxiety-ridden stage manner. Enzo spoke little English, and at the auditions, he'd been unable to follow Bill's simplest direction. Gerald often saw him sitting with Valentina, an exquisite dancer, whom he assumed to be Enzo's girlfriend or wife, and he wondered if she had insured Enzo's casting because they came as a pair. Or perhaps, given Bill's perverse notion of types, Enzo's awkward self-consciousness had been his trump.

Enzo, who seemed to have understood this direction, leapt on the tabletop and shouted, "I-EE-YA YAM."

"I—one syllable—*am*," corrected Bill, "and just speak it."

"I-EE-YA YAM," Enzo shouted, as if the words had been frightened out of him.

"We'll work on it," said Bill.

After a rough run-through of the new and rather complicated blocking, in which tempo changed so that some series of movements were played out in double time, others in legato, the actors, famished and tired, stared blankly at the director.

"It needs something else, no?"

"William," Martin said, "we are very far behind, at this point. You promised to block two scenes today and it is now well past the time for lunch, the actors look ill."

Bill raised the microphone to his mouth. "KA-BOOM!" His amplified voice echoed through the cavernous room. "Start the scene again. When a bomb explodes, KA-BOOM!, fall to the floor."

Gerald, hungry and worried about having to execute his laugh, was nevertheless excited by the way the scene was taking shape. The bomb element was precisely the sort of wild bird idea he'd seen Bill come up with hundreds of times to place a surreal twist on a commonplace bit of stage business. The actors practiced their falls to the hard marble floor again and again: "BOOM! BOOM! No! Not lyrical. Just fall. Straight down. Now hold for a count of fifteen. No, Otto! That's thirteen, stay down. Now get up. Slowly!"

"I heard they archive his *turds*," Jean declared.

The actors had finally been broken for lunch and the surly costume designer sat with them on the sunny patio of the palazzo. He was a big man with a basso voice. After a three-day period of abstinence, he'd reneged on his vow to Bill to control his drinking and resumed a steady consumption of red wine and public condemnation of nearly everyone. His assistants, the actors—especially women—and the entire production staff came under his attack, but his real vitriol was reserved for Bill.

Otto dragged a chair next to Jean. The sodden Frenchman and the fastidious German had lately formed an incongruous bond during dinners at the Arco Bellina. Under Jean's sour tutelage, Otto had become more talkative, giving voice to his own bitter agenda. ("When the Soviets controlled East Berlin, I had training, an assured position. I speak fluent Russian. But now, after *liberation*, I am treated no better than a dog.")

"Your Mr. Weiss only released you for lunch because he was summoned by the producer," Jean continued, his eyelids lowering and rising like a runaway theater curtain. "Fernando is very unhappy with the progress of the play. I mean, two fucking scenes in two fucking weeks? Really!"

"Che cosa?" Letizia said.

Jean sneered at her, then continued. "And those two scenes are shit! Shit! William *Weiss* should stick to fashion shows!" he said, referring to a lucrative alliance Bill had made with a prestigious Milanese designer.

"Why does not somebody tell him either direct the play or fuck off?" Otto said.

Gerald pushed his chair back noisily and moved to the steps under the shady archway, where Mima sat smoking a cigarette.

"Mind if I join you?" he asked.

Mima smiled. Gerald sat beside her and reached in his shirt pocket to pull up the last of the three cigarettes he now allotted to himself during the day. It was broken.

"Shit."

"Would you like a rolled cigarette?" Mima asked.

"Thank you," he said, taking the pack of tobacco she offered.

After moistening a finger to feel the sticky edge of the rolling paper, Gerald pulled just the right amount of loose tobacco from the pouch, spread it across the crease in the paper, and began to roll. The familiar motions reminded him of his college years. Which reminded him of a now ghostly enthusiasm for acting, early social anxiety, dropping acid, and a feeling of obscene health, all in the moment before Mima touched a lighted match to the perfectly rolled cigarette.

"How are your bites?"

"Almost all gone," he said, lifting his shirt and feeling silly for doing so.

"Oh, yes, they hardly show, just a few red spots. You still use the cream?"

"Yeah. Just to be safe."

"You want me . . . ?"

"No, I just did," he lied.

"Last night," Mima said, "Fabio and the German girl got very drunk. He did not return with us to Palermo. Did you perhaps see them at the Sociale?"

"No. But isn't Fabuloso, that's what Ariela and I call him, isn't he . . . ?"

"Homosexual? Yes, probably, but he's also young and stupid, and this woman made—how do you say?—an appeal to his vanity."

"Oh," Gerald said, wondering if Mima thought of him as "homosexual."

"I must ask you something and I hope you are able to

answer me with the truth. I think Bill does not like me. Do you think this is so?"

"No! He likes you. I mean, he doesn't dislike you—at all. But don't expect praise, he doesn't give any."

"Good. I can accept this explanation," Mima said, taking a last draw on the cigarette before flicking it onto the pavement.

After lunch, the company waited in the hot, airless theater for half an hour. Finally, Fernando and Annalisa, looking grim and businesslike, followed by Martin Lustinger, the production staff, and several members of the design team, took seats behind the long table, leaving one chair conspicuously empty. Fernando whispered to Annalisa, who took out her cell phone and left the building.

The actors were attentive at first, waiting for a word, but when none came, they began to lose interest and settled themselves along the wall and took out notebooks, books, or magazines. Zuzie began to vocalize quietly at the far end of the space, "Pah-pah-pah. Brrrrrrrrrr. Ta-ta-ta-ta," but stopped when Timothy, who now irritated her, joined in. In another corner, Ariela ran her moves with Holgar, who strutted about self-consciously.

Bill rushed into the theater wearing a pair of yellow Bermuda shorts, flip-flops, and a Palazzo dell'Arte T-shirt. All heads turned in unison to watch him flip-flop across the marble floor of the palazzo. The actors grinned, relieved perhaps that Bill's new dress code indicated the mood was not quite as dire as the appearance of the production staff had made them believe.

"Good afternoon, Bill," Fernando said, "you look very—

comfortable. I am so happy that you have chosen a shirt advertising our beautiful palazzo."

"Shut the fans off!" Bill barked at no one in particular. He turned to the actors, who had gathered around the table.

Bonnie rose to turn the fans off. Fernando stood.

"William, would you like to take a seat? No? Then, with your permission, I begin. As you know, we have a show to put on, and unfortunately, though we would all benefit from a much longer rehearsal period, we must put this show on in exactly seven days. The show was originally to contain ten scenes, three of which you have been working on, and which are, I am told, in very good shape. However, three is not ten—"

"It's a diSASter," Bill said, hurling the second syllable into a falsetto twang. His voice, even unmiked, had the effect of one of the bomb explosions in the Hell of a Party scene. "What am I going to do?" he asked after a short, stunned silence, as he searched among the faces for an answer.

The Italians, sensing that something extraordinary had been said, whispered among themselves. Fernando laughed uncomfortably.

"Now, Bill, it is usually the crew who mutinies, not the captain."

"I don't know what to do. *Someone!* Tell me what to do," Bill said. Once again, his gaze went from actor to actor. "Valentina? Vito? Otto? Zuzie? How do we get this thing opened?"

The production staff at the table looked down at papers or off to the side. Zuzie smiled down at her fingernails, Valentina bit her lower lip. The arrogant Otto looked like a frightened boy in a false mustache. Holgar's eyes drifted down Ariela's leotard where two half-moons of perspiration had darkened the fabric beneath her breasts.

"Ariela? Enzo?"

Enzo furrowed his brow and shook his head sadly as if a dying man had asked him for blood, and his was not compatible.

"Now, William, there is no need to involve the actors—"

"We have to postpone," Bill said, turning to face the producer.

"No, no, no," Fernando said with another little laugh, "that is hardly possible. It is not like opening a show in Rome where tickets are returned for a later date and the people can simply walk back to their homes. Our audience will have traveled here from all over Europe for the opening of an important arts festival, they cannot be told to cancel hotel reservations, to go back and return a week later."

"Why not?"

For a moment, the two men simply stared at each other.

"Excuse me, Bill?" Ariela's public voice, like her posture, was cool and formal, and Bill turned to face her. "Must we do all ten scenes?"

"Well . . . I mean, if people are coming this far we need to give them *something* more than two scenes and a prologue."

"Yes, but do you need all ten? Can we concentrate on, say, three more scenes? Or four?"

"It's an idea . . ." Bill wondered out loud.

Encouraged by Bill's willingness to listen to them, other actors began to offer suggestions. "Why not just rehearse more—into the night?," "Let's put in an intermission, to make it seem longer!," "Can we perform what we have twice?" As ideas were voiced, Bill began a slow pace in front of the table. Responding occasionally with a nod or chin rub.

Gerald watched from the shadow of the pillar. From tonight on, he knew, they would rehearse till they dropped. His eyes already burned with fatigue from missed sleep. He had no interest in offering his own suggestion to save the show; he didn't have one. Every William Weiss production required a level of chaos. Every rehearsal period reached the inevitable "what am I going to do?" stage, and at some point, Bill declared every show a "diSASter."

When he performed in his first William Weiss production, Gerald was shocked and attracted to the chaos. He'd only been in commercial, mainstream plays where hours were dictated by Actors Equity, but Bill worked outside the union where there were no rules. Rehearsals or "workshops," as they were called, often lasted into the small hours of the morning. Alcohol, cocaine, and pot openly fueled inspiration and temperament. In the final days before an opening, sleep-deprived actors, set builders, and prop makers moved about the theater like zombies.

"Gerald, It's a diSASter, no?"

At first, Gerald thought he'd only imagined Bill addressing him, but when he looked up, his eyes met Bill's. He smiled, hoping Bill would simply move on to someone else, but Bill's stare remained fixed.

"Yes," Gerald said.

"What?"

"Yes, the play's a disaster."

"Bill," Fernando said from behind, "he is making a joke, the play is not a disaster."

"Shhh," hissed Bill. "Gerald, what should I do?"

"You should quit the theater and open up an antique store in Greenwich Village."

Gerald thought he heard a gasp, several giggles, whispering, but his heart was beating too hard for him to be a good judge of audience reaction. Bill, whose recent weight gain was already emphasized by the T-shirt, stood with his hands bracing his lower back, which pushed his belly forward as if he were pregnant.

"Gerald," he said, with a barely concealed smile, "you are the *nas*tiest person on God's green earth. I mean the *nas*tiest.

CHAPTER EIGHT

When the company was released for a late dinner, the actors in the van wanted to go straight to the Arco Bellina. Only Gerald asked to be let off at the Sociale. After the long day, he wanted a shower, and the idea of doing so without roommates underfoot was more appealing than eating.

Bathed, refreshed, and changed, he walked through town toward the restaurant. Unlike New York, where even the moon could barely compete with the bright city lights, a dazzling cyclorama of stars shone against a deep blue sky over the dark streets of Bellina. Gazing up, he saw the stars appear to move in a great arc and sensed the tiny dot of himself rooted to the spinning earth.

"Let this moment be my last. Let gravity cease so I fly into the firmament and never take another breath," Gerald said aloud. He wrapped his arms around his body. "Or let me be twenty-one and gorgeous," he added, laughing, and continued on his way.

When he arrived on the little patio of the Arco Bellina, lit by paper lanterns under an arbor of plastic grapes, the other actors were already halfway through their *primo* courses and the

first carafes of wine had been drained. They were the only cus-
tomers in the restaurant at this hour, and the noise level suggested a rowdy family gathering. Only Ariela and Holgar sat
apart, eating in silence.

When Ariela spotted Gerald, she motioned him over. Gerald
cast a brief, longing glance at the line of tables pushed together
to accommodate the large, noisy group, but with a resigned
smile, he crossed the patio to sit with his friend—and her friend.

"There's the man," Holgar said.

"Hey," Gerald said back. He hated the locker-room intimacy of greetings like "There's the man," or "Hey, big guy,"
yet he knew Holgar sincerely welcomed his presence, if only as
a diversion from the posture-perfect silence of Ariela. Gerald
too had grown weary of Ariela's reserve at dinner, though he
was even more put off by Holgar's one-to-one relationship
with the wine and food. He glanced once more across the
restaurant at the others joking and shouting before pulling out
the third chair that always awaited him.

"You were brilliant today, Gerald," said Ariela, pouring
him a glass of wine.

"I thought so," said Gerald.

"Why is Timothy with that woman?" Ariela asked, following his gaze.

Timothy, having severed his allegiance to Ariela *and* Zuzie,
now shadowed Letizia, an Italian actress with straight auburn
hair hanging to the middle of her back. She not only played
Gotcha with Timothy, but occasionally put her arm around his
neck and kissed his ear, sending him off flapping and shrieking
down the palazzo patio, only to return a moment later for more.

Ariela bickered with Holgar over an additional carafe of

wine as Gerald watched Letizia, her legs stretched in front of her and the toes of one bare foot circling to the rhythm of an Italian pop song playing on a radio in the kitchen. She arched her spine away from the sticky plastic back of the chair cushion and, with one arm bent behind, held her hair off her neck, lazily fanning herself with a plastic menu. Her repose was full of constant movement, but so slow and languorous that, at a glance, she appeared still. Her hands, arms, and head floated like the notes of music from a snake charmer's flute and made Gerald sway in his seat. He wondered if Bill too had spotted Letizia's beauty, then remembered she'd been cast as Aphrodite in Cupid and Psyche.

"You can understand more about civilization from the way someone stands or moves than from all the books in the world," Bill said. And like Bill, Gerald had a nondancer's awe for effortless, beautiful movement. Letizia glanced up and their eyes met. Her parted lips relaxed into a slow smile, and she winked.

"What are you laughing at?" Ariela asked.

"Nothing," Gerald said, bringing his attention back to the table.

"But why *can't* I bring a carafe of wine back to the room?" Holgar asked.

Gerald glanced back to the Italian woman. Now, she leaned all the way forward in the chair, legs apart, head drooping low: the posture to clear dizziness, return blood to the head. Her long auburn hair cascaded down, nearly reaching the floor, revealing wisps of damp curls at the base of her scalp.

She must have sensed Gerald's attention return, for she lifted the long curtain of hair, looked up with wide eyes, and stuck out her tongue. Then she slumped back, laughing, arched suddenly when her shoulders touched the sticky plastic cushion, sat up, and then laughed again.

The others at her table looked over, smiling, waiting to be let in on the joke. Timothy, cued by Letizia's laugh, began to giggle, she put her arm around him and nuzzled his ear, eliciting from him a little shriek as he clasped his hands in his lap and began to rock back and forth.

"I bet she fucks him," Holgar said.

"What did you say?" Gerald felt he had never despised anyone so much.

"Zuzie," said Holgar, "she's met her match with that Vincenzo fellow. He's been working on her for days."

Vincenzo's shaved head emphasized his strong features and romantic profile. At the auditions, in his spandex bicycle shorts, he'd moved with the physical arrogance of a matador. Gerald had had no doubt he'd be cast in the show. But he was also a buffoon. Sitting next to Zuzie, Vincenzo played his part like a seducer in a silent movie, never letting his gaze leave the German girl's face, moving so close to speak that his lips seemed always to be reaching for her neck, her cheek, the lobe of her ear. If her attention strayed from him for too long, he reminded her of his presence with a touch, stroking her arm, or replacing a loose strand of hair. His absolute certainty of his own charm was more comical than sexy. Zuzie tried to ignore him by engaging in a conversation with Fabio, who sat on her other side. When Vincenzo touched her neck, she swatted his fingers away like a bothersome fly, but he was oblivious to the snub and his fingers returned to brush an imaginary crumb from her blouse.

"I'm leaving," Ariela said, standing up.

"Wait for me," said Holgar.

While Holgar pushed his chair noisily from the table, Ariela kissed Gerald's cheek. "Help!" she whispered in his ear before she left, Holgar trailing behind, struggling not to spill the open carafe of red wine he'd smuggled in his knapsack.

Left alone at the table, Gerald leaned back and lit a cigarette, listening to the musical chatter of the Italians. He was not alone for long, however. Ernesto approached, waving two fingers of his little priest's hand in front of his mouth. Gerald gave him a cigarette, and, mission completed, Ernesto hurried back to his table. Then Giovanni, excited from too much wine, sat down.

"I must ask you an important question about film acting," he began, pulling a chair close to Gerald.

Giovanni, barely twenty, was a fan of American movies. Knowing this, Gerald had, a few days earlier and in a weak moment, mentioned working with John Travolta. He was only an extra in the film and had never gotten near the star, but the exaggeration had made Gerald a movie expert.

"Tell me this," continued Giovanni, "I know I am pretty enough—no, this is for woman—I am 'andsome enough—but I must have the body, no?"

"You're fine," Gerald said. But in fact, the boy's self-assessment was correct. He *was* "andsome," but he still retained what might euphemistically be called baby fat.

"Never mind—this I can develop. But look," Giovanni said, pulling up his shirt to reveal an incongruous mat of soft fur that covered his torso like a shiny black T-shirt. "This is too much chest 'air for the American audience, no? I must have electrocution." He pulled his shirt back down. "See you later, okay?" he said, and returned to his table.

After Giovanni left, Gerald barely believed the conversation had taken place. He wanted to re-create the scene by repeating it to someone—"and then he said, 'I must have electrocution'"—but to whom? He'd have to wait until morning when he met Ariela in the courtyard of the Sociale.

Mima stood with her arms folded. "You would like to be alone?"

"God, no!" he said, "Sit. And let me tell you what just happened."

At first, Gerald found the retelling of his conversation with Giovanni unsatisfying. With Ariela he would have been able to widen his eyes, to describe the catch in his breath as the boy lifted his shirt, his impulse to run his fingers through the mesh of chest hair, and he might have ended with a campy phrase such as, "I nearly fainted!" But with Mima the story suggested something else, an adult's amused tolerance toward a child.

"These Italian men are the most vain in the world, just look around you," Mima said when he finished.

At the other table, Giovanni was now showing his hairy torso to Zuzie and Fabio.

"Come," she said, "sit with us and have some more wine."

Zuzie had finally moved away from Vincenzo to the other side of Fabio, and Gerald took her place. At one end of the table, he saw Ian talking to yet another beautiful Italian girl, whose name Gerald did not know. Daryl, who was speaking to no one, gave him a drunken smile.

"Gee-air," said Vincenzo, "how you are?"

"His name is Gee-air-*ol*," explained Vito.

"*Ger*—ald," corrected his wife, Eunice.

"Gee-air-ol," said Vincenzo.

"*Perfetto*," said Vito.

"No it's not! Sounds like Gee-*airhole*," Eunice said.

"That's all right. I hardly expect anyone to get my name right. I'm not sure I even know most of yours," Gerald said.

The other conversations had stopped, and Gerald felt he was being observed. He suspected his flip comment to the director this afternoon had made him somewhat of a curiosity.

"My name? My name?" demanded Ernesto.

"Oh, yes," said Gerald, smiling at the tiny mooch. "I know your name." He waved two fingers in front of his mouth. "It's Eh, Sigaretta Per Favore?, isn't it?"

Gerald was persuaded to go around the table to try and say the name of each person. He felt like the professor who becomes a "regular person" when he joins a table of his students at the local pub. Taking a quick survey, he realized he'd be able to name more of the men than the women, and, not wanting to appear biased, pretended to draw a blank on Vito's name. He was going to do the same with Ian, but the boy seemed to purposely leave for the bathroom before Gerald could make his little joke. When he tried to name everyone again, a carafe later, he had no trouble.

"Say to Valentina, '*Fammi una pompa*,'" Vincenzo whispered to Gerald.

"What does it mean?" he asked.

"It mean 'How did you enjoy the food, Valentina?'"

Knowing full well he was asking for a fuck or a blow job, Gerald delivered his line with convincing innocence. Valentina screamed and the others laughed.

"What? What did I say? '*Fammi una pompa*.' Isn't that

'Did you enjoy the food?'" More laughter. But the effort to have fun was exhausting.

When the waiter came out to collect the vouchers, Vito began to argue with him about getting more wine, but it seemed a good-natured exchange, performed more for show than purpose.

"I'm not tired," Eunice said, "let's go to the *acqua calda*." The suggestion produced an enthusiastic response from the others as they gathered bags and knapsacks.

"What's the *acqua calda*?" asked Gerald.

"A stream coming from underground that is very warm and full of that stinky stuff. What is it? Oh, you know—what's in the water, Vito?"

"Sulfur."

"Oh, I don't think I'll come," Gerald said.

"You must," said Vito seriously, "it is very healthful."

Is it common knowledge that I need something healthful? Gerald wondered.

"How far away is it? How would we get there?" he asked, hoping to find an appropriate excuse.

"Not far," said Vito, "thirty, forty minutes. We take the van and Enzo can take a few people in his car."

Gerald looked at Daryl, who stood by supporting himself on a chair back.

"Don't worry, I drive," Vito said. "Come, Daryl, give me the keys."

The mood of the group was lively. The Italians were keen to impress the German and American visitors with the wonders of the *acqua calda*, but Gerald found the persuasive efforts of such enthusiastic guides daunting. As they left the restaurant, he anticipated the moment when too many bodies would try to fill too few places in the van. Then he could yawn, plead fatigue, and free himself. He envisioned the relief of a solitary walk back to the Motel Sociale and a pillow under his head. But as the group reached the parking lot and he turned to make his excuses, Giovanni grabbed him by the arm.

"The front, Gee-air-ol must sit in the front to see the beautiful hills of Sicily!" With a hand on Gerald's back, Giovanni literally lifted him into the front seat next to Eunice. Ginger climbed onto his lap, and as Vito backed the van out of the parking lot, she searched the scratchy car radio until she found a station playing an American pop song. "Young American," she sang, "I want to be a young American."

After an hour's drive, two wrong turns, and a loud disagreement between Vito and the macho Vincenzo, the van turned onto a gravel road. The night was dark and Gerald could see almost nothing except the pitted road illuminated by the car lights. Suddenly, Vito turned the headlights off, plunging them into total darkness, and the others screamed in unison begging him to turn them back on. They passed a few other cars parked along the grassy border of the road.

"The river is just there, but you can't see because it is below the road. We look now for a place away from other people who have also come for the *acqua calda*," Vito explained, as he parked the van in a deserted spot along the shoulder of the road.

The passengers got out. Gerald shook his sleeping leg. He felt chilled and wished he'd brought a sweatshirt. He should never have let the others bully him into coming, nothing was more important for him now than sleep.

No one had mentioned a bathing suit, so Gerald assumed

underwear or nothing was the fashion. Luckily, he was wearing a modestly baggy pair of boxer shorts.

"Take off your shoes or they get very muddy."

Giovanni was right. As Gerald made his way barefoot down the steep embankment, he felt the cold mud ooze obscenely between his toes. He also smelled an acrid stench, like the rotten-egg smell of a high school chemistry lab, but stronger, so unbelievably strong the odor seemed to thicken into a taste, which made him push his tongue against his upper teeth.

The actors inched their way down the embankment until they reached a wide stream covered by a layer of ghostly mist. Water fell over the edge of a flat rock into a pool below, creating a small waterfall. Letizia was the first to pull her dress over her head, step out of her underwear, and, with her arms raised, wade into the stream. As her body sank beneath the mist, into the black water, she released a guttural sigh of pleasure. The others fumbled out of trousers, shirts, skirts, and underwear and waded into the sulfured pond, exhaling their own ecstatic sighs.

Gerald folded his clothing, including his boxer shorts, and laid them in a neat pile on top of his sandals. Letizia's sigh had seemed to tug at something rooted deep inside him: a tension, an untruth, a piece of the illness. But a fear, pale and familiar, crept into his abdomen. The dank sulfuric smell made him doubt the cleanliness of the water. What new bacteria waited to attack his compromised immune system? The smell was awful, he felt he might be sick and lowered himself down into a sitting position, but when his hands pressed into the slimy bank, the need to vomit increased. Instinctively, he started to cover his mouth, but realizing his hand was muddy, he scuttled forward, crablike, to wash it in the stream. The water was warm, and he forced himself farther in until it covered him to his neck. The comforting warmth seemed to leach the fear from his gut. He stood and waded in quickly until he had to stand on tiptoe to keep his head above the water. Then he held his breath, lifted his feet from the muddy bottom and embraced his knees, somersaulting into the pungent warmth. Uncoiling, he broke the surface and drew the cool evening air into his lungs, pressing the drops from his face and hair with his hands. He ran his palms up and down his sides, imagining the odorous minerals were etching off the last of his rash, an allergic reaction to the Sicilian sun.

Other bathers appeared as disembodied heads floating atop the steamy black surface. Otto, with his absurd handlebar mustache, crouched with Valentina beneath the waterfall. Nearby, Zuzie and Fabio lightly supported a floating Giovanni. His penis, looking like a small mushroom, bobbed above the surface of the water.

"Ahhhhhh," Giovanni moaned.

"Eeeeyahhh," echoed Valentina.

"Mmmmm," Eunice hummed.

"Ahhhh."

"Ohhhh."

"Ummm."

The bathers continued their chorus of moans until they reached an orgasmic pitch and broke into laughter. Occasionally, laughter and voices from upstream could be heard above the splash of falling water.

Gerald floated on his back. Above, framed by the black silhouettes of trees, a fingernail paring of a moon and a billion stars appeared to swirl as if stirred by a giant's wooden spoon.

"Dov'è Ariela?"

Gerald's toes reached for the muddy bottom of the stream. "With Holgar, I guess."

"Such a shame," Vito said, and drifted away.

Gerald was angry with Ariela. Why had she attached herself to . . . anyone? She was missing this beautiful experience. Tomorrow, he thought, I'll tell her about the *acqua calda*, and make her sorry she didn't come.

Several bathers had moved downstream and he could just make out heads bobbing under the low-hanging branches of a black-silhouetted tree. Soundlessly, in slow-motion movements, he half floated, half swam through the warm water until he was close enough to recognize three heads melded together. Fabio, Zuzie, and Giovanni didn't notice him as they clung to each other in an awkward three-way embrace. On the other side of the stream, he saw two heads just visible above the steamy surface of the water and heard the amorous panting of Letizia and Ian.

He felt he had to get away from the tangled lovers and was dog-paddling back toward the waterfall when someone splashed him. He wiped the water from his eyes and saw Ernesto grinning expectantly, hoping to engage him in a water battle.

"Get!" he snapped, as if the little man were an annoying pet. "Get!"

Gerald moved back into the deeper section of the stream, but the little man-dog paddled after him. Gerald swam toward the sheet of falling water. The flat rock was only a few feet above, and he wanted to pull himself up, but the surface was slippery, and his grip would not hold. As his fingers slipped off the rock and he fell backward into the pool of water, Ernesto surfaced for air a few feet away.

"Here, Gee-air-ol. We help," said a voice nearby.

Before he could protest, Vincenzo and Vito grabbed him under the arms—*"Uno, due, tre,"*—and propelled him up so he was able to pull himself onto the plateau above.

As Gerald lay on his back on the moss-covered stone, so many of his senses were called into play. The moss was a soft, slippery pillow. The flowing water bubbled around his body like tiny warm fingers. Above the water, his face, chest, stomach, were moist and sensitive to the least stir of a breeze. The odor of sulfur, still strong, had the presence of an animal. Staggering, he thought, as he looked up at the stars, and cringed at the inadequacy of the word. But his mind was really on the romantic couplings below. Of course, the *acqua calda* was the perfect place for a sexual encounter. How exciting to fondle and be fondled, hidden—well, almost hidden—in this warm sulfuric womb. He splashed warm water onto his torso, spreading it over his chest and abdomen like lotion.

"May I join you?"

The voice was quiet, intimate. Gerald raised his head. Mima was beside him. Her wet hair, pulled back from her face, emphasized her strong features, her prominent nose, and the overdrawn arch of her eyebrows. As Gerald, she was in her late forties, and in a company of actors in their twenties and early thirties, the two had begun an easy friendship. He was glad to have her company now, but their nudity embarrassed him. Her breasts were large with dark nipples the size of—Gerald searched his brain for the right coin—Susan B. Anthony dollars. He thought he saw her glance down at his penis and squelched the impulse to cross his legs. He was relieved when she lay down beside him. For a while they were both silent, staring up into the starlit sky.

"You must not take me wrong," Mima said finally, "but when an experience is so beautiful, for me . . . is also a little sad if I am not sharing it with someone."

"My friend," he began. He feared the salutation might sound false so he repeated it. "My friend. I know exactly what you mean. "

"Do you have someone special?" Mima asked. "Someone you could wish to share this beautiful evening with."

"But I'm sharing it with you."

"Yes, I know. And I am very glad for this, but I mean—"

"He died two years ago."

"I'm so sorry."

They lay silent for a moment staring at the stars.

"Did you see many things together?" Mima asked.

"Not so many."

"And he died of . . . ?"

"Yes."

Gerald and Damon had not been lovers. They'd tricked once, become buddies, and for years phoned each day to gossip and find out who'd gotten lucky. When Damon became ill, he made Gerald a set of keys to his tiny studio apartment. Gerald came over to tidy up, or coerce Damon into eating some infinitesimal amount of food. When Damon was hospitalized, Gerald visited regularly and scheduled the visits of friends. It was Gerald who called Damon's parents (against Damon's wishes) when the doctor informed him, "It's time."

Damon's death changed his relationship to Damon's family in an unexpected way. The parents approached him with great sympathy, as if he were the grieving widow. A mutual friend offered to stay over "so you won't be alone this first night."

When Gerald referred to Damon as "my friend," he knew people heard "my lover," and he didn't correct the misconception. In fact, he *had* loved Damon, truly mourned his death, and their everyday communication had made Damon the closest thing Gerald had to a lover. The following year, when Gerald himself became ill, he found the misconception a convenient excuse for his gradual unwillingness to leave his apartment or to explain his lingering unemployment. "I still need time," he said, to turn down a dinner invitation; "My lover died," he explained when asked what he'd been up to.

"Do you miss him very much?" Mima asked.

"Very much," Gerald said.

"And you, Mima, who do you miss?"

"For nine years, nearly ten, I worked with a company of actors based in Mexico City. We lived communally, like paupers, really, but happy paupers. I was in love with the director, but he was gay."

"You didn't know?"

"Yes, I suppose I did, but it didn't matter. He was so many things for me, that part of him seemed minor." Mima laughed. "I know this sounds naïve, but all of us in the company were a little in love with Georges."

"Sounds like Bill."

"No. William Weiss—you see, I cannot even call him by his first name as you do—one always wishes for a word of praise from him, but that is not love."

"No," Gerald said.

"Our director was generous with his praise. We were a family. He wrote our plays and the parts were, you know, designed for us. It was a great artistic experience, but not always so much a great emotional experience, not at the end, anyway."

"Let me guess: the actors began to get jealous of each other. Some parts were better than others, and if everybody was a little in love with Georges, some actors began to feel he loved them less."

Mima turned her head to look at Gerald. She smiled.

"Yes, you are very good. This is exactly what happened. For a while I was never so happy to work. The parts George wrote for me always demanded more than I knew I had. But then, as you say, new members came into the company and he became, I don't know, excited by them—the way he once had been excited by me. I felt he was beginning to use me always the same, and not in such good roles. I felt that worst of things, unnecessary."

"And so you left."

"Eventually, but this took another two years. It was like leaving something religious—an order of priests. And even then his spell over me was so strong, I had to escape without saying goodbye."

"You ran away?"

"When I had tried to leave before, he talked me out of it. There were always tears—most of them his—and promises and apologies. So I just left without telling anyone. It was after the final performance of a play in Mexico City. When I returned to Palermo, I felt I had made a terrible mistake. There was little work. At least with Georges, I was always performing."

"And now?"

"Better. Palermo is my home. It is still hard to find work here, but I have a nice apartment and a small house on the sea, which I inherited from my family. My life is good. Of course, I miss Georges still. At least, I miss the intensity such devotion brings."

Another splash sent sulfured water into Gerald's eyes. When he sat up to rub them, he heard Ernesto giggling from the bank. Mima hissed something in Italian. As Gerald's vision cleared he saw Ernesto slink back to the pool below.

"I can't stand this one," Mima said, "such a little fool. And with so little work, he gets the job. It makes me ill."

"Yes," Gerald said, "and I actually thought he was sort of cute and charming, at first."

"With Ernesto and me, it is like opposites. When people meet him, he is little and charming. Then they begin to know him and he becomes repulsive. I think I am a little repulsive to people at first, but they like me more as they know me."

Gerald did not know how to respond to her accurate self-perception.

"But you," she went on, "you were kind from the beginning." She laughed. "Perhaps you were feeling a little desperate because of your sun rash. I am going into the water below once more, then back to the van. I wish to dry off and have a cigarette."

After Mima left, Gerald stretched his arms over his head. He felt tired and wondered what time it was. He sat up and scooted to the edge of the rock, letting his legs dangle in the sheet of falling water.

"Gee-air-ol, come down 'ere," Giovanni said.

As Gerald stood, he momentarily lost his balance on the mossy rock and gave a little shriek.

"Careful, love," Eunice called from the pool below.

"Thanks," Gerald said, carefully tiptoeing to the bank.

He rubbed his arms in the cool air. The *acqua calda* had been wonderful, but he needed *some* sleep before tomorrow's rehearsal. How long did the group plan on staying? Looking along the bank for his clothes, he heard his name whispered. He squatted down by the water's edge and saw six or seven of the bathers had formed a massage line.

"Come back in, join us," said Letizia, who was at the end of the line.

Gerald eased himself back into the water, waded behind Letizia and began to give her shoulders a light rub. He felt someone move behind him, and before he could turn, two hands were kneading the muscles in his shoulders. He could tell by the size and strength they were male, but whose hands were they? Vito was in the line in front of him, so were Ernesto and Otto. Vincenzo? A posturing, macho straight guy? But with Italians, who knew? Gerald's shoulders began to relax under the firm touch and his head drooped forward. The hands moved down his shoulders to his biceps. They slid down to his wrists, pulling his arms into the water. "Eh?" Letizia asked, starting to turn. The hands released Gerald's arms and Gerald quickly resumed Letizia's massage.

The front of the line began to break up. Letizia moved away with a little murmur of gratitude. The hands kneading his shoulders slid down his back, under his arms, pulling firmly down his sides in a shaving motion. They moved to the small of his back. The pressure was strong and Gerald felt himself falling forward, but a supporting arm wrapped around his chest, while the other hand continued to knead the muscles along his spine. The man's body brushed against his, and

Gerald felt the coarse texture of hair. Giovanni? No, Gerald could hear Giovanni's voice coming from the bank. The arm locked around Gerald's chest moved down to his abdomen, pulling his hips back.

"Umm," he moaned, but suddenly he felt silly in the arms of an unidentified masseur and laughed. The man responded quickly by pulling Gerald in tightly. The pressure of an erection against his back quelled Gerald's amusement. He tried to scan the area to see if they were being watched, but heads blurred together, indistinct above the misty surface of the water.

It's Ian, Gerald thought with a start, we've been arguing, and this is his way to apologize. Now it made sense. Though Ian was straight, he prided himself on having no sexual hang-ups, or looked at from another angle, his vanity urged him to be all things to all people. But he and Ian had hardly spoken. Would Ian really be rubbing his dick against Gerald's backside? Was it a cruel tease? No, this touch was too genuine; no one could fake an erection.

"I-ee-ya . . ." his stranger whispered, "I-ee-ya . . . like . . . ah-you."

Gerald leaned back and felt coarse body hair against his skin. Besides, Ian was smooth. He twisted his head round. Enzo's big, serious face stared back at him.

"I-ee-ya like ah-you," he repeated.

"Umm," Gerald said, turning back.

This meant he wasn't Valentina's husband? Right? Enzo held Gerald with both arms, his fingers retaining only the slightest pretense of massage as they traveled over Gerald's chest and stomach. Enzo. What was his last name? Enzo! He might have gone through the entire company and never guessed.

With his back to Enzo, Gerald pictured the man's face: large nose, thick lips, prominent forehead, and coarse, convict-short hair that lay on his scull like a black cap. Completely masculine and typically Southern Italian, like a portrait found in the ruins of Pompeii. And now, that very nose, those big lips, were brushing the back of his neck, his ear.

"I-ee-ya like ah-you."

Enzo! Enzo! Gerald felt weightless as he pivoted in the man's embrace, like a ballerina. Enzo's features were enormous at close range.

"Enzo."

"Shhhh. My car—after."

"What?"

"Eh, when we leef, eh, you, eh, ride-ah my car."

"*Si, si,*" whispered Gerald.

Someone splashed nearby and the men separated. Gerald heard Mima's voice.

"Ah, just a little," she said, moving in front of him.

"I thought you went to dry off," Gerald said.

"A little lower down the back. That's it, yes."

Mima let her head fall forward and leaned back into Gerald's hands. He glanced round, but Enzo was gone.

"Ow, not so hard," Mima said.

Vito, standing on the bank of the river, announced, "The van leaves in *cinque minuti*—five minutes."

When Mima turned to face him, Gerald panicked, thinking she meant to embrace him and thus discover—and misinterpret—his arousal. But she leaned forward to kiss his cheek. "Now, are you glad you came to the *acqua calda?*" she whispered.

"Yes," he said, truthfully, "very glad."

• • •

"Why do I have to ride back in the van?"

Though Valentina spoke to Enzo in Italian, Gerald easily guessed the translation and he feigned sleepiness, bestowing on Valentina a dotty smile as he climbed into the back of Enzo's little tin can of a car. Ginger and Ernesto sat on either side of him and were asleep within minutes. Eunice, who had been assigned by her husband, Vito, to keep Enzo awake on the ride home, sat in front jabbering away like a dutiful copilot.

Gerald had never felt so awake. The cool air from Eunice's open window numbed his face and stung his eyes. He shut them and wrapped his arms across his chest, remembering how Enzo had held him in the water. Within this hour, he thought, he'll kiss me. How long had it been? The feeling of excitement already tinged with a sense of loss was so familiar. I'm still a romantic slut, he thought, I'm already in love with him and I don't know his last name. No, he thought with a start, this isn't "being in love," it's being alive—that's what I'd given up.

Eunice and Enzo were arguing in the front seat when Eunice turned to give Gerald a translation.

"I don't know what he's doing, I told him he should drop you off first, since you're on the way. Now, he's got to take us, *then* take you, *then* come all the way back. It makes no sense."

Gerald hoped that Enzo's circuitous route would continue to make no sense to Eunice. He didn't want anyone to know he was going off with Enzo. Partly, he was honoring Enzo's caution, but Gerald also understood that much of the excitement of an assignation is due to its secretive nature. Nothing poisoned an encounter faster than the good-natured teasing of friends.

Gerald was shivering with anticipation as Enzo kept the motor running in front of the little villa where the Palermo actors rented rooms. When the other passengers were inside, he climbed into the front seat, and Enzo, glancing nervously toward the building, put the car in gear and drove away.

As the little car rumbled through the empty streets of Bellina, Gerald inched his leg close to the gearshift, and Enzo's hand came to rest upon his knee. He reached out and stroked Enzo's arm, brushing against the grain of coarse hair, then smoothing it back, as if he were petting a contented housecat.

Enzo drove slowly down a badly lit side street where ugly stucco houses abutted the pavement. In the dim light, Gerald made a quick study of the man's crude, irregular face: the dark cross-hatching of beard, the great nose, the close-set brown eyes under a single, unruly eyebrow, and the sensual inner-tube lips. When Enzo stopped the car and turned off the motor, Gerald leaned in for the kiss.

"I go pee-pee," Enzo said, getting out of the car and looking back over his shoulder as he performed a comical little prance down the road. A dark circle widened in front of him as he stood with his legs apart, his back to the car. Gerald quickly reached into his knapsack, searching blindly through a tangle of rehearsal clothes, scene pages, vitamin bottles, deodorant, sun cream, moisturizer, a yogurt container, and an apple until his fingers closed around the smooth surface of a tube. He opened the tube and squeezed a line of paste on his index finger. As Enzo shook off the last drops of pee, Gerald brought his finger to his mouth and vigorously rubbed across his teeth—but the texture was all wrong and the toothpaste tasted like petroleum. "Shit," he hissed, running his tongue back and forth across his greasy teeth. He lifted the tube into the light: Shine-Eez; he'd bought the cheap "hair control" in New York, but found it too greasy to use. As Enzo walked back to the car, Gerald shoved the tube back into the knapsack, pulled out a rehearsal T-shirt and ducked below the dash to spit.

"Better now!" Enzo said.

There was a small wet spot on the front of his trousers.

"Good!" Gerald reached back into his bag and felt for the bruised apple. He bit into it, then offered the clean side to Enzo. "Hungry? Nature's toothbrush, you know."

"Yes, I-ee-ya yam 'ungry." Enzo held Gerald's wrist and looked into his eyes as he bit into the fruit. A bit of apple flesh fell from his mouth to his chin. " 'Ungry for you."

He leaned forward until his cushiony lips covered Gerald's. Gerald wanted to surrender himself to the warm wet mouth, but the taste of petroleum made him self-consciously tighten his lips against Enzo's tongue. Opening his eyes, he saw, just beyond Enzo's head, a curtain drop in the window of the house next to which they were parked, and he pulled back, half expecting a popping noise as their mouths parted.

"Enzo, someone is watching us."

"Eh?" He spun toward the window. "You, eh, me, eh, go someplace else. Very, very beautiful—in the hills—not so far."

As they drove past the Palazzo d'elle Arte gates, up into the steep hills surrounding Bellina, Gerald devoured the apple and threw the core out the window. His mouth still tingled, but he thought it was the kiss not the hair cream. The empty highway wound up and up. Gerald put his hands behind his head to let the air through the open side windows rush over him. He shifted his glance to study Enzo's face. He was like a character out of a Jean Genet novel with his prison-short hair and rugged features. Suddenly, a chilling wave, like nausea, passed through Gerald. He dropped his arms down and pressed his hands between his thighs. This was the feeling he had the few times before he'd "gone up" on stage, when suddenly, he didn't know the next line. Should I tell him? Now? Before we kiss again? He foresaw Enzo's expression, unibrow raised in alarm, eyes narrowed in disgust, big lips opening in soundless disbelief—followed by a polite but firm rejection.

Enzo looked over and blew Gerald a kiss. Gerald's arms were covered in goosebumps.

Near the top of the hill, Enzo turned off the highway onto an unpaved road, which dead-ended in a field of some dried, brittle crop. He stopped the car, turned off the motor, engulfing them in an abrupt silence. A chilly wind blew through Enzo's open window. He rolled it up and with a little shiver, rubbed his arms.

"Freddo!"

The two men leaned across the gearshift to meet in an awkward embrace. Enzo's mouth tasted like mouthwash. That's not fair, he must have sprayed when I wasn't looking, Gerald thought. But he forgot the slight as Enzo's soft tongue slid into his mouth. "You have a better chance of winning the lottery than infecting someone with a kiss," his doctor had told him. But that meant there *was* a chance. He felt a sharp pain in his side, as the gearshift pressed into his ribs. He pulled back and, with what seemed to him a stagy laugh, pointed to the gearshift. I'm communicating with him like he's the village idiot, Gerald thought.

"Enzo . . ." His voice sounded unused, and he cleared his throat. "Enzo, we have to be careful."

Enzo's eyes widened.

"*Si!* If the others find out . . . ayeee!" he said, striking his temple with the palm of his hand. "Especially Signorina Valentina. She think she own me, though we never—well, once, but we was very drunk and never again . . ."

"No. I mean, we have to be safe. You know, safe sex?"

"*Si, si,*" Enzo said, pulling Gerald close, sandwiching the shift between their bellies.

As Enzo pulled Gerald's T-shirt up and over his head, Gerald wondered if he'd understood his warning. He pulled Enzo's T-shirt off and put his hand on Enzo's crotch, thinking that if he kept the lead sexually, he'd be better able to navigate their amorous course around the whirls and eddies of unsafe sex. He tried to undo Enzo's belt, but the fancy designer buckle was as impossible to open as a Chinese box. When Enzo took his wrists, lifted Gerald's hands to his face and kissed his fingers, Gerald noticed the windows were opaque with fog, and the car was as claustrophobic as a hothouse.

"We go out, yes?" Enzo said.

Gerald could see Enzo more clearly outside. He found his unsculpted build, so unlike the pumped torsos of American gays, perfect and sexy. Usually taut with muscularity himself, he hadn't worked out in months and felt soft and unappealing. To avoid close scrutiny, he put his arms around Enzo and pulled him in tightly.

"You'll get cold," he said.

He pressed his nose into Enzo's neck and inhaled. The faint scent of sulfuric water from the *acqua calda* made him dizzy. He began to kiss Enzo's chest, and when, for a moment, he couldn't find his nipple, remembered seeing Mima's—but that seemed days ago. He moved down the line of hair that bisected Enzo's torso, his "treasure trail," clipped like a Florida lawn to uniform length. Some convict, Gerald thought, but even this mild sign of the man's vanity touched him. Encouraged by a moan, he continued his southward journey and, squatting, hooked his fingers in Enzo's belt loops and pressed his face into the stiff fabric of the new pair of American jeans. The childish pleasure in taking out a man's penis—like unwrapping a present he already knew pleased him—made Gerald want to take his time. He searched beneath the denim strip until his tongue touched a cold metal button. Would opening a pair of 501s with one's teeth appear too professional? Take too long? Was it even possible?

The headlights of a car rounding the curve of the main road streaked across the dried field. Enzo pulled away quickly, almost knocking Gerald to the ground. When the car passed, Enzo thrust his hands deep into his pockets, grinning sheepishly. Gerald's knees made a cracking noise as he stood. He grinned back, but remained a few feet away. Enzo glanced down the road, making sure the car had passed, then embraced Gerald stiffly and maneuvered his back against the car.

"Sorry, I thought . . . you know . . . *polizia!* "

Enzo had no trouble with Gerald's belt buckle. The cautioning hand Gerald placed on Enzo's shoulder did nothing to dampen Enzo's enthusiasm. Gerald tried to surrender himself to Enzo's skills, but his pleasure felt tainted with villainy. Enzo, cowed no doubt by Gerald's waning hard-on, stood up. But when they kissed, Gerald felt the electricity go back on. Pants fell to ankles, hands worked, and they continued to kiss until Enzo came with puppy-dog moans, and Gerald came a minute later.

The men were quiet on the drive back. Enzo started to speak, but grew shy and silent when his English faltered. Gerald wondered if he was disappointed with the sex. Don't worry, he wanted to tell Enzo, this is only the beginning, tomorrow I'll buy condoms. But did Enzo consider Gerald callback material, as he and Damon used to refer to tricks they'd consider seeing more than once? If tonight had just been about my safety, Gerald thought, I would have let you fuck me until the cum shot out my ears. He smiled at the thought of trying to translate *that* sentiment to Enzo.

Gerald put his hand over Enzo's. The empty streets and shuttered homes of Bellina appeared deserted under the first faint light of dawn. He brought Enzo's hand to his lips at a traffic light. By the time the little car turned onto Gerald's street, the first long rays of the sun were washing over the ugly cinder-block walls of the Sociale. Enzo kept the motor running.

"I-ee-ya see you *domani*," he said.

"No *domani*—today," Gerald corrected.

"Ho, my God! *Si!* To-dayee." Enzo withdrew the hand Gerald had been absentmindedly stroking. "To-dayee! I forget."

He held his stomach and rocked back and forth with laughter like a madman. Gerald got out of the car. "Ciao then." He walked backward a few steps, then turned to go into the Sociale.

"No *domani*—to-dayee," Enzo called to his back. The gears engaged and as Gerald turned to watch the car move down the street, he realized he'd forgotten his knapsack.

"Enzo! Wait!"

The car braked noisily. Gerald ran to the driver's window.

He bent down and was about to ask for his bag when the goofy, expectant expression on Enzo's face caused his breath to catch. It was only seconds, but seemed like several minutes that they clung to each other in a long, defiant, daylight kiss.

"I-ee-ya, eh, like ah-you," Enzo said as he passed the bag out the window.

"I like you, too," Gerald said, noticing his lover's eyes flick nervously back toward the motel.

CHAPTER NINE

Enzo?" Ariela repeated, "Enzo? The one who looks like he just got out of jail?"

"Shut up" Gerald hissed, "and don't you tell anyone, especially not Holgar."

They were in the theater warming up, Ariela using a chair back for a barre.

"So, Auntie . . ." Ariela pliéd into a deep second, "who was the rooster and who was the hen?"

Gerald was sorry he had told her. Sorry, at least, that he hadn't waited, as he'd planned, until the lunch break.

Zuzie, Holgar, Ian, and Otto ambled into the theater, followed by Timothy. They dropped their bags and excess clothing along the wall. Zuzie, Otto, and Ian placed their mats as far as they could from Ariela and Gerald and began a series of bends and stretches. Holgar unrolled his mat beside Ariela's chair, lay down, and curled up with one arm shielding his eyes from the light. Timothy came over and began an awkward imitation of Ariela's ballet exercises.

"Good, Timothy!" Ariela said, as a faint smile lit her otherwise impassive face. "And where is everyone?"

"Who?" Timothy asked.

"The actors from Palermo."

Timothy stopped exercising and brought his wristwatch up close to one eye.

"It's all right, Timothy. Italians are always late."

"Why?"

"Because they eat a lot and talk a lot, and because *some* of them stayed up *all* night."

"Be careful, dear," Gerald warned, trying to keep his tone casual.

If Ariela sensed his anxiety, she'd tease him ceaselessly. Just then, the Italians trooped in, many of them carrying little plastic espresso cups or food.

"Ariela!" Timothy said, shaking his hands in the air. "Italians!"

Enzo entered eating a brioche. He glanced at Gerald but immediately looked away and followed Eunice and Valentina to a far corner of the room. Ariela balanced on the ball of her foot and extended her free arm in a delicate arc above her head. Gerald sighed, stood, stretched his arms in the air, then flopped over at the waist. Between his legs, he saw an upside-down Enzo, stalled mid-change in dance belt and sandals, carrying on a conversation with Valentina. As Enzo lingered in the skimpy attire, one hand on his hip, Gerald began to feel dizzy and had to break the sexual spell cast by his Sicilian Adonis by dropping to a crouch, and letting his head hang between his knees. When the blood had returned to his head, he looked up at Ariela, who in a balletic gesture extended one hand to the heavens while the other hand casually reached down to pull the drawstring at the waist of her rehearsal skirt. With a little shimmy of the hips, the skirt slid to her ankles (leaving her in a leotard) and she held the pose, until she dissolved onto her mat in a fit of giggles.

Two days after Bill had declared the play a diSASter, the cast and production team were in good spirits. Changes had been made. Three of the seven unrehearsed scenes had been dropped, and it was agreed that the efficient Bonnie could, with the aid of an early video, take over the blocking of a four-character scene while Bill worked on two larger scenes. That left only one other scene, a solo monologue/song performed by Timothy, culled from material he'd been using for years.

The plan gave everyone hope for some semblance of an opening. But Gerald wondered about Bill's other changes, especially a time-consuming alteration of the entire playing space.

Originally, *Rivers, Saints, Space* was planned as a proscenium piece. The stage, made from units, had already been built and bleacher-style seating was to be set up in front. But Bill decided the platform and the bleachers polluted the integrity of the vast, empty, cathedral-sized room. Never mind that four rehearsed scenes had been staged for proscenium; now he wanted each scene to unfold in a different area, with a mobile audience able to view the action from any direction.

"And I want sand," he told Fernando, "over every inch of the floor."

"But Bill, it would take several tons of sand to cover the floor of this room, it is the size of a soccer field."

"Let me see a sample first," Bill warned, "it's got to be the right color."

"And Bill, pardon me for asking . . ." Fernando smiled at

the men and women sitting silently at the table. "Where will the audience sit?"

"Do they have to sit?"

"Well, yes, I think—"

"We could give them camp stools," Martin suggested.

"Or they could stand," Bill said. "Let's rehearse!"

Bill sat at the long table flanked by Daryl and Annalisa. Polaroids, one of each actor, were spread out in front of them. Bill pointed to a picture and Daryl, wearing his art-handler gloves, placed it in its allotted row. Annalisa had been asked by Fernando to monitor rehearsals and to insure Bill remained on schedule, a task no man or woman was really equal to, but Annalisa displayed a natural sensitivity to artistic temperament by simply staying out of the director's way. Bill, with his facility for recognizing intelligence, demanded she sit next to him. ("Annalisa! Come over here! No, not there! Here! Right next to me!") He consulted her on every decision from casting to bathroom breaks.

They concentrated, now, on assembling a cast for Famiglia, a scene played at a table with the members of an archetypal family: mother, father, daughter, daughter's boyfriend, maiden aunt, grandfather, and family dog.

During the selection process, the actors stretched, studied blocking notes, and opened bottles of *acqua minerale*, but they were acutely aware of each Polaroid shuffled into this or that pile.

Little Ernesto made no pretense of being otherwise occupied and stood at attention, a few feet from the table, gazing worriedly at Bill and his assistants. Finally, Annalisa spoke to him and he slunk uneasily away, casting backward glances at the single, glossy photo he recognized as his own. After a final consultation with Bill, Annalisa announced the roles.

"Vito, *padre*—the father; Letizia, *madre*—the mother; Mima, *zia*—the aunt; Ernesto, *cane*—the dog; Enzo, *ragazzo*—the boyfriend; and Gerald, *nonno*—the grandfather.

Gerald worried he wouldn't be able to concentrate with Enzo so near, near enough to touch. His breathing became shallow, his pulse quickened, and his mouth got dry. Sexual fantasies cluttered his mind. He avoided looking at Enzo, because when he did, the man's face, his lips, black tightly curled hair, his dark fawn's eyes, crashed over Gerald like an ocean wave, leaving him weak and with a painful longing. This is just what I don't need, he told himself, even as he kept a vigilant awareness in case Enzo should glance his way to give him some sign of like desire.

Despite his fears, the afternoon's rehearsal went well for Gerald. Only once during the rehearsal, as he'd sat, half listening to Bill admonish Vito ("No! You've got to be aware of the space *behind* your head!"), did his nostrils fill with the sharp smell of the sulfuric waters, and he looked to see if others were reacting to the odor (no one was). Otherwise, he had surprisingly little trouble paying attention. Bill's directions were clear and precise. The family members entered the playing space, each in the exaggerated style of the character he or she played. The drama unfolded in silence around a long table.

The style of the piece was surprisingly literal for Bill, and Gerald found his direction fascinating, even when he was not involved. The comic entrance of the dog undercut the dancelike, expressionistic movements of the mother. A heroic confrontation between the father and the daughter's suitor gave way to a dance of sexual repression by the maiden aunt.

Bill brought in David, a composer he'd often worked with, to play taped sections of music written for *Rivers, Saints, Space*. It was oddly romantic music for a William Weiss piece, full of lush, repetitive chords. The performance level, as the actors began to learn their moves and execute them along with the music, reached an almost religious intensity.

"No! No! No! I don't want *acting*," shouted Bill. "Just do the moves." He assumed a wide-eyed look to indicate the over-enthusiastic expression worn by several of the performers. "Don't just play to the house, be aware of the space in *back* of your heads!"

Gerald and Ariela smiled at each other; they knew Bill's phrases by heart.

"And be aware of the space between your arms and your torso, your head and neck, the space between your fingers, your toes." Bill slowly paced the length of the room, pressing his palm against his lower back. Earlier he'd sent Daryl for Tylenol. Once, he accidentally stepped out of a flip-flop and a look of confusion passed over his features after his foot came down upon the marble floor. "When is the sand coming, Annalisa?"

"On Wednesday, Bill."

"I need to see it first." He limped a few feet forward, before turning back to slip into the flip-flop. "All of civilization is apparent in the way you stand. When you move, you tell us more than all the books in the world. It's all right here."

Bill's face relaxed, and the hand that held his back floated to his side. His large frame seemed to grow taller. He calmly executed a complicated bit of his own blocking. Even in the patterned shorts and T-shirt he appeared regal, imposing.

"And don't think so hard, it shows in the face. Think with your body, not with your brain. Don't telegraph what you're going to do next. When you turn your head left, turn right." He released the high-held position and pressed his palm into the small of his back. "It doesn't have to make sense. Daryl! Aspirin!"

When Bonnie broke them for lunch, Enzo left without a glance back.

"I'm going to the canteen—see you on the patio," Gerald told Ariela.

When he'd waited for her before, there had been nothing but olives and tomatoes left when they arrived at the canteen. "That's all I want," she'd said, "it's too hot to eat." Gerald had been furious; meals were important for someone in his condition.

The midday sun was blinding as Gerald emerged from the theater into the cobblestone courtyard of the Palazzo dell'Arte. He didn't see Enzo in line at the canteen, but when Gerald came out to the porch area with his tray, he discovered Enzo alone in front of a plate licked clean of food. He was shirtless, eyes closed, arms behind his head, and his face tilted up toward the sun. Mima called from a neighboring table, bringing Gerald out of his reverie, and he joined her and sat with his back to Enzo, but he could still picture the man, a few feet behind, the curly black hairs under his arms glistening with perspiration.

"You look rested," Mima said. "The *acqua calda* is very nourishing, no?"

"Yes, but rested? I didn't get much sleep last night."

"No one did from what I hear."

"Oh? What did you hear?"

"Not so much really. Giovanni has been bragging about his three-way with Fabio and the German girl. Then the sloppy American boy with the long hair—"

"Ian?"

"Yes, Ian with Letizia. Many matches were made last night, I call it 'the night of many hands.' "

"Do you want an espresso?"

"*Grazie, no,*" Mima said, "I think I go back to the theater and take a little nap."

Gerald returned to the café, and when he came out, placed two espresso cups on Enzo's table and sat down. The metal seat of the chair was burning hot, and Gerald tugged the hem of his shorts down to protect his legs. This was the absolute worst time of day for him to be in the sun. Already, the heat stung the vulnerable areas of his face: nose, forehead, lips, and the insides of his elbows and the backs of his hands. Enzo's eyes opened.

"Are you tired?" Gerald asked him.

Enzo sat forward as if he'd been caught napping during a history lecture.

"Am-ah I-ee-ya . . . ?"

"Tired?" Gerald repeated.

"Oh, *si, si!* Eh, you?"

"Yes. Very. But I also have a sort of weird energy left over from the evening."

"*En-ar-gee?* No, me neither. I have need—how you say?— a small sleep?"

"A nap."

Gerald felt as if he were having the awkward conversation

while trapped in a kiln and was relieved when Bonnie came out to hurry them back to the theater.

During the afternoon's rehearsal, Lars came into the theater and stood by the entrance. The designer looked like a wild man with his tangled halo of blond hair and a two weeks' growth of reddish beard. He wore the same blue work shirt and jeans he always wore, but they were caked with dried clay. He crept in and hovered behind Bill.

"Not now, Lars," Bill said.

"Ah, Bill, I must—" Lars stammered.

"I'll come by the studio after rehearsal."

Lars stepped forward in his big work boots. "It is finished," he said.

Bill stared at him for a moment. "The head?"

"Yes," Lars said, picking a bit off clay of his shirt.

"Well, let's go see it then," Bill said, getting up from the table. "Everyone! Come!" he commanded, and the actors dropped their party poses and followed the two men out to the design studio.

All the actors and most of the crew crowded into the Swede's studio for the impromptu unveiling, staring expectantly at the sheet-covered shape on the worktable. When Lars yanked the sheet away, they stared at the sculpture in awestruck silence, while Lars dug his fists deep into his pockets and stared down into the gravel floor. The head was magnificent. Serene and Buddha-like, the slanted eyes were barely opened. Asian features and the hint of a smile playing on its clay lips gave the face a curious but worldly innocence: wise infant or ageless being? The group broke from its reverie with applause and congratulations, and the sculptor's face boiled red with pride and embarrassment.

The actors, rehearsing later than usual, were on a break. The big double doors leading onto the back patio had been opened to allow air in. The patio would double as a dressing area during the show and the actors lingered on it now. Beyond this patio, the hill continued to rise another sixty feet. A goat herder, herding his small flock home in the dusk along a wide path encircling the crest of the hill, stopped and squatted on a rock. His goats stopped too and stared stupidly down, but seemed unimpressed with the crowd on the patio. The tiny bells around the animals' necks tinkled as they bent to pull bits of dried grass from the ground. Above, an early scattering of stars foretold a brilliantly clear night sky.

Gerald took a cigarette from his pack, but replaced it when he saw Enzo approach.

"Allo." Enzo smiled at him and he smiled back. "Eh, you, eh, very good *nonno.*"

"Nonno?"

"Old father, how you say?"

"Grandfather."

"*Si.* " Enzo's raspy laugh sounded like it was pumped out of a damaged accordion. He brought his mouth close to Gerald's ear. "I-ee-ya would like to be with you tonight."

The smell of perspiration and cologne wrapped around Gerald like a pair of strong arms.

"I thought you were mad at me," Gerald said.

Enzo clutched his chest above his heart with both hands. "I-ee-ya? Mad at you?"

"It's just, we haven't talked since . . . last night. You haven't even looked at me really . . ."

"Valentina, that *puttana*, she know."

"But so what?" asked Gerald.

"A big mouth! You understand?"

"But what does it matter if she tells everyone? Who cares?"

"Who cares? Loo-ees! My, eh, friend. Everybody know him. English, like you, He is director, eh, of the dance company in Palermo. Valentina, Letizia, Fabio, all dance for him. Also, he teach at school of Vito and Eunice . . ."

While Enzo spoke, Gerald tilted his head back imperceptibly to track the man's musky scent. He inhaled slowly, precisely, distilling the human from the chemical smells, the animal bouquet beneath the lime aftershave. Though he heard Enzo, understanding came as an echo, a beat off the soundtrack. Friend? English? "Your boyfriend thinks I'm English?"

"No! No! Lewis, he does not know of you. Very bad. Very bad. But we no more, eh, sex . . . not for a long time. But he still love me, he say, so I stay and never, until I see you . . . until we . . . last night."

As he spoke, Enzo's hands mimed emotions for which he had no English equivalent: prayerful imploring, a heart clutched with love, the jabbing finger of accusation. Sometimes his close-set eyes widened until his pupils resembled the dots of exclamation marks.

Of course, nothing about Enzo was really new: swollen lips, rough five o'clock shadow, prominent nose which, this close, showed oversized pores. But now the prison tough had a boyfriend, gossiped, worried about scandals. He's even a little effeminate, Gerald thought. This unmasking didn't make him less sexy. In fact, the complexity, like the comingling of cologne and perfume, made Enzo even sexier.

"Enzo, follow me."

"Che?"

A trapezoid of light fell through the open doors of the theater onto the trodden earth of the back patio. The tinkle of bells mingled with the chatter of actors standing about smoking and drinking bottled water. As the crowd looked up to see the goat herder and his herd move on, Gerald strolled casually along the wall, then quickly turned round the corner and raced down the side of the building where wood for scaffolding was stored. He stepped behind a brace of two-by-fours and leaned against the wall, trying to calm his breathing, as he waited for Enzo to join him.

The darkness calmed him and focused his desire, reminding Gerald of nights before the epidemic, spent in the dark coupling spots of downtown Manhattan. All gone, gated, patrolled, during the initial public fury over GRID or Gay Related Immune Deficiency, as it was then called. He pictured his favorite spot, a covered pier along the river—a dilapidated hull by day—that had in nights past resembled a ruined cathedral, the moonbeams shining through its torn metal roof illuminating a supplicant kneeling on rotted boards before his priest. Gerald had not sat in his little neighborhood park for a year—well, lately it was locked at ten—but once upon a time, he'd spent summer evenings in a half-block of badly maintained paths, bushes, and trees transformed at midnight into a pocket of Sodom.

"Those places were just filthy and dangerous," Gerald had said to Damon, who still pined for the days of easy, outdoor sex. But his friend would probably never leave a hospital bed again, much less troll the Rambles in Central Park. Compassion for Damon prompted Gerald to malign the cruising spots, though he still despaired to see an expensive high-rise replace the parking lot in the meatpacking district, where once he'd climbed into the empty cab of a parked truck to spend a pre-daybreak hour with a handsome stranger.

But where was Enzo?

"Jer-al!" Enzo whispered.

"Where were you?"

"Your friend Ariela watch me very close, I 'ave to go the other way, all the way ah-roun."

Enzo laughed nervously, pressed himself against the building with his hands in his pockets and his arms close to his sides, then leaned forward to peek around the boards.

"No one can see us," Gerald said.

He moved in front of Enzo, kissed him. After the emotional jangle of the day—rejection, resentment, longing, frustration—Gerald wanted a cleansing passion, like making love after a bad quarrel. He pulled Enzo's T-shirt free from his trousers and ran his fingertips over the coarse hair bisecting the man's thin torso. His other hand felt for Enzo's cock beneath his jeans.

"I-ee-ya have something to tell you," Enzo whispered.

"Me, too," Gerald said, deftly opening Enzo's fly with one hand.

Enzo placed his hand upon Gerald's in halfhearted protest, but then transferred it to Gerald's crotch and began to fumble with his zipper. Lack of time and impropriety of place heightened Gerald's excitement. At the same time, the hasty grope felt no less romantic than a lazy Sunday in bed with a lover.

As Enzo released sighs of pleasure, Gerald listened with an actor's ear, for any sign of indicating (as opposed to really feeling) emotions. Every sigh and moan from Enzo rang slightly false, but maybe overacting was a part of his character since he invested the most banal exchange—asking for the time, greeting a friend—with summer-stock enthusiasm. What really took Gerald out of the zone (as his West Coast acting guru described the state) were the false notes in the melody of his own passion: he was thinking about other things.

It's the second time. I have no excuse for not telling him my status, Gerald thought. And if he rejects me? The chain of thoughts interrupted Gerald's ardor like speed bumps in a mall inhibit drag racing. Now even his erection seemed indicated. Casual laughter and voices drifting from the patio made him more self-conscious. Their spot was fairly dark and the boards hid Enzo, but Gerald stood butt-naked in view of anyone who peeked around the corner.

A woman screamed, followed by panicked shouting.

"Is that the party scene?" Gerald whispered.

Enzo and Gerald yanked at their pants like culprits caught in a vice raid and rushed from their hiding place back onto the patio, faces flushed, looking sheepishly about them. It was empty. Voices, shouting in Italian, came from within the theater.

"Someone 'as been 'urt!" said Enzo.

They ran through the open double doors. Some of the actors and members of the tech crew stood gathered at the far end under the sound and lighting scaffolding. A flimsy guard rail, tellingly broken in the middle, dangled in two pieces over the edge of the platform.

"Someone's fallen," Gerald said. He stood frozen in the

middle of the room, while Enzo ran to join a group that stood
staring down at the base of the scaffolding. Gerald saw Mima
nearby and went to her.

"What happened?"

"He had some kind of attack and fell off the platform. Not
so high, but the floor is made of marble. There is much blood
under his head," Mima said.

For an instant Gerald thought she was talking about Bill.
His eyes quickly darted about the room until he saw the
director standing near the curtained entrance to the theater.
Next to him, Annalisa pressed a palm into her forehead as she
spoke on her cell phone.

"Who fell?" Gerald asked Mima.

"Valerio Lights."

The two Valerios, one did sound and the other lighting,
were actually addressed as Valerio Sound and Valerio Lights.
Valerio Sound was a beefy, T-shirt and work-belt man with an
unlit cigarette constantly dangling from his lips. His cousin,
Valerio Lights, was tall and thin with a soft beard that grew
above his top lip and along the sides of his jaw, framing baby-
smooth cheeks. He wore glasses, appeared scholarly, and
exuded root shyness. He often peered down from the scaffold
during rehearsal with genuine interest.

The staccato blast of an Italian ambulance horn wailed up
the hill and the crowd stepped back from the scaffolding as if
proximity made them suspect. Gerald saw that Vito, who stood
near the front of the crowd, held a pair of delicate wire glasses
between his thumb and forefinger. Many of those who had
been kneeling near the fallen man stood. Gerald moved forward, and with cinematic timing, the group broke to reveal

Valerio Lights, his head in a wine-colored halo of blood. Someone had tried to wipe some of the blood and smeared it in a crosshatched tic-tac-toe across the marble floor. A roll of paper towels lay nearby.

"Has any person thought to go outside and direct the driver of the ambulance?" asked Otto irritably.

As he moved away, Gerald stepped forward like a spectator at a street parade filling a vacated spot. He stood directly above the fallen man, the toe of his sandal inches away from the smeared blood. Valerio's eyes were open but something was wrong with their gaze. One eye was as inert as a marble, the other flicked side to side as if on a desperate search. For a moment, this runaway eye locked into Gerald's, but by the time Gerald knelt and put a hand on the man's arm, the frenetic eye had continued on its frantic search.

Valerio Sound returned with a blanket. His hands were shaking. Gerald and Vincenzo helped him cover the man on the floor. Valerio Sound sat back on his haunches. His lips—from which no cigarette now hung—trembled as if he might cry. He spoke to Vincenzo who translated for Gerald.

"He say that Valerio Lights is the son of his father's brother—his . . . ?"

"Cousin."

"*Sì.* He say he never see 'im fall, just hear the wood break and then he look down, and . . ."

A gurgling sound came from the fallen Valerio's throat followed by a release of saliva that ran down his cheek. Gerald took a handkerchief from his back pocket, wiped the man's mouth, and mumbled in a soft, rhythmic chant, "Shhh, it's all right. Everything is all right. You don't have to do anything.

Just breathe, just breathe." The man probably spoke no English, but all Gerald could offer was the lilt of bland reassurance.

The ambulance team belied any generalizations about Italian inefficiency. Two men and a woman from the Bellina emergency unit worked over Valerio Lights with silent authority. They placed a C-shaped pillow under his neck and quickly bandaged his head before rolling him gently onto a gurney. Valerio Sound accompanied his cousin on the long ride to a Palermo hospital.

The room was quiet after Valerio had been removed. The actors stood in small groups whispering or consoling each other like mourners at a funeral. Letizia and Valentina cried softly and an occasional sniffle or sob would erupt from one or the other of them.

Gerald began to shake. He wanted to go outside again, but the stage manager guarded the back door and told him to "please wait for instructions." His mouth was dry and he went to his bag to get a bottle of water. Enzo came over and stood beside him.

"Terrible, no?"

"Awful," Gerald said.

"You think he . . . ?"

"No way of knowing. You okay?"

"Yes! Why not?"

Gerald thought Enzo's reply odd, but decided it was the language.

"Can we eat together later at the Arco Bellina?" Gerald asked. Enzo looked confused. "You—me. Dinner?"

"Si, si, I-ee-ya want to be with you," Enzo whispered.

Another commotion started across the room. Letizia had

succumbed to full, hysterical sobbing and Valentina had followed suit. Enzo pulled away from Gerald and ran over to join the other Italians already comforting the women.

Ariela came up to Gerald.

"They act like he's already dead," she said.

When Annalisa came in with a bucket of water and a mop, Vito and Vincenzo took them from her and washed the floor until only a shiny, unscuffed area of marble remained to remind the company of Valerio's fall. Bill moved back to his place behind the long table.

"I know this is difficult," he began. "Microphone!" When the mike arrived, he resumed. "It's very, very difficult to continue, but we're behind and I don't think we can afford to lose an evening. Does anybody have a problem with rehearsing? Good. Then take five and get into places for Famiglia."

"At least he didn't say 'Valerio Lights would have wanted us to rehearse,'" Ariela said.

Rehearsing was difficult. A grim mood still hung over the room as the actors tried to invest themselves into the roles of the family members. Ernesto, as the dog, made the company laugh, hopping awkwardly to the table, holding his hands as paws, limp-wristed, under his chin and delivering his *woof* with great sincerity. Enzo, as the suitor, executed his moves with the rococo flourish of a nineteenth-century actor. Ariela looked over at Gerald and raised an eyebrow. The more Bill directed Enzo, the more Enzo embellished his acting.

"The space in *back* of your head, Enzo!"

"Che cosa?" he whispered to Vito, looking even more confused after being given a translation.

Enzo struggled to restrain his cartoonish movements, and

Gerald felt his agony. Tonight, I'll explain Bill's style of acting to him—after I tell him I have AIDS.

Annalisa reentered the theater and spoke to Bill who put his hand up to halt the rehearsal. She was smiling as she faced the actors.

"Valerio will recover. He is not completely out of danger, but he will recover."

The company applauded and cheered in genuine relief. Then Annalisa continued.

"A small tumor near his brain caused a seizure, and that is why he fell from the scaffolding. Apparently, the doctors feel the tumor can be removed. Otherwise he has a wound on his head, a small skull fracture, and a broken shoulder."

Gerald thought of the frantic look in Valerio's eye and wondered if "a small skull fracture" was underplaying a bit.

"The good news *is*," whispered Ariela, who had come up beside him, "he has a brain tumor."

"Rehearsal tomorrow at ten sharp," Bonnie said, when the company was released. The actors rushed to gather their belongings like fifth-graders at the final bell. Gerald also rushed to get his knapsack. He wanted to stop off and take a shower at the Sociale before meeting Enzo and the others for dinner at the Arco Bellina, but he needed to explain to Enzo that he'd be at the restaurant a little later.

"Oh!" he gasped, when he looked up and Bill was standing over him.

"Did I scare you?" Bill asked, looking pleased.

"Yes."

"What are you doing?"

"Nothing," said Gerald, with a sinking heart.

In the old days, Bill, an insomniac, would call Gerald in the middle of the night to ask, "What are you doing?" followed by, "I need you, here." "Here" might be home, a restaurant, or another city. The other company members had long since learned how to say no, or simply didn't pick up the phone after midnight. But Gerald always acquiesced.

"Come to dinner with me."

"Sure," Gerald said.

"Meet me in front of the actors' canteen, I just have to go upstairs to send a fax. Daryl!"

Gerald hunched over his knapsack, pretending to look for something, until he was sure Bill had left. He wanted to gather his thoughts before telling Enzo he'd made other plans. Surely he'd understand you can't just say no to *Bill!*

Enzo was waiting for him in courtyard.

"I have to go to dinner with Bill," Gerald said.

"Bill? Oh! Will-yam Weiss."

"I don't want to."

"No, you must!" Enzo insisted. "Maybe after. How long you be?"

"That's the trouble, when you have dinner with Bill, you never know," Gerald said.

The others had left in the van or were on their way down the hill into Bellina. The courtyard was empty. The sky, fulfilling its early promise, was clear and star-filled.

"But I-ee-ya must be with you tonight," said Enzo, with an unappealing pout. A light went on in Bill's second-story office.

"Meet me by the fountain"—Gerald mimed the gushing water—"in the square"—he drew a square in the air—"around midnight"—he flashed ten, then two, fingers.

Enzo smiled. "I-ee-ya wait for that."

"*Enzo!* " Valentina stood at the edge of the courtyard with her hands on her hips.

"Oops," Enzo said, "see you." And he ran off toward the parking lot.

While Gerald waited for Bill in front of the Café dell'Arte, he tried to imagine his evening. They would eat at the Tavola Bella, the other restaurant in Bellina. Bill usually dined there with Annalisa and Fernando, but tonight Fernando had obviously made other plans, and Gerald had noticed Annalisa shake her head apologetically when she spoke to Bill earlier, not long before Bill approached Gerald with the dinner invitation. Bill never ate—or did anything, for that matter—alone.

Gerald was worried about getting out of the restaurant in time to meet Enzo. He could confess the situation to Bill. "I have a date," he could tell him. But he knew Bill would not leave it at that. "A what? A date? With who? What kind of date?" No one liked gossip more than Bill and no one was less capable of keeping a secret. No, he couldn't tell the truth. "I'm tired. I've got to go to bed," he'd say, and then leave in time to meet Enzo.

Gerald looked at his watch. After eight. Bill could keep him waiting for eternity.

Obviously on a mission, Daryl ran by.

"Daryl!" Gerald shouted.

"Bill left his address book in the theater," Daryl said without stopping.

"Wait! Tell him I'm going, I'll meet him at the Tavola Bella."

If he went home first he'd be able to take a shower and pick up aspirin. He always got a headache after an evening with Bill.

CHAPTER TEN

As Gerald started down the hill he saw the single taillight of Enzo's car winding down the gravel road. The car reached the bottom of the hill, then rattled onto the modern four-lane highway bordering the town. Gerald felt a sting of separation and comforted himself with the thought of the rendezvous by the fountain in the town square. The tall spiderlike sprinklers inched across the vineyards spitting arcs of water. In an olive grove, midway down the hill, the leaves glowed silver.

Gerald smiled thinking of the pleasures that lay ahead: a shower, a drink—not wine, but a real one, a vodka—dinner with Bill, sex with Enzo. Of course, he had to escape Bill in time to meet Enzo, had to spill the beans about his HIV status, then, if Enzo hadn't bolted after the health alert, Gerald had to find a place for them to go—and hadn't he sworn off alcohol? It seemed only the prospect of a shower remained untainted by anxiety.

Still, as he veered off the circuitous road to cut through an untilled field, he was struck by the absurdly joyful turn in his life. This time last year he was thirty pounds underweight and didn't expect to live, much less feel anything like physical attraction again. Now he was racing down a hill in Italy under a canopy of stars. He felt filled with—if not love, what?—love for Bill, in his Bermuda shorts and plastic thongs, love for Enzo, with his earnest expression, his heavily stubbled features and adolescent odors, and even a little love for himself, for his legs and feet half running, half sliding down the last hundred feet of this hill. He felt his strength again, as he pumped the sweet Sicilian air into his lungs, flung out his arms like wings, and sang out in the full, supported voice of an Italian tenor, "*Nessum Dorma, Nessum Dorma. Tu puree o Principessa . . .*"

Even the tepid drizzle of a shower at the Sociale felt invigorating to Gerald. He put on black jeans and a snug black T-shirt, but then remembered a fashion article that advised "mature" men never to wear *two* tight articles of clothing, and changed from the jeans into a pair of roomy khakis.

On his way out, Gerald noticed one of the louvered doors ajar at the far end of the courtyard, the room where Valerio Lights stayed.

The Sociale appeared deserted. The staff had gone home and the actors were at the Arco Bellina. Gerald walked to the open door. The room was empty, the unlucky lighting man's things already removed. Gerald sat on the edge of a mattress, thin as his own, but raised on a metal frame. The bed was stripped, the sheet and pillow left on the floor. Gerald picked up the pillow and cradled it in his arms, like an infant. Then he placed it at the end of the mattress and left, carefully closing the louvered door behind.

Instead of turning toward the double-gated main exit,

Gerald turned left, around the corner from Valerio's room, to an emergency exit kept locked from the inside. He slid back the bolt, went out and closed the gate behind him. He tried it once more from the other side to make sure it was not locked. No one will see us come in, he thought, and Enzo and I can have a room. He hurried down the street to meet Bill.

Both the Tavola Bella and the Arco Bellina had outside dining patios under ivied trellises. But the ivy at the Tavola Bella was real, not plastic, and no noisy laughter disturbed the atmosphere. Two middle-aged Italian couples sat near the entrance, chatting over afterdinner espressos.

Bill had already arrived and sat in the back studying a magazine under the rose glow of a paper lantern. The bulky manila folder in which he kept drawings and notes was placed beside him on the table. He looked freshly showered and shaved. His large, fine head, with its receding hair clipped military short, was bent over a magazine. He'd changed into jeans and a short-sleeved, plum-colored shirt, so dark it was almost black. A black sports coat was draped over the back of his chair.

Bill was so absorbed in the magazine he didn't notice Gerald come in. Gerald watched from the doorway as Bill stared at the left, then the right page, turned a page and lowered his hands back to his lap, before giving the same considered attention to the next two pages. He might have been examining a rare book in a monastery library. But as Gerald crossed the patio, he saw it was the silly gossip magazine Letizia had been reading at rehearsal, an Italian version of the *National Enquirer*.

Bill liked to look at pictures. It didn't matter if the pictures were in a pricey art quarterly or a supermarket tabloid, he approached them in the same studied manner. He appeared not to read text, but occasionally picked up on some pop phenomenon and would ask Gerald without irony, "Is Madonna talented?," or "Did O.J. Simpson really kill his wife?"

Sometimes, an image was morphed onto the stage: a white jungle, for instance, inspired by a vodka ad, or the Siamese twins he'd seen in the *Sun*.

Suddenly, in one clean rip, Bill stripped a page from the gossip magazine and placed it in the folder.

Gerald checked his watch: a little after nine. Two and a half hours was more than enough time for a late meal and would leave him time to meet Enzo at midnight. But getting away would not be easy. Bill hated to be alone and demanded continual company—*one more minute; one more drink*—a witness to every moment, right through his last insomniacal minute of consciousness. Courage, Gerald warned himself, be firm.

The proprietress, a large frowning woman hovering at the back of the patio, anxious to place the final food order, started toward the table when she saw Gerald approach. Bill rose with a great moan, and in a dramatic display of exhaustion, collapsed into Gerald's arms.

Bill was one of those legendary people said to average an hour or two of sleep per night. It was true he rarely went to bed before four in the morning, but then he never got up before ten or eleven and was notoriously hard to wake for early appointments. Still, his output of plays, museum installations, and fund-raising events was enormous by anyone's standards and he was nearly always in a state of jet lag.

Gerald struggled to support the larger man's weight as the

unsmiling signora looked on. "I haven't slept *one* night since I got here, not *one* night," Bill moaned.

When they were seated Bill asked Gerald, "Can you drink wine?"

"Sure, great," Gerald said, picturing a cool vodka tonic with a slice of lime.

"Miss, a large carafe of red wine, please."

Gerald stared up at the woman. He could taste the chilled vodka at the back of his throat and willed himself to speak— *Signora, per favore, una vodka*—but the words didn't come and with a little thrust of her chin she retreated to the kitchen. The slam of the screen door felt like a slap, setting off a tiny shiver of despair. He always turned so fucking will-less around Bill, which was part of the reason he'd had to leave School for Life. Oh, well, Enzo will be drinking wine, too, he thought, absently stroking the hair on his forearm.

When they were left alone, Gerald found it difficult to look at Bill. There was always something slightly unbelievable about just being with him. They'd known each other for years, but Gerald was always aware of *William Weiss*, the great director, when he was in his presence, which unsettled Gerald. It took time to bridge that gap between familiarity and adulation before Gerald was able to compose himself, step back from the edge of hysteria.

"Why are you smiling?"

"I don't know," Gerald admitted. "Sorry." He giggled and felt his face flush.

Bill stared at Gerald quizzically.

"An awful tragedy today, no?" he asked.

For a moment, Gerald was not sure if Bill was referring to the lighting man's fall or the state of the play. "Awful," he said.

159

"Did you know him?" Bill asked.

"By sight. He sat up on the platform during the rehearsals. Seemed interested in the show."

"What did he do?"

"Lights. And follow spot, I think."

"Did anyone see him fall?"

"I don't think so." Gerald felt he might giggle again.

"Where were you?"

"On the back patio."

He pictured Enzo and himself next to the lumber with their pants down, and for a startling moment, feared the image might be telepathically communicated to Bill.

"Where did they take him?" Bill asked.

"To a hospital in Palermo," Gerald said. He covered another wheezy laugh with his napkin while Bill stared.

"Memo to Daryl: Send flowers, find out which hospital from Annalisa. Memo to Annalisa: Follow spot replacement. Needs to start immediately. I don't want someone to come at the last minute. Another memo to Daryl . . ."

Gerald patted his pockets frantically while his eyes, watery from held laughter, scanned the table for a pencil.

Once Gerald had filled in for two weeks when Bill was between assistants and had felt completely unsuited to the task, but ever since, Bill, whose mind never completely left his work, felt free to dictate memos.

"Find out from Fernando if whoever runs the Peggy Guggenheim museum in Venice has been invited to the opening—I think it's John Hohnsbeem. His number is in my directory."

"Bill, wait, I don't have a pencil."

"Why not?"

Bill pulled a mechanical pencil from his pocket. When he opened the folder to get a sheet of paper, Gerald saw that the page torn from the magazine was a picture of Princess Diana standing next to the pope. He'd read or heard Princess Diana was in Italy to raise relief money for a recent disaster. Bill picked up the page and cocked his head to one side.

"She's interesting, no? Sort of trashy. She could be anyone—a suburban girl—who becomes a princess."

"Well, hardly suburban. She was *Lady* Diana before they married," Gerald said, frantically jotting down the memos Bill had dictated.

"Memo to Daryl: Find out if Diana is still in Italy. Invite her to the opening."

"Why not invite the pope, too," Gerald suggested, with a smile.

Bill looked at Gerald.

"Do you think he'd come?"

The signora arrived with the carafe and stood waiting for the men to order. Bill poured red wine into Gerald's glass and refilled his own. "To your health."

"To yours," Gerald added quickly.

"Gerald! Would the pope come to see my play?"

"No, I don't think he'd have time. Bill, the signora wants us to order."

"Why not? Miss, would the pope come to my play?"

"The kitchen close soon, signore," said the woman, gesturing toward the screen door.

"*Il pesce, per favore,* " Gerald said.

"Memo to Daryl: Invite the pope."

"*Finito!* " she barked, in reply to Gerald's order. The only entrée choice left was veal.

"I don't eat veal," Gerald muttered into his menu, though, in truth, he'd eaten veal three times that week at the Arco Bellina. "*Pasta e insalata mista. Grazie.*" Just as well, eliminating a course might hasten the meal and get him to the fountain in the square by midnight. He smiled thinking of the dark empty room and the side gate by which he and Enzo could sneak into the Sociale unseen.

Bill ordered spaghetti, veal, and another carafe of red wine and asked that their salads be brought before the entrées. Then he handed a pencil and paper to Gerald. "Another memo to Daryl . . ."

Gerald pressed his palm over his watch as if he might stop time as Bill casually pulled a piece of lettuce from the plate with his fingers, and nibbled it between sips of wine.

"I thought rehearsal went well today," Gerald said, pushing his empty salad plate to the side.

"Famiglia works?"

"It's my new favorite scene in the play."

"Timothy's monologue is very beautiful, no?"

"Always."

"I mean, you see all these people . . . *acting* . . . then this boy comes out—well, I know he's not a boy anymore—he comes out and looks at the audience, looks at the people on stage, just *behaves* . . . naturally. He's curious! It's amazing to see real curiosity on stage, no?"

"Yes, he's fascinating to watch," Gerald said as Bill put another bit of lettuce in his mouth. "Am I acting too much?"

Gerald didn't mean to ask the question, didn't even want an answer. He knew better than to ask about his performance. Bill, who might be devastated by a bad review, predict diSASter for every play, or worry out loud over his artistic standing in America, had no tolerance for other people's insecurities. But dinner alone with Bill, the time constraint, his impending tryst with Enzo, had set his nerves on edge, and tonight, stupidity seemed to be his natural element.

"It's all just too much for me," Bill said, without looking up.

What's too much for him? Gerald was left to wonder. My acting? My audacity?

"What's going to happen after Family?" Gerald said, determined to introduce a subject other than himself.

"I don't know . . . something."

"Something? That should reassure Fernando."

Bill examined his salad.

"The first five minutes and the last five minutes are the most important moments in a play. The first five get their attention and the last five leave them with a final impression." Gerald had heard this dictum before and knew Bill was meticulous with the opening and closing scenes. "I've got the first five minutes. I think the Prologue works."

"Do you have anything in mind for the end?"

"A singing hermaphrodite."

"Oh, somebody sings?"

"Well, not really sings—some final text to music, a prediction. The hermaphrodite sings the future into being." Bill looked up at Gerald. "I need someone who can handle language."

"Yes?"

163

The other performers came from dance backgrounds. Gerald, with his commercial theater background, was the obvious choice for a speaking role. Of course, there were no stars in a William Weiss production, but Bill often gave a moment—a bit of stage business—to an individual performer. Maybe that was why he'd invited Gerald to Sicily, he needed someone who could speak.

Instinct warned Gerald away from early enthusiasm, but the evening was rich with promise, the wine adequate, and optimism came as naturally as his next breath. A hermaphrodite! What might he wear? Would it involve gaffing like drag queens did? Taping genitals into a formless bump? He could call an acquaintance who did drag to find exactly how it was done.

"Will the text be in English?"

"It will have to be, Dede Dorsch is writing it."

"Dede Dorsch?" Gerald asked with surprise. Dede was a rich Texas lady who invested heavily in Bill's work. She'd produced one of his plays in Dallas. At an opening-night barbecue thrown at her ranch-style mansion, Bill had politely admired an abstract painting. "It's an *original!*" Dede screamed in her high Texas twang. "All the paintings in my house are *originals!*" Bill had repeated the line until it became mythic among the Weiss group. "Does Martin know Dede's writing the last speech?"

"Not yet."

"Why Dede, Bill?"

"She wants to be more involved. Maybe it'll be good, at least we know it'll be *original!*"

Bill's perfect imitation of the woman's high-pitched screech sent Gerald into a fit of laughter. The diners at the other table looked over at them.

"Even if the text is no good," Gerald said, blotting his eye with his knuckle, "a good actor can make it work."

"Umm," muttered Bill.

As Bill took a charcoal pencil from the folder and began to sketch on a sheet of paper, Gerald leaned back in his chair to study the ivied canopy. The night sky was visible through the latticework. He closed his eyes. The overture from *The Marriage of Figaro* drifted in from the kitchen; Unlike the Arco Bellina, the Tavola Bella tuned its radio to the classical station. A scraping of chairs, the Italian couples were leaving—*"ciao, signora, ciao, ciao"*—and then were gone. *Squeak, squeak.* Bill's pencil worked busily upon paper. Gerald opened his eyes. From upside down the drawing looked like a figure draped upon the elongated branch of a leafless tree. Other figures floated around the tree.

The acting gears in Gerald's mind began to turn. He saw himself, a being of either sex, languishing in the tree, now vulnerable, now virile, adjusting the image like a new hat, angling the brim down over his brow, pulling a curl free. His head exploded with ideas: *Forget the drag. I won't play him—her—like an androgynous freak in a Fellini movie, but as a pair of opposites: now a man, now a woman.* Again, he stroked the hair on his forearm. *A psychological gesture to trigger my—the hermaphrodite's—masculine side?* Should he tell Ariela about the new role? Or Mima? How do you say "hermaphrodite" in Italian? *Hermaphradita?* Best not say anything, it might sound like bragging. A small cloud of doubt passed over his optimism. Playing a character of indeterminate sex wasn't much of a turn-on—or was it? Enzo might find Gerald's—the hermaphrodite's-dual sexuality provocative.

The wine had a metallic taste. Bill's pencil continued to squeak across the paper. The drawing had taken on an ominous chiaroscuro effect. Gerald picked up the gossip magazine and opened right to the article titled *"Il Papa e La Principessa."* The text blurred, as if he were reading through tears, but it was just his farsightedness. He ran his finger along the uneven tear in the magazine's binding. *I-ee-ya like ah-you.* Why couldn't Gerald believe Enzo? He closed the magazine. *He likes me, he likes me, he likes me.* The chant had a depressing ring—like a New Age affirmation.

Gerald pushed his salad plate farther to the side and glanced toward the kitchen. The signora, who had been standing sentinel behind the screen door, swooped out to clear the empty plate.

"Not yet," Bill said, when she went for his. "Another carafe of red, please, miss."

Gerald looked up at the woman, imploring her with his eyes to bring the next course and hurry the meal. She glanced down at him, unmoved, he thought, and returned to the kitchen. But almost immediately he heard an encouraging clatter of plates and she burst through the door to deliver the pastas. Bill pushed the bowl to the side and continued to rub his charcoal pencil into the paper.

"Bill, don't let your food get cold." Gerald tapped a spoonful of grated cheese over the spaghetti.

Bill placed his drawing in the folder, pulled the bowl of pasta forward and salted it heavily. Gerald was starving. The steam from his plate carried a warm, buttery smell of tomatoes and garlic. Now he wished he had ordered the veal, too. Especially since he wouldn't be leaving before Bill finished and would have to sit through his *secondo* course, anyway.

Gerald recovered some of his enthusiasm for the evening as he ate. He could even imagine telling Bill the truth: *I have a date.* Well, that sounded a bit teen romance. *I'm meeting someone.* Of course, Bill would want to know who and why and what had happened so far. Was it wise to share such intimate information? Was it fair to Enzo? Maybe Bill would think it unsafe for Gerald to have sex at all? Or unethical?

"Last night, I went with some of the actors to this warm sulfuric stream where we all bathed . . . naked."

"Do the actors like the play?"

"Yes, I think so."

"You *think* so?"

"I mean, they like it. You had them a little worried today when you called it a disaster."

"I said that?" Bill asked, smiling.

"You know you did. You always say the play's a disaster."

"I do?" Bill, looking pleased, turned his attention to the pasta.

"Last night got pretty wild." Gerald took a sip of his wine. "I call it 'the night of a thousand hands.'" Bill's fork halted midway to his mouth.

"A thousand hands? That's a nice image, what does it mean?"

Gerald described the warm waters and their amorous effect while Bill continued to eat.

"Who else?" he asked, after Gerald had told of Valentina and Otto's underwater exploits.

"Fabuloso—Fabio—and Zuzie were doing *something* under the water. But I think Fabuloso is queer. And Giovanni, who I'm sure is queer, joined them for a menage à doubtful."

"Which one is Giovanni?"

"Baby fat, cute face, very hairy. In the Prologue he's third from the left. He came up to me a few nights ago, in the Arco Bellina, lifted his shirt and asked me if he needed *electrocution* . . ."

Gerald babbled on, unable to resist Bill's enthusiasm for gossip, but at the same time, he listened to himself with disgust. Bill's interest was largely prurient, he'd never use the information against anyone, if, in fact, he even remembered it tomorrow. But still, discussing the personal matters of his fellow actors with their director cast neither them nor him in a flattering light. And didn't Bill question the credibility of a first-hand narrator who left himself out of an orgy scene?

"Really? He's gay? Who else?"

"Enzo—you know, '*I-ee-ya yam*.'"

"He's gay? How do you know?" The signora brought the wine to the table and they stopped talking. Her lips were pursed, as if she had listened and disapproved of their conversation. When she left, Gerald continued.

"I know about Enzo because *he* met someone at the *acqua calda*, too."

"What about Holgar?" Bill asked.

"What?"

"Was he there?"

"No."

"Is he gay?"

"Bill, he's sleeping with Ariela."

"Umm." Bill twirled his fork in the bowl of spaghetti and delivered a neat bale to his mouth.

At midnight, Bill pushed his untouched plate of veal to one side.

"Then . . . this big bird . . . the suicide bird . . . flies in a diagonal line across the stage and disappears into the earth."

Bill scribbled scenes from the long-running "hit" play he'd opened two years ago in Paris, while Gerald pulled and twisted bits of his paper napkin, turning it into a moist spiky ball. "Pull your chair next to me so you can see," Bill demanded.

Gerald tried not to scrape the chair along the floor as he scooted next to Bill. The other diners had long since left. The signora stationed herself a few feet from their table and stared down on them with her look of permanent displeasure.

"I saw a video of the whole play this summer, Bill." Gerald heard his tone of exasperation and tried to recover: "It was incredible."

"It's become like—I don't know—*The Phantom of the Opera* or *Cats* in France, you can't get a ticket."

"Bill, I think we need to leave."

"Miss, another carafe of red, please."

"No, signore, you *go* now!" She slapped the bill on the table and angrily snatched up the plate of veal.

Gerald shot up from his chair, knocking into the paper lantern above his head.

"You are very rude!" he shouted back at the woman. During the momentary silence that followed, he noticed the radio in the kitchen had been turned off.

"You come too late!"

"*So?* We work late—at the Palazzo dell'Arte," Gerald flung the name at her like a dart. "Which probably accounts for most of your summer business." Gerald had seen the Tavola Bella's advertisement in a program from a concert given at the palazzo: "Pleasant dining, before or after the theater."

"No! Not true! We no need your business! You come too late, everyone go home. I go home, too."

Though the signora had her hands on her hips, Gerald could tell that, like most bullies, she backed down with direct confrontation, and her delivery was less sure.

"Does she want us to leave?" Bill asked pleasantly.

"I don't care what she wants," Gerald said. His voice seemed to him to boom into the quiet evening, as if he were projecting for an outdoor drama. He tried to modulate into a normal tone. "We'll have one more half-carafe of wine, *please*, signora."

He and the woman faced off like gunfighters.

"Never mind," Bill said. He put his pencil down, pulled out his wallet, and dropped a credit card on top of the check. "There, miss." The signora immediately grabbed it and went inside.

Gerald sat. Adrenaline pumped through his body. Why had he become involved in a stupid restaurant drama? Sometimes he blamed an outburst like that on his acting career. After all the indignities and rejections, no wonder an actor carries a chip on his shoulder the size of a showboat. And it wasn't even about the rude signora, but about counting minutes, watching Bill linger through dinner, ordering more wine, pulling another sheet of paper from the folder.

Gerald wanted to meet Enzo more than ever, to feel a pair of strong arms around him until the petty scene ebbed from his mind and body. Bill smudged in a final shadow with his middle finger and carefully placed the drawing in the folder as the signora returned with the receipt. "Grazie, signori," she cooed, as if this final transaction marked the end of a pleasant visit.

"Are you going back to the palazzo?" Gerald held the sports coat and folder Bill had left at the table. "Why don't you get the taxi that hangs out in front of the bar?"

"Where're you going?" asked Bill.

"Home to bed," Gerald said as Bill began to walk down the center of the road.

"Ariela is very very very beautiful in the play, no?"

"Yes, she is—Bill, I have to go the other way."

Gerald planned to circle back to the town square as soon as he was out of Bill's sight.

"The way . . . her arms . . . as Psyche . . . like a goddess . . . I don't know . . ." Bill stopped to pose with his arms lifted in a crooked fifth-position *port de bras.* "Very very very very beautiful, no?"

"*Bill,*" Gerald pleaded, "I need to go to that way."

"All right," Bill said. He stopped and looked up and down the empty street. "Taxi!"

"I told you, there's one in front of that bar that stays open late, You know, the one that's shaped like a figure eight lying on its side. It's just a few blocks down."

"Have one more drink with me."

"*Bill.*"

"One more drink." Again, Bill began an unsteady but determined course down the center of the street.

It was already midnight. Gerald walked uneasily beside Bill debating whether to simply turn and run in the opposite direction shouting his goodbyes, when Bill dropped a heavy arm round his shoulders. "You . . . you're very very very beautiful in the play," he mumbled, resting his cheek on the top of Gerald's head. Gerald, half supporting the larger man, transferred the coat and folder and snaked his free arm around Bill's waist as the two of them stumbled down the empty street.

When they entered the Bar l'Otto, a cheer went up from the actors gathered round little tables or leaning against the bar. Vito, Eunice, Letizia, Valentina, Zuzie, Ian, Ginger, Giovanni, Fabrizio, Mima, and Holgar—nearly everyone was there, except Enzo. They hugged and welcomed Bill with drunken camaraderie as he slumped over the diminutive Ginger and moaned, "I never sleep, Ginger, help me."

Ordinarily, Gerald would be thrilled to make an entrance with Bill, enjoying his status as the director's friend. But now he shrank back, staying near the door, so he could sneak out before someone engaged him in conversation. He gave the room a last check.

"Will you have a drink?" It was Mima.

"I can't. Bill and I already finished three carafes of wine, I need to go home and sleep."

Gerald excused himself and slipped out the door without saying goodbye to Bill. As he ran down the street the sound of his shoes echoed on the pavement.

Two teenagers sitting on the edge of the fountain locked in an embrace didn't even look up when Gerald ran into the square. The fountain was off, though water still dribbled from the mouth of a serpent wrestled into submission by three putti. Gerald walked quickly past as if he meant to continue across the square, but realized it was useless to pretend he was going somewhere when no one watched or cared, so he stopped and sat on a curb.

Perhaps Enzo, feeling awkward in front of these young

lovers, had left. Perhaps he'd made some excuse to the others—
"No, no, I go home to sleep"—which didn't allow him to show
up later at the bar. Gerald pictured him pleading fatigue,
stretching his arms above his head with a stagy yawn. Enzo's
bad acting was so sexy.

Gerald felt empty, sad, and very tired. Lying down on the
pavement seemed preferable to moving. He'd never felt this
tired in his life, a frightening fatigue that made him wonder if
he could get back to the Sociale alone. The motel was only
about a mile and a half away, but the taxi stand in front of the
bar was closer. He shuddered at the idea of running into any of
the group again, but he had to take a taxi home. He passed by
the teenage couple again and saw their hands kneading each
other's crotches.

The few blocks, covered quickly on the way to the square,
seemed to take ages to retrace. Finally, he saw the neon Bar
l'Otto sign at the end of the block and the taxi waiting outside.
But just as he quickened his pace, he heard, "Taxi!," and Bill
stumbled out. Gerald was about to shout—his motel was on
Bill's way—when Holgar also stumbled out of the bar. The big
German glanced back at the bar as Bill opened the car door,
then he quickly climbed into the back seat, followed by Bill.
With a grinding of gears, the taxi started up the block toward
the highway and the palazzo. Gerald turned down the street
toward the Sociale.

CHAPTER ELEVEN

G erald awoke late the next morning with an awful coating on his lips and tongue and a dull headache. Timothy and Daryl were not in the room. He dressed quickly and went into the courtyard—it was empty, and the staff was clearing breakfast from the table.

"Buon giorno. Un caffè, per favore?" The woman set the pitcher back down on the table. Gerald poured cold coffee and milk into a glass and drank it down.

He trudged up the hill under an overcast sky, the first since his arrival in Sicily. The symmetrical rows of olive trees, the grape arbors, even the gravel road under his sandals appeared softened, grateful for this respite from the heat and brilliance of the sun. The coffee had eased his headache and he was able to think more clearly about his predicament. A knee-jerk panic forged during freshman year at drama school reminded him he was late for rehearsal. He tried to compose an excuse, but his mind kept circling back to the truth: I needed sleep.

Gerald had arrived late at the fountain last night and he knew he had to apologize to Enzo. Although he thought Enzo, who knew he was having dinner with Bill, might have waited a little longer. Bill wouldn't require an apology. Gerald had often taken a French leave—one without a goodbye—upon the occasions when Bill was particularly relentless in trying to hold him. Bill's follow-up inquiry was usually, "What happened you?" To which Gerald would give an evasive or silly answer. But might last night's leave jeopardize his frontline position to play the hermaphrodite? Probably not, Bill didn't hold grudges. In fact, Gerald suspected, the director never really thought about people who weren't physically present. And last night he'd had Holgar to occupy his mind.

Gerald should not have been surprised about Holgar, given Bill's record for seducing heterosexual men. One Christmas, during a brief stint as Bill's assistant, Gerald had spent an entire day shopping for the wives and children of the straight men with whom Bill had had "something" over the years. Whatever Bill used to lure these men to his bed—artistic genius?—was a currency so acceptable, none of them, or their wives or girlfriends, ever complained or seemed remotely ashamed about the affairs or drunken evenings in bed with the director. "Would've been my first and last hayride with a man," a macho stagehand in Pittsburgh revealed, "but we were both too drunk to get it up."

Bill never bragged, but he often confessed conquests to Gerald like a smitten schoolgirl. "Gerald, I'm in *love*! I've never been so in *love*!" Of course, *love* never pulled him off a workaholic international trajectory set well into the next decade, but he was constant (in his fashion) and retained an affectionate rapport with his heterosexual harem long after the affairs ended.

Gerald searched for the water bottle in his bag. His leg muscles ached, and he thought he might have a low-grade fever.

He'd left his Tylenol back at the motel, but Mima might have some. He continued his climb, contemplating last night's deep fatigue. I'm battling a virus—capricious, tyrannical—a virus that demands its due for every missed hour of sleep, every moment of anxiety. Had stopping the pills amounted to suicide? Recovering even a little health over the last months had been such a slow, step-by-step process. Had he thrown it away? How long before I get sick again? he wondered. A month? A week?

Outside the palazzo, actors sat along the low wall of the patio. Enzo was chatting with Valentina. Gerald was not ready to socialize, but he hoped Enzo might smile or wave, show some tiny sign of pleasure at his arrival. Ian was also on the wall, stretched out with his head in Letizia's lap, and Zuzie, Fabio, and Vito were at a table nearby, drinking espresso. Why weren't they rehearsing?

"Early lunch?" Gerald asked Otto, who was about to walk past without a greeting.

"The fucking rehearsal is stalled for the installation of the fucking sand," Otto fumed, twirling the end of his handlebar mustache like a villain in a penny dreadful.

Gerald hurried across the interior courtyard and into the theater. A dozen Italian workmen were shoveling a mountain of sand, dumped in front of the double doors, onto the marble floor. Some of the workers were field workers he'd seen in the grape arbors and olive groves. What must they think of this arty project? Shoveling a beach into a chapel? As he was about to leave, Bill came in wearing the flip-flops and shorts and followed by Annalisa. He passed by Gerald, halted in the middle of the room and stared at the mountain of sand.

"NO! NO!" Bill shouted.

The workmen paused with their shovels and stared at him. "STOP RIGHT NOW!"

A number of them, unable to understand, or because they'd already been given instructions, started back to work.

"I SAID STOP!" Bill turned to Annalisa. "*ANNALISA! TELL THEM TO STOP!*"

"*Arresto!* " Annalisa called to the workmen. "*Un momento.*" They stuck their shovels into the sand mountain and sat down. "Bill, I'll get Fernando."

"*What* did I tell him?" Bill said, stepping gingerly across a sandy area of the floor as if he were treading through sewage. "*What* did I tell him?" He looked about the room and spotted Gerald. "I can't leave *one* thing, not *one* thing to anyone else. *What* did I tell him?"

Gerald was unsure what had been told or why Bill didn't like the sand, but he felt some response was required.

"Do you hate it, Bill?"

"*Yes*, I hate it, look at the color! Don't *you* hate it?" Gerald had the eerie feeling Bill was addressing him without having yet recognized him.

"It's too . . . beige . . . or something, isn't it?"

"*Beige? Beige?*" Bill paced at the edge of the sand-covered floor. "It's *JONES BEACH!* "

"Bill?" Annalisa had returned, with Fernando and a few members of the production staff.

"Bill," said Fernando, walking toward Bill with open palms to show he'd come unarmed. "Is there a problem with the sand?"

"GET IT OUT! I WANT IT ALL OUT, TODAY!"

The workmen watched Bill kick through the sand with his flip-flops.

"Bill," Fernando said, with a little laugh, "I thought you wanted the sand."

"*What* did I say? *What* did I say? Show me a sample. I want color—red, gold—*why* wasn't I shown samples?"

"But Bill—"

"NO! I want it OUT! NOW!"

"But Bill, are you sure colored sand is so important? It sounds very expensive—"

"NO! NO! Not another WORD! This play is a *visual* experience, not a day at the BEACH! *Why* do you think I asked to see samples? To waste your time? Get it OUT!"

"But Bill, sand is sand and—"

"I WANT THE BEACH SAND OUT AND RED SAND IN HERE BY THE END OF THE DAY!"

The workmen sitting on the mountain of sand were smiling.

"Now Bill," said Fernando, as if he were trying to placate a child or a madman.

"I WANT RED SAND ON THIS FLOOR BEFORE I START REHEARSAL!"

When Bill left the theater, Fernando's charm rapidly waned. He shouted something at the workmen, whose expressions grew grim as they picked up their shovels and brooms and set to work. Then he turned on Annalisa. Gerald couldn't understand what was said, but heard Fernando's accusatory tone. He remembered Annalisa's frank kindness at the doctor's and wanted to defend her—assigning blame for any of Bill's capricious demands was absurd—but there was nothing he could do. Fernando's rant came to an abrupt end, and he started toward the door, shooting an angry glance at Gerald as he passed.

He'll never forgive me for witnessing his humiliation, Gerald thought, vowing to stay out of the producer's way.

The actors, hovering just outside the theater and pretending to be absorbed in scripts and newspapers, knew something was amiss. Gerald's appearance had the effect of an "at ease" command, and they dropped their poses and rushed toward him.

"*Che cosa?* What happened?"

"Bill wants red sand."

The Italians began to translate and discuss the news among themselves. Enzo stood at the back of the group next to Valentina.

"*Fuck*," said Otto, to no one in particular, "this means there will be no rehearsal for the present? *Fuck!*"

Ian sneered and turned away as if he blamed Gerald for the sand fiasco.

"Red sand?" Zuzie cooed. "Does such a thing exist?"

Gerald wanted food. He started toward the café when Enzo caught up to him in the covered archway leading to the porch.

"Eh, this, eh, bad news, eh?"

"I don't think so. Bill pulls these tantrums all the time, especially during opening week, but I think he's right about this one. Besides, it just means we have the afternoon off."

"But the play!" Enzo slapped his forehead. "*Dio mio!* So much not yet, eh—so much to do!" Enzo had dabbed over a small blemish near the fold of one nostril with a beige cover-up several shades lighter than his complexion.

"Oh, well, it's only a play," Gerald said.

"What? Only a play?"

"I'm so sorry we didn't meet last night, Enzo," Gerald began.

"I-ee-ya yam sorry, too. I-ee-ya . . . very drunk! Vito, Zuzie, walk me, eh, how you say? For sober! Look at my watch—*Dio mio!* I-ee-ya no know how happen."

"You never got there?"

"I want, but—"

"Doesn't matter."

"Tonight?"

"No, I need to sleep." Gerald wasn't angry. In fact, he wasn't even thinking about Enzo, but about the drugs he'd stopped taking. They were sugar pills—or poison—he was sure of it now, and he was right to stop taking them.

"You no want?" Enzo's big lips pressed into a pout, and he lowered his head.

"I'll talk to you later," said Gerald, curling his fingers into a soft fist, which he brushed lightly down the front of Enzo's shirt. He started down the steps. "Bye for now."

He really is the world's worst actor, thought Gerald. If I turn around, he'll still be standing like that, like a punished dog.

Ariela and Timothy were sitting at a table in front of the café.

"Bill hates the sand," Gerald said.

"Oh, no! Bill Weiss hates sand?" Timothy cried out.

"Do you know who Bill was with last night?" Ariela asked.

"Yes, I saw them leave the Bar l'Otto."

"Oh, no, Ariela! Bill hates sand!" Timothy said.

Gerald and Ariela began to laugh.

"Come on, Timothy," said Ariela, "let's get some food and go have a picnic with Gerald before it rains."

The actors were given a three hour break, and a rehearsal was called for late afternoon. They arrived back at the theater, contented after long lunches and naps, but their calm was soon broken.

"The run-through begins at five-fifteen sharp," the stage manager informed them.

"What? Run-through? But no one told us," they cried.

"Fernando wants to see the show. Do the best you can."

Bill had demanded red sand and this was Fernando's revenge. The play opened in a mere five days; at least two of those days had to be spent on tech elements: lighting and sound. It was a producer's right to demand a run-through, to see what had and hadn't been accomplished. But this would be the company's first run-through, and first run-throughs, important as they were for the actors and the director, were inevitably chaotic.

The actors scrambled for scripts, hoping to refamiliarize themselves with scenes left unrehearsed for days. Gerald and several of the other men in the Prologue begged Eunice to run through the precise blocking with them. Because of her good memory and clear accurate notes, she had become something of a team captain: "No, love, that bit, covering the right eye with the left hand, doesn't come till the end, right after the silent scream."

Ariela, using a chair back for a barre, calmly went through the same dance warm-up she used for any other rehearsal. When Holgar, script in hand, approached her, her gaze did not veer from the distant point upon which she focused, nor did she pause in her warm-up routine. Holgar, left to go over the Cupid and Psyche blocking on his own, stormed away.

At five o'clock, Bill arrived and spoke to the stage manager who announced, "People, we will begin in fifteen minutes. Please use whatever costumes are available."

A collective moan went up from the actors. They'd had fittings but the clothes were still basted with pins or needed adjustments for size. Gerald immediately left for the costume shop, hoping to arrive before the crowd turned the shop into bedlam.

"This fucking Mister Weiss—who the fuck does he think he is? Fredrica, bring me more pins!" Jean, after a long, wet lunch with Otto, had just been informed about the run-through with costumes.

Gerald could smell the liquor on his breath.

"You tell your Mister Weiss your Hell of a Party costume isn't finished and if he doesn't like it he can go fuck himself, thank-you-very-much."

If Jean had been a less able designer, his bad behavior would never have been tolerated. But he, along with two local seamstresses, had managed to create several costumes for each of nearly twenty actors on a laughable budget.

Jean handed Gerald two plastic packages.

"What are these for?" Gerald asked.

"Tights! One black, one white. Would you rather go naked?" Jean asked, giving Gerald a lascivious wink. "Give him a dance belt, Fredrica—probably a small. And write your name on it, we don't have extras."

Tights? Gerald hadn't worn a pair in twenty years, and then he was of an age and shape to get away with them, but now? He stood in the corner in his underwear, clutching the new pairs of packaged tights to his chest.

"What's the matter, Auntie? You look confused."

"Ariela, I have to wear these tights," Gerald whispered. She started to giggle. "It's not funny!"

"All the men will be wearing them," she said.

"All the men, except for me, are in their twenties, I can't wear these." Ariela took the packages from him.

"Put these on first, the white ones, then the black."

"Wear both? Why?"

"Because if you undertight with white, your legs will look bigger." Gerald gave her a skeptical look.

"And what about Beds, when I have to wear the white?"

"Just hope the lighting is low."

Gerald put both pairs of tights on and looked in the mirror. The white tights, under the black, did seem to flatter his legs, but the crotch came too low.

"I look like I have no dick in this dance belt."

"I see a little bump there," Ariela said.

Holgar had changed into his white tights and stood, bare-chested, in front of a mirror, while Jean and the other seamstress, a girl who could have been no more than eighteen, fitted him in a vest made of wire mesh. His sturdy Prussian legs needed no undertights. Jean knelt before him to fasten a row of mesh with pliers. Gerald wondered how Jean could concentrate with Holgar's impressive bulge inches from his face.

"Holgar looks like he's smuggling a gourd in those tights," Gerald whispered to Ariela. "What's he got down there?"

"Ask Bill," Ariela said.

Gerald looked at his friend to gauge the seriousness of her reply, but her face gave nothing away.

"Oh, Ariela, they were both so drunk they probably just passed out," he said.

"I don't care, it gives me a good excuse to get rid of him."

Her olive skin shone under the sheer pale dress in which she would dance as Psyche. She stuffed her rehearsal skirt into her bag. "I wish they would both drop dead. I'll fix your tights, but you need to pull your tea set up, and that I won't do."

"Tea set?"

"That's what my mother used to call it. When the dog licked itself, she'd say, 'stop washing your tea set, Alia.'"

"Thanks for comparing my tea set to your dog's," Gerald said.

He reached down into the uncomfortable dance belt and pulled his genitals up flat against himself. Ariela pulled and tugged at his tights until the waist had nearly reached his nipple line, then buckled his belt high on his torso and wound the tights over the belt down to his waist. He would never look like Holgar, but he was pleased with what he saw in the mirror: slim, nice-looking, handsome even, and confident. I should be an actor, he thought.

The run-through went better than anyone expected. And though it was stop-and-go, it gave the actors (and the director) a sense of what was needed to turn the still loosely structured scenes into a play.

Gerald didn't go the Arco Bellina after rehearsal. Enzo would be disappointed, but then Enzo had never made it to the fountain in the town square. Besides, with less than a week left until the opening, Gerald needed time to focus on work and catch up on his sleep. Luckily, he'd bought yogurt, cheese, meat, rolls, an orange Fanta, and a bar of good chocolate at the grocery. After a light dinner, he'd write out a list of his scenes and costume changes and go to bed early.

Though the sun had set, it was still light when Gerald dragged the chair from his room onto the cement veranda circling the charmless Sociale courtyard. He'd given up on the Henry James and borrowed a book of E. M. Forster short stories from Eunice. When he returned with the book, Ian, who had also brought a chair out, was sitting across the courtyard, holding a paper bag. His long hair, still wet from a shower, was combed back from his face. He wore a pair of baggy shorts and a clean white tank top that emphasized the tan he'd been cultivating on the palazzo patio during rehearsal breaks.

Ian looked up and gave a robotic smile which Gerald read as both greeting and sneer. Gerald called back a jokey, exaggerated *bone-a say-ra* in a country twang and the two men sat, on opposite sides of the scorched courtyard, in silence. Ian took a hard roll from his bag, ripped a section off with his teeth and began to chew while absently rubbing the big toe of his bare foot.

"That your dinner?" Gerald asked.

"Yeah," replied Ian, looking at the roll. "This and a banana."

Gerald opened his bag and withdrew the packages of meat and cheese neatly wrapped in waxed paper.

"I bought so much stuff," he said.

Ian looked up with his head tilted to one side, wearing a weary expression, as if Gerald had meant to gloat.

"Is it too rude to extend a dinner invitation on such short notice?" Gerald asked.

Ian shrugged and dragged his chair behind him as he crossed the courtyard, cutting two shallow furrows into the dry soil.

"I'm honored," said Gerald, standing as Ian arrived. He unwrapped the packages of meat and cheese and passed them to Ian. "Fanta?"

"I don't want to take yours."

"I'd actually prefer water, I've had nothing but soda, coffee, and wine for three weeks."

"Tell me about it."

Ian raised the nearly full orange Fanta and drank until the bottle was empty, then burped.

"Bless you," Gerald said.

Ian was about to take a bite of the sandwich, but stopped.

"You don't like me, do you?" he said.

"What are you talking about? I like you," Gerald said, conscious of his defensive tone of voice.

"Yeah, sure. That's why you yelled at me at the airport, and why you and Ariela roll your eyes whenever I come around." He took a bite of the sandwich.

"Ian, you're right, I behaved badly at the airport. But you were acting like such a pushy know-it-all." Gerald tried to eat, but his hand, holding a slice of cheese, fell back to his lap. "I haven't done much socializing for the last couple of years and I've turned sort of . . . impatient. Sorry."

"Forget it," he said. "Why aren't you eating at the Arco Bellina?"

"I don't want to drink, I want to go to bed early, and I'm sort of avoiding someone," Gerald said.

"Can I ask you a question? Are you fucking that Fabio guy?"

"I'm not fucking anybody." Gerald found himself a little flattered by Ian's question. "And especially not Fabio. He's seeing Zuzie, isn't he? *And* Giovanni? When would he have time for me?"

"He didn't fuck Zuzie, I asked her."

"Would she tell you the truth?"

"She said he couldn't get it up until—what's the other one's name?"

"Giovanni."

"Until Giovanni came in on the picture. They're both faggots." He looked at Gerald. "You know what I mean, they're, like, pretending they're not."

"It's not my favorite word."

"Okay, okay," Ian said.

The sky, just over the slate roof of the Sociale, was blue with the ghost of a three-quarter moon still low on the horizon, but directly above them the blue had darkened, almost to black. Gerald, even in long pants and a long-sleeved shirt, felt the chill in the evening air and wondered how Ian could sit in shorts and a tank top. When Ian finished his sandwiches, Gerald unwrapped the bar of chocolate, broke off half and gave it to Ian on a bed of tinfoil. Gerald bit into his half and the release of bittersweet flavor upon his tongue was a simple, but deeply satisfying, sensation. They finished the chocolate in silence.

"Enzo," Gerald said quietly, "that's who I'm avoiding." Bits of chocolate stained Ian's bottom lip, and Gerald reflexively wiped his own mouth.

"Who?"

"Enzo? You know, the *I-yam* guy."

"You're kidding! He doesn't even look gay!"

"And he said something similar about you."

"What?"

"That you don't look straight."

Ian's brow rose quizzically then fell. "Oh, fuck you."

"Well, can you see how what you said might be condescending?"

"You're always trying to teach me something, *that's* condescending."

Gerald folded the chocolate-bar wrapper into a tight little origami package. "Touché," he said.

"So why are you avoiding that guy? Did you have a fight?"

"No, our relationship hasn't advanced quite far enough to have a fight."

"Is it because you guys haven't found a place to do it? Letizia and I can't find *any* place. I wanted to do it in one of those olive groves on the way to the theater—after dark—or just in some field, but she won't do it unless we get a bed, and we both have roommates."

"Enzo has a car, but yes, there is the place problem."

"I doubt if Letizia would do it in a car."

"I just find it . . . too complicated to be drooling over someone right now. Enzo takes up too much energy. I want to concentrate on the play."

"Tell me about it. I don't have a fucking clue what I'm doing in most of the scenes.

"So Ian, why aren't you eating at the Arco Bellina? Did you and Letizia have a fight?"

Ian rolled a ball of tinfoil between his palms. "Got to meet Bill later," he mumbled, not looking up.

"You're meeting Bill?"

"Yeah, after his dinner with Fernando."

"What's the meeting about? Do you know?"

"Said he's figuring out the last scene, he wants me to play some part."

"What part?"

"I don't want to say."

"Why not?"

"It's embarrassing. Oh, what the fuck—it's like a eunuch or something."

"A hermaphrodite?"

"Yeah."

Gerald put the uneaten meat and cheese back in the bag. He tried to take a deeper breath, but it stopped in his chest as if the lower half of his lungs were inert.

"When did he tell you that?"

"Last night after rehearsal. He's having dinner with Fernando and Annalisa but he wants to meet late for a drink. Now that's someone I'd like to fuck—Annalisa!"

"Well, I'm going in. I want to look over some scenes. Congratulations on getting the role."

"Thanks. You think he'll ask me to cut my balls off?"

"That's a eunuch, not a hermaphrodite. Night, Ian." Gerald took his chair inside and shut the louvered doors behind him.

The electric lights in the courtyard shone through, illuminating the floor with yellow strips of light. Gerald lay down fully clothed on his mattress and pulled the thin paisley sheet over himself. He heard Ian drag his chair back across the courtyard, heard him burp again.

How vain I've been, he thought, how ridiculous to think Bill was giving me that part. Five days until opening, two weeks of performance, and then . . . He tried to picture his home, to make himself feel homesick, but couldn't. Homesick for what? Family? They were all dead except for a paternal aunt in Florida and a few cousins he didn't keep in touch with. His *chosen* families (as gay men and runaways referred to their city friends) were mostly dead (except for Barbara) or dropped in an attempt at social housecleaning during his illness. Was he homesick for his home? A midtown studio apartment in New York above an Irish bar?

CHAPTER TWELVE

When Gerald awoke he remembered Timothy and Daryl coming home from the Arco Bellina, but he couldn't recall getting out of his clothes, which lay in a heap on the floor. Then he remembered the conversation with Ian, which triggered a little shiver of despair, but drove him out of bed and into the bathroom to claim the shower before his roommates got up.

"Where were you last night?" Ariela sat on the edge of the cement walk in front of her room with rehearsal notes in her lap. The other doors around the portico were still closed.

"What time is it?"

"Six-thirty, no one is up yet."

"And no coffee for another hour. Do you want to go to the espresso bar in town?"

"No, I'm going to walk to the theater for an early warm-up. Want to come? We can get coffee at the café, later."

The cloud covering of the previous day had vanished, giving in to yet another clear, sunlit sky. "Are you all right, Gerald?" Ariela asked as they walked up the hill to the palazzo.

"Why?"

"You look . . . tired?"

"Probably because I slept ten hours."

"Are you maybe a little thin?"

Gerald felt a cold dread. He hadn't been on a scale in weeks. He thought back to his morning shave, when he'd been alarmed by his reflection. When had his face grown so gaunt? Over the spring and summer, he'd struggled to regain weight. He'd actually been successful and proudly showed his love handles to his doctor. "Look," he'd joked, lifting his shirt to pinch the half-inch of extra flesh. "I need lipo." There was nothing to pinch now, and he knew how quickly a missed meal or a couple of days without an appetite could morph into the point of no return. He wanted to reason his fears away: my weight feels normal, this is what I've probably weighed for most of my life, and I'm just vain and preoccupied with my appearance. But now Ariela had noticed, too.

He and Ariela were both perspiring when they reached the top of the hill. Gerald had set a hearty pace to show Ariela his fitness. The café was not yet open, so they went straight to the theater.

Once inside, they found themselves standing at the edge of a golden-red desert. Sand, raked to a smooth perfection, covered most of the area, with only a narrow path around the perimeter of the enormous vaulted room.

"It's like a red sea," whispered Ariela, "beautiful."

"They must have worked all night. We better not walk on it," Gerald warned.

"Why not?" Ariela said, as she stepped out of her shoes and onto the sand. Gerald ran along the edge of the room to a barrel of rolled rubber mats. He took two and, careful to step in Ariela's footprints, joined her in the middle of the room. They unrolled both mats side by side upon on the sand.

"Go ahead," Ariela said, stepping on a mat, "I'll follow you."

Gerald stood with his feet together at the front of his mat, closed his eyes and took a deep breath. He still felt warm from the walk up the hill as he stretched his arms into the air, arched back, then bowed forward to place his palms upon the ground. He heard Ariela beside him, her inhalations and exhalations accompanying his own as they went through the yoga sun salutations. The exercises relaxed the muscles in his back, his neck, and his calves. But after only ten minutes of yoga, Gerald felt the fatigue return. Well, I walked up the hill, too, he reminded himself. Next to him, Ariela was balanced on one leg in a standing split, the other leg extended up, her head near the floor, torso pressed into the straight, standing leg. She resembled, in her stillness, a Brancusi sculpture.

Gerald lay on his back and closed his eyes: corpse pose. He fell asleep and dreamed of Valerio Lights, standing at the edge of a high platform, ready to swan-dive headfirst into the marble floor. As he was about to leap, he looked down at Gerald. Now Gerald was on the platform with him. The young man with the soft beard and wire-rim glasses smiled sweetly as he took Gerald's hand. "Don't be frightened," he said. Together, they dove down, down into a cushioning sea of warm, red sand.

"The café's probably open. Want some coffee?" Ariela asked. She was sitting in a cross-legged position on the mat.

"Was I snoring?" Gerald asked.

"A little," Ariela said.

"Just a second." Gerald ran across the room for the rake, which had been left leaning against the wall by a workman. As he and Ariela stepped through the red sand, he drew the rake behind them, erasing their footprints.

In the sunlit courtyard separating the two buildings of the palazzo, Gerald stopped and put his arms around her. "Thank you," he said, "that was really wonderful. I was so unhappy earlier. I mean what, besides yoga, can change you, every molecule of you, so utterly?"

Ariela gently pulled away from his embrace.

"A martini?"

Gerald and Ariela worked on their notes over coffee. Even in the scenes in which they played no role, actors were often required to move a set piece or hand someone a prop. It was important to nail these assignments down now, before tech rehearsals, when actors were of secondary importance to lights and sound.

Gerald bent over a piece of paper with a worried expression. Ariela sat next to him with her notebook open, while she looked thoughtfully off into the distance and sipped her espresso. Neither of them cared for this part of the process, writing or studying notes. They both preferred physical intuition and muscular memory, distrusting anything heady when it came to learning a part.

But Gerald was especially wary of depending on his memory during these days of erratic sleep. When he did sleep, his dreams had an exhaustingly real feel that bled into a half-waking consciousness. Waking was like swimming up through murky water toward air and light, and every day it seemed to take a little longer to reach a functioning reality. He wrote out his stage business, scene by scene, in bold letters, easily read without glasses. He'd tape it somewhere offstage and probably never use it, but knowing it was there reassured him.

In the parking lot, wheels crunched over gravel; the actors had arrived.

"Oh, God," Gerald sighed.

"Me, too," Ariela said, "I'm not ready."

Gerald gathered his things and pushed his chair back. "I'm going to hide for a while."

"What if a certain someone asks for you, Gerald?"

"Holgar? Tell him thanks for last night and I can still taste him at the back of my throat."

"Very amusing. Don't be late for rehearsal."

Gerald knew the actors would come from the parking lot, around the front building and up the steps onto the patio, so he hurried through the arch into the courtyard in order not to be seen. He could hear them chattering and laughing on their way to the café. Vito and Eunice were having a row, but he couldn't tell if it was real or in fun. The tinkly, modulated laugh belonged to Zuzie. That bitch starts early, he thought, then wondered, Who's the bitch?

His temporary euphoria from the yoga had evaporated, just as the cool, moist morning air had given way to an uncomfortable humidity, and he felt exhausted.

He was thinking about where to rest when he looked up and saw the dormer windows in the roof of the front building. Except for the costume shop and the café, Gerald hadn't explored this building. Bill, Martin, Annalisa, Fernando, and Lars had apartments on the second floor, but what was above, on the floor with the dormer windows?

The door into the building was on the parking lot side, just where he'd heard the actors chattering on their way to the café, and he peeked around the corner to make sure they'd gone. The side door was open. Inside, a wide, curving staircase led up from a small vestibule to the apartments on the second floor. The stairs were covered in deep green carpet, and he climbed them soundlessly up to a wide hallway with six doors, three on either side. Each door had a brass holder containing a card with the occupant's name written in an elaborate script. One card read *William Weiss, Regista,* and underneath was taped a piece of paper with *DON'T DISTURB!* scrawled in Bill's hand. The card on the door across from Bill's read *Martin Lustinger, Drammaturgo.*

Gerald tiptoed down the hallway reading each name card— no one up here was sharing a room—and then tiptoed back to the staircase. He was about to descend, when he noticed a door he'd missed on the other side of the stairs. It had no name. He tried the handle; it was unlocked. He twisted it slowly. Inside was another, more narrow staircase, this one uncarpeted. A first flight of steps turned abruptly into a shorter, second flight that led to a set of double doors fitted with ornate brass handles. He pressed down on one of the handles and opened the door onto a sun-filled library of glass-covered cases filled with impressively bound books. On both sides of the room slanted walls inset with windows reflected the mansard roof, as seen from below. But at the far end, in an anachronistic architectural touch, a large picture window had been cut in from ceiling to floor. He'd never seen this window from below because it was visible only from the far, unused side of the building. The view looked onto blue sky over the tops of trees on an untended side of the hill and made the room feel like a bibliophile's tree house. An oriental carpet, worn thin in spots, but still brightly flecked with scarlet, indigo, and gold, covered most of the dark wood floor. A long wooden table, with a straight-backed chair behind, suggested a scholar's solitary contemplation of rare volumes of Italian verse, or the daily calligraphic tasks of a monk. Had the large globe cradled at an angle upon a carved pedestal of dark wood offered the monk a view of the world beyond the Mediterranean? A fainting couch, upholstered in a glossy forest-green fabric, gleamed in a canopy of sunlight, in front of the big picture window.

Gerald had never heard anyone mention this hidden library. A musty unused smell suggested the room rarely saw visitors. From the dormer windows on the one side he could see the courtyard between the two main buildings, and on the other, the patio in front of the café. Looking out the patio side, he saw Ian lying on his back on the low wall looking up, and stepped away quickly, not wanting to be spotted.

It was then that he noticed a small door slightly hidden behind one of the glass bookcases. He went over, opened it, and sighed with pleasure at the tiny room, no bigger than a closet, whose solitary furnishings consisted of a bowl-sized sink, a commode, and a full roll of toilet paper.

As Gerald pulled a book from one of the glass cabinets, and closed himself in the little closet (there was even an inside door latch), he felt that at least *one* dilemma, in a situation fraught with dilemmas, had come to a satisfactory resolution.

The actors, even the Italians, arrived at the theater before the final warning call from Bonnie. They removed their shoes and stood shyly around the perimeter of red sand like bathers at a pond's edge.

"*Bella, bella,*" whispered Valentina in reverent tones. "The earth turns red with the blood of martyrs. William Weiss! He is a genius!"

"Red sand," Mima said curiously, "where did he get it?"

Ernesto, the tiny cigarette mooch, put his toe into the sand as he glanced around with a sly smile. When no one seemed to notice this, he placed a foot squarely in and then the other.

"No, Ernesto!" cried Valentina. "You must not!"

Bill strode in briskly followed by glum Daryl and efficient Bonnie. At the edge of the sand, he halted them with an upheld hand before he, himself, trod on, leaving a wake of flip-flop prints. He stopped in the center of the room and, hands on hips, turned a slow three hundred sixty degrees to survey the space. The actors, full of silent expectation, watched as Bill slowly bent to scoop up a fistful of the red sand. With his clenched hand held out from his body, he let the grains sift between his fingers, then opened his hand to reveal a palm coated in eerie red. Once more, he turned slowly in place, round and round, this time with an open hand as if he were pushing against the air.

Genius at work, all he needs is a bucket and spade, thought Gerald, still smarting from Bill's casting of Ian as the hermaphrodite. Bill turned faster and faster, like a Sufi dancer, until he stopped suddenly, looking surprised to be in this room, with these people.

"Who can spin?" he asked, when he had regained his composure. Letizia and Eunice giggled self-consciously. "Ariela, can you spin?"

Ariela walked onto the sand and began to turn slowly, but she had trouble staying in one spot.

"Wait."

Bill motioned to Daryl, took his bottle of water and poured it onto Ariela's open palms. She bent forward and pressed them into the sand. "Hold your hands in front at the beginning—like this," Bill said, "and focus on the thumbs. Then gradually move your hands outward, but keep the focus point where your thumbs were and you won't get dizzy."

She began again, gradually increasing the speed, until she was spinning smoothly.

"Okay," Bill said flatly, "that's enough. Practice. You have to learn to hold the focus for a long time. Everyone should learn to do that, I may use it later." Bill turned to Bonnie. "The table's not here."

Several of the other actors ran to set up a production table at one end of the room, while others moved onto the sand to try the spinning technique. Vincenzo, Otto, and Holgar turned the dance into a competitive event to see who could twirl the fastest until each succumbed to dizziness and fell. At a signal from Bill, Bonnie clapped her hands.

"People! We will begin where we left off—with Famiglia. Get in place. *Avere fretta!*" Bonnie said.

Vincenzo muttered something under his breath that made the other Italians laugh. Though Bonnie was not fluent enough to understand, she knew the comment had been aimed at her, and her face, under the baseball cap and frizzy hair, went pink.

"BONNIE! What's taking them so long?" Bill's voice had its usual unsettling effect on the company, and they hurried to get in place.

Gerald was still at the side getting out of his shoes and socks.

"Gerald! What's the matter with you today? You're holding everyone up!" Bill called out.

"I'm coming," Gerald said.

Bill used Balinese "sticks," teak dowels the size and shape of the cardboard center in a roll of toilet paper, to start scenes. The sticks, when hit together, made a resounding click. Enamored with the sharp finality of the sound, Bill was also fond of hearing them during a scene, and increasing the tempo if a performance lagged. Bonnie now held the sticks aloft, waiting for Bill's signal to begin.

The choreography appeared simple. In the beginning of the scene each family member entered the playing space in a stylized character walk and took his or her place at a long table. The daughter and her suitor skipped in with youthful ardor, the papa strode in with paternal authority, the *madre*, proud and long-suffering, walked regally, the dog on all fours, and the *nonno*, bent with age, moved slowly and deliberately.

The *nonno* was the first to move into the playing area. Gerald stood in his place trying to clear the sting of Bill's voice from his mind. Why had he been singled out? Bill's admonishing tone had made him self-conscious and he imagined all eyes upon him as he stood in place waiting for the click. He knew he must be perfect, but he was unsure if the soft thud he heard signaled his entrance, and he started uncertainly on his walk to the table.

"No! No! Stop!"

Gerald froze.

"Why haven't you learned to do this yet?" Bill said irritably, and snatched the teak sticks from the stage manager. He struck them against each other sharply to make the loud resonant click, then handed them back. "Is that really so difficult?"

Although relieved that Bonnie, not he, was the object of Bill's scorn, Gerald also felt for the girl. Bill was notorious for singling one person out as a repository for his frustrations. Daryl had originally been the whipping boy, but he'd managed a sort of immunity by cloaking himself in a fog of alcohol. Bill, momentarily bereft of a vulnerable target, found Bonnie.

Bonnie's anxious manner and pathological need to please made her a perfect candidate for Bill's ire, but what really decided her fate were her clothes. She wore Bermuda shorts and colorful shirts, the same resort wear, in fact, that Bill had lately adopted. But there was something about Bill, even in flip-flops, that suggested austerity and commanded respect. Bonnie, on the other hand, seemed determined to offset a humorless managerial efficiency with a saucy blouse tied at the waist and a long-billed baseball cap perched atop the unruly frizz on her head.

When the stage manager's outfits, often newly purchased from local tourist vendors, began to appear, Gerald had expected a reaction. Bill had once humiliated a dancer for appearing on stage with her hair down instead of pulled into a tight bun. When Bonnie arrived at rehearsal in a blouse emblazoned with *CIAO!* printed in bold letters over the boot of an Italy rendered in the red and green colors of the flag, Gerald had thought to warn the girl of an inevitable attack, but the truth was, he wasn't all that fond of her himself.

When Bonnie struck the sticks together a second time with the same muted click, she stared down in horror at the objects in her hands as if they had somehow betrayed her. She hit them together again and again, but could still not produce the same confident tone Bill made. When he put his hand out, the chastened stage manager handed him the sticks and bowed her head, pretending to busy herself in the production notebook.

"Places, and . . ." Bill hit the sticks together with a dynamic clack and the actors began.

Well past time for the lunch break, Bill was still not halfway through Famiglia. He'd spoken harshly to Gerald twice more. Once for fidgeting and once for missing a cue. Gerald had missed the cue, but he'd only just learned it, and as for fidgeting —who wasn't fidgeting while Bill microdirected Ernesto, as the *cane,* whose only task was to sit up and beg for a table scrap. Honestly, Bill acted as if there were *weeks* of rehearsal left instead of days.

When Bill left to take a phone call, and Annalisa mercifully broke the actors for an overdue lunch, Gerald rushed out of the theater. He crossed the courtyard, slipped around the side of the front building, through the double doors and up two sets of stairs to the secret library.

Despite the oppressive heat in the room, he felt a wave of relief as he closed the door behind him and hurried toward the fainting couch. He'd have to go back down to the canteen soon if he wanted to eat, but just to lie here with his eyes closed, even in the stifling hot air of the library, was more appealing than food. Every moment was precious. The inviting couch seemed to have been waiting for his return. Alone, free of any necessity for social interaction, Gerald's relief was as palpable as a drug.

Midday naps weren't such an unusual occurrence in Italy, of course, where nearly everyone rested after lunch. But for a workaday American, especially a New Yorker, a midday sleep was synonymous with old age, depression, or indolence, and even when Gerald was unemployed (most of his life), he'd avoided sleeping during the day. Over the last debilitating year, he'd reluctantly succumbed to long naps and eventually came to relish that point in the late morning, the only time of day his building was not darkened under the shadow of Midtown skyscrapers, when the rays of the sun fell across his bed, and he could curl up like a cat in the warm spot.

Gerald fell into a dreamless sleep on the fainting couch and might have gone on sleeping if rivulets of sweat had not begun to fill the creases of his neck and run down beneath his collar. He opened his eyes, sat up quickly, and rushed to the window. The patio was empty but he heard a clicking sound coming from somewhere below. What time was it? Had rehearsal begun? He looked at his watch but couldn't remember when they'd been dismissed for lunch. It didn't matter, he was late.

As Gerald turned the corner of the building to cross the courtyard to the theater, he saw the stage manager, facing the wall with her back to the sun, hitting the Balinese sticks together with grim determination. He tried to pass quickly without notice, but Bonnie turned and spoke.

"You're late," she said, "they've started."

Gerald smiled, determined not to appear anxious about the time.

"It's only a play, Bonnie. Besides, how can they start, you've got the sticks?"

"It's an extra pair. Hurry up, Bill was asking for you."

"I was hiding." He started toward the theater, stopped and turned back to Bonnie. "You know why you were having trouble with the sticks this morning?" he asked. She looked up cautiously, as if expecting an insult. "You got caught in the 'up there' syndrome."

"What's that?" she asked suspiciously.

"It's when someone is up there trying to do something and everyone's watching. It happens to us all, we just go brain-dead, lose all ability to take direction or understand what anyone is saying." He smiled.

"I didn't go brain-dead," she said.

"No, but you know what I mean, it happens to actors all the time. You tell them to go left and they turn right. And the worst thing is, everybody who's not 'up there' can see exactly what you're supposed to be doing."

"I'd like to see any one of them try to do my job."

"Well, I'm sure they couldn't—nor would they want to. It's just how the phenomenon works. You can watch someone else and know exactly what he or she should do. And it's not just in theater. I saw a game show where they asked this really intelligent woman, 'What's the largest city in Asia.' She answered 'China,' and the audience all groaned—and of course, the woman knew she flubbed, but she's up there so she's like in a cloud."

"So, you all know how to make these fucking sticks work?"

"I think I do." Gerald resisted the urge to take them from her. "See, I think you were trying to make more sound by hitting them harder, but Bill holds them loosely. Yeah, like that. And then you just hold one still and hit it with the other one."

Bonnie held them in clenched fists.

"No, just keep them loose, and just hold this one still and hit it with the other one."

She took a breath, exhaled, and hit the sticks together with a resounding click.

"See, you got it!"

Bonnie dropped her arms to her side and looked at Gerald.

"He hates my guts."

"He doesn't hate you. But he is—for the moment—picking on you."

She leaned back against the stone wall of the building, her face shaded by the bill of the cap.

"You know," she said, "this is the first time I've ever done this kind of work."

"Really? You've never been a stage manager?"

"Never. In college I stage-managed a play, but I'm really a biochemist. I've been working for the last ten years in a lab at the University of Wisconsin, and I needed to get out and do something different. I had this Italian friend who knew Fernando, so I wrote and told him about the one college production I stage-managed, and he gave me the job. I'm sure it's because he can pay me less than a real stage manager."

"I would never have known you weren't real."

Bonnie stuck the sticks in the pockets of her shorts. "You better get to rehearsal."

"I will, but no hurry—might as well be hanged for a sheep as a lamb."

Gerald turned for a moment to feel the sun on his face. It felt nurturing, but he hadn't put on sunblock this morning and worried about the spots recurring this close to opening.

"You know, Bonnie, Bill would have taken the sticks from you even if you'd clicked them together perfectly."

"But why?"

"Because he wants to do everything himself. If he had his way, he'd be playing all the parts, and he'd be the stage manager. He was determined to be the stick-clicker."

"You know, I kind of got that impression, I mean why make such a big deal out of it."

Gerald looked with curiosity at the new Bonnie, not the uptight stage manager with bad social skills, but the biochemist who came to Italy to take on a job for which she had no experience. He admired her bravery. Maybe one day he'd give her some wardrobe advice, but this wasn't the time.

"Okay, see you inside," he said.

When he was halfway across the courtyard, she called to him. "It's Tokyo."

"What?"

"The largest city in Asia is Tokyo."

"I don't remember what the right answer was."

"I just told you, it's Tokyo."

When Gerald slipped into the theater, the family was already in place at the table. Daryl, his eyes closed, sat in for him in the grandfather chair. Bill was correcting Mima's movements. The actors facing Gerald all saw him enter. Enzo, his posture rigid, stared at Gerald with wide eyes. I'm not that late, Gerald thought, as he shook Daryl's shoulder and reclaimed his seat. Ariela gave him a cryptic smile. Enzo remained saucer-eyed, but his expression was not astonishment Gerald realized, but rather, concentration: he was acting.

"Let's go back to the entrance of the mother," Bill said.

Gerald thought his late entrance had gone unnoticed, until Bill, about to bring the sticks together, stopped. "Where were you?"

"Napping," Gerald said.

"Napping?" Bill repeated, as if unfamiliar with the term. "Well, don't nap."

Clack! went the teak sticks and the *madre* began her proud, resigned dance.

Chapter Thirteen

By now, the big vaulted back building of the palazzo-turned-theater had become a second home for the performers. Nesting against pillars and along the walls, they littered the floor with backpacks, bags, paper bags, bottles of water, tobacco, empty espresso cups, notebooks, books and clothes, and made impromptu beds of exercise mats with sweaters or shirts balled into pillows.

Rehearsing is, above all, a physical business and the space had a lived-in smell, even though the performers, for the most part, were fastidious about personal hygiene. Toothbrush and paste, soap, moisturizer, deodorant, were the integral elements of an actor's day kit. But by late afternoon, all the perfume in Italy could not disguise the human smells. No one minded. The job demanded a sweaty intimacy, and an individual's smell was worn like a clothing accessory—a scarf tied at the neck, a leather wristband.

The actors had also gathered makeshift costumes, props, and set pieces from the shops and grounds of the palazzo and brought them into the space: woven baskets, two beach balls, several broomsticks, paper fans, plastic champagne glasses, empty eyeglass frames, a baby doll, a toy snare drum, seven pairs of heavy-duty electrician's gloves, a velvet cape, wooden crates, folding chairs, a hollow door used as a palanquin to transport a deity. These items were set in places convenient for an entrance.

The actual playing area, lately defined by the red sand, remained, by some unspoken set of rules, pristine. Shoes (except for Bill's flip-flops) were always removed before entering. Like monks in a Zen monastery, several of the performers had taken it upon themselves to rake the sand smooth at the start of rehearsal and between scenes.

But suddenly, in the final days before the opening, the familiar intimacy of the theater changed. Lighting and sound technicians arrived. Scaffolding, this time with secure railing built around the perimeters, appeared overnight, and a motorized cherry picker hoisted a lighting man fifty feet up to secure instruments to beams and attach colored gels to Fresnels. The actors, mindful of Valerio Lights' fall, watched with trepidation or turned away until the machine's arm returned its passenger to earth.

Designers and their assistants brought in real props, set pieces, and costumes from the shops, and just as often plodded back across the sand with them when Bill demanded changes. A second wooden plank, secured upon yet another set of sawhorses, was added to the production table. More chairs arrived to seat the burgeoning crew. Civilians, rich patrons of the festival invited by the producer or director to witness the *actual* making of a William Weiss piece, stayed until beads of sweat appeared on their tanned foreheads, the heat began to wrinkle their linen suits, and their smiles went slack with the stop-and-go boredom of a typical rehearsal.

For the actors, the added technical elements and the invasion of outsiders was a mixed blessing. A lorgnette, a feathered fan, a gilded throne, could add excitement and verity to a performance grown stale through repetition. The use of sound—lush opening music for Prologue, bomb blasts for Hell of a Party, or an atmospheric tape of nocturnal insects to accompany the Cupid and Psyche scene—acted as emotional filler and revitalized artistic imaginations. And though the tech crew were members of the production family, they still counted, in the eyes of the performers, as audience. Rote gestures, reimagined through the eyes of a shop assistant, gained focus and power. Concentration improved under the surveillance of the prop master and performances grew sharp.

This captive audience was often difficult. The Italian stagehands, in particular, yawned openly during afternoon rehearsals, or slept in full view of the cast, and even though more people were watching, less attention was paid to the actors. Bill stopped constantly to correct a sound cue or inspect a new prop or costume. With the technical elements to deal with, he sometimes offered only terse, glancing comments to actors—"More interior!" "Less hands!" "No! No! No!"—as if he had despaired of the possibility of real improvement this close to an opening. But then, for no apparent reason, he might lavish twenty minutes on some bit of blocking minutia: "No! No! More space between the thumb and forefinger! Air between the arm and the torso. Do it again."

Tempers never flared in front of the director, but offstage threats were as common as double espressos.

"If I am acting too much," hissed Zuzie, "then perhaps next time he hires a plumber."

"I won't wear a parrot's face," Letizia cried, referring to a beak Jean had attached to her face. "Bill don't say I'm a bird, he say, *like* a bird."

Gerald observed the onstage mayhem and the backstage emotions as a man on high ground observes the flood below, safe for now but with an anxious eye on the rising water. He knew his finite energy must see him through opening night. No, he wasn't ill, nothing like last year, but something was, well, off.

Still the first one up at the Sociale, Gerald had lately, during those early hours, found himself in an alarming fog of fatigue. He was dazed and forgetful. Twice he'd forgot to bring his script to the theater. He left his dance belt in the room and had to make do with his boxer shorts bunched under his tights. He continually forgot the yogurt and cheese bought to sustain him through the long afternoons and evenings only to discover them days later, spoiled, in the communal fridge.

After sleeping through a lunch break, he no longer trusted himself to take an unattended nap in the third-floor library and substituted brief meditations with his legs folded into a penurious lotus position that precluded drifting off. The private bathroom was still a joy, but he'd been spotted by a cleaning lady on his way up the carpeted stairs to the second floor and she'd spoken sharply to him in Italian. Though he'd smiled and continued on his way as if he had business being there, he was still afraid that she'd make some kind of fuss later. And once, about to enter the building, he ran into Fernando and slunk back to the canteen rather than risk discovery.

Another aspect of Gerald's energy-conservation program involved Enzo—or rather, avoiding Enzo. He even tried to avoid thinking about him, visualizing his mind as a running river and the Enzo-thoughts as leaves floating past on its current. This basic meditation technique worked in the short term, but required more vigilance than Gerald could sometimes muster. In the middle of rehearsal his lips would begin to burn from remembered kisses or his concentration drift as the muscles in his back loosened under the memory of Enzo's strong hands massaging him in the sulfuric waters of the *acqua calda*. Swallowed semen, deep salivating kisses, ejaculating cocks—the bodily fluids began to flow unbidden into Gerald's daydreams as memory slipped into fantasy. He tried to wrench his mind from the sex scenes back to the flowing river, grown black and glutted shore to shore with rotting leaves. I'm not a monster, he chanted to himself, I'm not, I'm not.

The actors stood silently in place while Bill set sound levels during an excruciatingly boring Hell of a Party rehearsal. Gerald held an empty plastic martini glass by the stem, rotating inch by inch until he sighted the star of his conflicted fantasies. Enzo stood as still as a wax figure, a Popsicle stick as cigarette holder dangling between his two fingers. His shirt was in the costume shop having its buttoned front Velcroed for quick change. Bare-chested under the tuxedo jacket, his skin glowed against the satin lapels of the formal wear. His short hair had grown in the last weeks, and he'd begun to gel the dark curls flat against his head. His head was lifted, the large nose held high like some grand object upon a platter.

Gerald stared. Each time he looked at Enzo, he felt as if he'd forgotten how attractive the man was: the doe eyes, the ridiculous fullness of his lips, the swarthy coloring (Sicilian olives caught in sunlight). Actors nearby stood slack-jawed with boredom—Vito's eyes were closed as if he'd mastered sleep standing up—but Enzo, with his earnest concentration, stood out like something raw and beautiful.

A recorded blast shook the speakers. Several of the actors shrieked in surprise. Nervous giggles followed.

"Fall!" Bill shouted. "Fall! No! No! Not like a sack of potatoes. Slowly! Gracefully! Again!"

Bill cued another bomb blast. Still shell-shocked from the first loud boom, several of the partygoers faltered and descended in slow jerks like drunks. Gerald, on his way down, twisted balletically, to make sure his jacket was between him and the sand and, at the same time, keeping Enzo in his line of vision.

"Gerald! Stop dancing!"

"What?"

"HOLD!" Bill commanded, then turned to discuss new cues with the sound engineer.

The actors lay motionless upon the ground, some closed their eyes to catch a minute's sleep. The sand had dried under the harsh stage lights, producing a fine moisture-leaching dust. Gerald hated the feeling on his skin. The tips of his fingers felt especially dry and he surreptitiously licked them. Fifteen feet away, Enzo also lay on his side, upside down from Gerald. At first, seeing Gerald, his lips widened into a relaxed, provocative smile, as his eyes wandered slowly down Gerald's body. He looked back up and grinned suggestively. I'm not a monster, Gerald thought, as he let his gaze drift past a rectangle of chest and abdomen framed by maroon suspenders, over a pleated cummerbund, onto the shiny fabric of tuxedo pants where, if his eyes weren't playing tricks, a satin crease shifted slightly. Enzo pushed the tip of his tongue between his lips, then moved it in a slow circle like a street-corner prostitute. The man's an idiot, Gerald thought, as he contracted his pelvis in a futile effort to readjust his awakening penis in the confining dance belt.

"Stay down for a count of . . . thirty-seven," Bill called to the actors, "then get up. Slowly! Otto is in the middle. *Everyone!* Take your cue from Otto."

The actors rose, the prerecorded audio background of piano music and cocktail chatter resumed, and Enzo was blocked from Gerald's view by Valentina and Otto who had stepped toward each other in a stagy tête-à-tête. Despite Gerald's precautions, sand inside his T-shirt scratched his still-tender flesh, and as he reached under to brush away the irritating granules, his arousal waned.

As the afternoon rehearsal continued, most of the actors, standing or sitting in place while Bill set sound and light levels, entered into a private space somewhere between ennui and sleep. Annalisa entered the theater with an armful of papers.

"*Per favore,*" Valentina pleaded, holding her hands together in an attitude of prayer as Annalisa passed.

"In a second," Bill muttered, when Annalisa whispered to him over his shoulder.

"Just ten minutes. Look at poor Valentina," she said.

Valentina wrapped one leg around the other and hopped up and down in a mime of desperation. Bill appeared startled. Had one of the marionettes suddenly come to life? He put his pencil down, leaned back in his chair and rubbed at his face like a cat.

"All right, ten minutes. *Daryl!*" Daryl loped across the sand in his heavy shoes. "What do these say?" Bill asked, handing him Annalisa's papers.

"Uh, this is from the opera house in Salzburg: 'Dear Mr. Weiss, alas we are unable to honor your request for an additional one hundred chorus members . . .'" Bill was already on his way to the door as Daryl, still reading, followed.

A collective sigh rose from the actors, as they slumped out of their stiff Party poses, pulled off headdresses, loosened cummerbunds, and removed tuxedo jackets. When Bonnie turned on the big standing fans, too noisy to run during rehearsal, Ginger, Eunice, and Letizia grabbed the hems of their evening gowns and ran in front of them, leaning into the blasts of air, like carved figures on a ship's prow. The others headed toward their bags to get a cigarette or a snack before drifting out into the sunlit courtyard. Gerald was still in the playing area brushing the sand off his trousers when Enzo approached.

"Very sexy, this party, no?"

"Yes, and I usually don't like parties."

"No?" Enzo asked, his eyebrows tenting into a troubled arch. "Why?"

"But I liked this one," Gerald added quickly, regretting his silly attempt at humor, which had only made communication seem less possible. The bright Fresnels aimed at the playing area went out and the unlit chapel assumed the heaviness of an overcast day.

"Uh, cigarette, please," Enzo asked.

"Enzo, you smoke?"

"Sometime."

"It's rolled," Gerald said, miming the action, "I'll get my tobacco."

"*Sì.*"

The sand, still warm from the powerful stage lights, cooled

noticeably as they stepped beyond the recently lit playing area
and walked off the artificial beach to get their sandals. Gerald
noticed that his sandals, recently purchased in town, appeared
touristy next to Enzo's worn leather ones. Above them, the
new lighting man sat on his scaffold typing cues into a com-
puterized lighting board.

"My bag's on the other side, I'm just gonna . . ." Gerald
said.

"*Si*, I-ee-ya wait outside, eh?"

"Okay, see you outside."

When Enzo left, Gerald took his tuxedo jacket off and
hung it over the back of a folding chair near his things. He
reached into his bag and pulled out a little Handi Wipe™
package—about the same size as a wrapped condom. He'd
never considered packing condoms when he left New York.
The three in the drawer of his bedside table had been there for
years. He unfolded the moist Handi Wipe™ and swabbed gently
under his arms and over as much of his torso as he could reach.
The quick wash was refreshing even if the chemical scent was
reminiscent of bathroom disinfectant. Of course, with Bill, this
ten-minute break might stretch into a half hour, or an hour, or
even an afternoon. He glanced down at a tube of toothpaste to
make sure it *was* toothpaste before squeezing a quarter inch
upon his tongue and swishing it around his mouth with a sip of
bottled water. What would Enzo think of his secret library? he
wondered. After a fruitless search for an empty coffee cup in
which to spit, he swallowed the chalky toothpaste water,
quickly pulled his T-shirt back on, grabbed the package of
tobacco, and hurried out of the theater.

The cobblestone courtyard between the two buildings was

empty. Perhaps Enzo had misunderstood and was waiting for him on the patio, perhaps he'd gone to the canteen for an espresso. How annoying. Now, they'd have a hard time escaping the others. As Gerald crossed the courtyard, the late afternoon sun made his skin feel prickly the way it did after a day at the beach. He heard shouts coming from the patio and quickened his pace until he reached Mima sitting on a shaded step underneath the archway.

"What's going on?" Gerald asked, wanting to look for himself, but feeling obligated to stop. "Who's shouting?"

"Oh, it's Jean. He is very drunk and he makes a scene in front of the costume shop. I don't want to watch." Gerald glanced down the steps in the direction of the shop. "Go. See for yourself. Of course, he appreciates an audience," Mima said.

"I guess I will just go see what's going on."

Gerald ran down the steps two at a time. When he turned the corner he saw the actors gathered in front of the costume shop, and Enzo was not among them. Costumes and bits of clothing lay strewn across the patio. A bolt of black fabric flew out of the shop door followed by Jean.

"You can tell your *Mister* Weiss I am having the costume parade now and he is very welcome to attend."

Valentina stepped forward to pick up a dress.

"No! Don't anyone touch a thing!" With an awkward pirouette, Jean lurched back into the shop and returned almost immediately with an armful of felt cloaks, which he flung to the ground. "And there will be no more changes after today. If the great genius is not pleased with what he sees—which, my dears, is exactly what he asked for—then let him learn how to use a sewing machine and make the fucking costumes himself."

Gerald edged behind the group and sat next to Ariela on the low stone wall.

"Quite a show," she whispered.

"Drunk?" Gerald said.

"Of course, but I'm not talking about Jean. You and Enzo, during Hell of a Party, that was quite a show."

"What? What did you see?"

"I saw Enzo lick his lips."

Gerald glanced down to one end of the patio, then the other. Where was Enzo?

"I don't know what you're talking about," he whispered back. "All you think about is sex. You must be in heat. Maybe you should invite Holgar back to do whatever it is he does."

"What makes you think I haven't?"

Zuzie, standing in front of them, turned and offered one of her twinkling smiles. Gerald was too polite not to smile back, but Ariela's expression remained impassive.

"Did she hear us?" Gerald whispered. Ariela shrugged. "Ariela, do you think anyone else saw Enzo and me?"

"What does it matter, Auntie, we'll be out of here in a few weeks. We'll never see any of them again." When she kissed her finger and placed it on Gerald's cheek, it felt like a slap.

Gerald had given so little thought to going home. In fact, he'd almost grown used to the invasion of comfort and privacy that had characterized the last three weeks. But Ariela was right, it would end soon. In a few weeks, he'd be back in his own Midtown studio apartment with one or two more empty summer weekends to endure until Labor Day. Then fall, his favorite season in New York, when the city returned to a frantic normalcy. And then dreadful winter. He had no prospect of employment, but after his recent illness, he was technically disabled and therefore eligible for assistance. But after Bill's call, he persuaded himself he needn't go to one of those awful bureaucratic places where sick people were treated like freeloaders. Could he now? Yes, of course. If there was any lesson to be learned from the past few years, it was that there were few indignities he could not brook.

Where was Enzo? He went over their last conversation. "I'll meet you outside," that's what he'd said.

Gerald stood on the wall for a better view, just in time to witness Jean drop-kick another fabric bolt, sending it unraveling down the patio. The two seamstresses were visible behind the sliding glass door of the costume shop. The younger one, a shy local girl who treated the actors as visiting royalty, spoke only when spoken to, and kept her head lowered during fittings, stared wide-eyed and unblinking, as Jean hurled more clothes out the door. The older woman looked on with weary contempt.

Bill appeared with Bonnie at the end of the patio. As Jean stood puffing in the doorway with his hands on his hips, Bill walked down, wading among the clothes and fabrics strewn upon the cobblestones. He paused to lift a garment with his toe.

"There!" bellowed Jean, smacking his hand against the doorframe with a crack that made the onlookers wince. "I make the costume parade! You like? And now, no more changes!"

His face was a bloated and ugly mask, as tics of doubt, terror, and fatigue played over his eyes and mouth, betraying the defiant glare he struggled to maintain. Behind the bravado, Jean appeared deflated and tired; the alcohol-fueled anger had already begun to dissipate.

As Jean and Bill faced each other, the actors too remained silent, motionless, and desperate, for once, not to upstage the leading players. The young seamstress cowered in the background like a hostage, her hand pressed against her breast as if her heart might leap out. Beside her, the older woman sat motionless. A smile seemed to play across her mouth (usually a vise for straight pins) as if she'd begun to enjoy the little farce that had enabled her to rest her arthritic fingers.

"And I make them all on no fucking budget! Do you understand me, *Mister* William Weiss? I say, no more changes! No more changes!"

Jean's eyes, no longer able to hold a single focus, maniacally scanned the audience for support.

In a voice so quiet that Gerald had to strain to hear, Bill spoke. "I know you're overworked, Jean. We all are. And I think the Hell of a Party costumes look great."

Bill stared down at the costumes scattered along the patio. "I'll need to see the rest of these things *on* the actors. Do you need anyone down here for fittings?"

"Of course, I need everyone," bellowed Jean. He seemed to recall why he was angry, which made him appear less drunk. "You add this new scene, with new costumes which must be made and fitted. We don't buy them off a store rack, you understand?" he said in a more reasonable tone.

New scene? This close to an opening? The actors cast uncertain glances at each other. Perhaps the real drama was still to come.

"Bonnie," said Bill, "send the actors to Jean a few at a time. I don't need everybody in rehearsal."

"Humph," Jean snorted.

"All right, people," Bonnie called out.

Bill turned to go, but stopped and turned back. "Oh, Jean, when the women come in, could you look at the Party dresses? I think they're all about an inch too long."

"That's because they were wearing shoes when we measured them! Then you decide, no more shoes!" Jean shouted.

"Yes!" Bill said, as if the costumer had offered a helpful suggestion. "With the sand, barefoot is better." And he disappeared around the corner of the building.

"Cunt!" spat Jean under his breath.

Gerald glanced up and saw, in a dormer window of the library, a face—Enzo's—looking down at the scene below. In the first moment of recognition, he felt violated. How did Enzo know about his secret hideaway? He wanted to expose the trespasser, to call out and point like a grade-school tattletale.

"What new scene?" the actors asked, gathering around Bonnie. "Who's going to be in it?"

"If they ask where I am, say I went to the bathroom," Gerald whispered to Ariela.

"Where *are* you going, Auntie?"

"To the bathroom!"

Gerald walked quickly down the patio and then ran up the archway steps, into the courtyard between buildings. Ian was sitting on the edge of the useless dry fountain, his face lifted to the sun.

"Hermaphrodites don't have tans, darling."

Why was he being campy with Ian?

"This one will," said Ian. "Where are you going?"

"Parking lot, I left something in the van." He hurried around the corner of the building, checked to make sure he was alone, and went in the side door. The hall was empty. He bounded up the stairs and to the library but stopped at the door. There were things to remember, things to say. When a floorboard creaked, he opened the door. The room was as hot as a sauna. Enzo leapt up from the daybed.

"How did you know about this—?"

"Where was you when I-ee-ya—?"

The questions, spoken in the same moment, lost their sense and both men laughed as they moved toward each other and embraced. Gerald felt like a moisture-absorbing sponge as his T-shirt dampened with the sweat that glistened on Enzo's chest. He opened his mouth against Enzo's neck and tasted the brine on his skin. His fingers explored Enzo's back, lingering over a range of pimples between his shoulder blades. This intimate contact with a blemished Enzo filled him with a tenderness so intense, he imagined it taking on a form like the mist from the vineyard sprinklers, enveloping them both. He leaned back and gazed into his Enzo's eyes.

"We were supposed to meet in the courtyard. Where were you?"

"I-ee, eh, toilet. Come out, no you. I-ee-ya see you—one day—come up here, but no you. I-ee-ya hear Jean, look down." Enzo pointed toward the window overlooking the costume shop.

Gerald didn't care where Enzo was or why he wasn't in the courtyard. He'd only spoken to pry himself apart from his own alarming emotions. But with Enzo so close, so available, his joy was replenished, he felt grounded again, playful, and he halted Enzo's chatter with a kiss.

They broke the kiss for a moment when Enzo pulled

Gerald's damp T-shirt over his head. Gerald, laughing and panting, grabbed at the shirt. "No, Enzo, wait. We've got to go now. We've got later—tonight."

"You don't want . . . ?" Enzo's big lips pushed into a pout.

"No, let's meet tonight after rehearsal. Here, or . . . wait, shhh!"

The wooden stairs creaked, Enzo jumped back, and Gerald barely got his T-shirt over his head when the door opened.

The housekeeper stood with a Dirt Devil in one hand as she held them in her offended gaze. She can't do much cleaning with a Dirt Devil, Gerald thought. In his haste he'd put his T-shirt on backward, and the neckband pressed uncomfortably against his throat.

The housekeeper seemed to be cursing, but Enzo answered her in an impressively authoritative tone. She slammed the door behind her when she left the room.

"What did you say?" Gerald asked, pulling his T-shirt off and pulling it back on right.

"I-ee-ya say she must knock because we are rehearsing."

"And she believed you?"

"Eh, no."

CHAPTER FOURTEEN

"Why don't you go in first, I'll be there in a minute," Gerald suggested as he and Enzo crossed the courtyard to the theater.

Arriving with Enzo didn't worry Gerald, but they were both shaken by the housekeeper's intrusion, and Gerald felt neither of them was up to more subterfuge. He waited a few minutes after Enzo went in, then followed.

Luckily, Bill had not arrived. The actors were dotted about the sandy playing area practicing their spinning techniques with varying degrees of skill. The scene was chaotic as one or another spinner lost focus and spun out of control. Little Ernesto looked mad, his eyes wide, focused on some invisible point. Suddenly, he lost his footing, flung his arms out for balance and shrieked comically. When he came to a standstill, he smiled nervously at Gerald, but quickly reassumed his earnest expression and started, once again, to turn.

"All right, people," Bonnie shouted, "everyone should be out of Party clothes and ready to rehearse Saints. If you don't know what saint you're playing, you need to talk to Martin."

"What's going on?" Gerald asked Ariela, who was sitting

against a wall taking tiny nibbles from an apple. "Why the spinning fever?"

"Bonnie says we'll use it for the new scene. And we're all going to be saints," she said, offering him a bite. "I'm Saint Theresa, the little flower."

Gerald stretched his mouth open wide and took an enormous bite.

"Ohshur," he said, his mouth full of apple.

"It's true! And you'll be Mary, of course."

Gerald began to laugh, sending bits of apple flesh into the air while Ariela looked away in mock disgust.

Leaving his sandals at the edge of the sand, Gerald crossed to the production table where Martin Lustinger sat with books, papers, and a full ashtray. Martin looked like a man who'd been up for several nights. The strain of working showed in the tiny muscle tics that rippled under the sallow skin of his face. His eyes were red, he was unshaven, and the hairs in his nostrils and ears wanted clipping. Martin raised his head from the papers he'd been studying and smiled, displaying a row of small nicotine-stained teeth.

"And you are?"

"I don't know yet."

"No," he said testily, "I mean who are you? What's your name?"

"Oh! Sorry, it's Gerald."

It wasn't really odd that the dramaturg, largely concerned with the historic and literary aspects of the play, didn't know his name. Besides, he and Gerald had never spoken directly. Still, Gerald thought, I'm in the play, and he has been at most of the rehearsals.

While Martin ran a yellowed finger down the photocopied cast list, Gerald stared at a flaky patch of skin on the dramaturg's head where his scalp showed through his thinning hair. Under Gerald's nose, an unfiltered cigarette burned in a small metal ashtray brimming with butts. Gerald waved away the smoke.

"I have stayed up the whole evening. So, I have trouble deciphering the words—even if the handwriting is mine," said Martin, with a little hiccup of a laugh. "Ah, yes, here you are! You are Saint Augustine, the great fifth-century bishop. You are familiar with Augustine?"

"I've heard of him."

"I should think so, his writings are well known. I have jotted down a few important facts: pagan father, Christian mother, Saint Monica, inherited wealth, married, bishop in North Africa—"

"Can I read about him for myself?" Gerald asked, interrupting the stream of biographical detail and picking up *The Penguin Dictionary of Saints*, which lay open on a pile of books.

"Wait," Martin said, "I must give you a line."

"A line?"

"William Weiss wants each saint to speak a line of dialogue. Let's see . . ."

Martin picked up a beautiful bound book with a gilded cover, like the books in the glass case in the secret library. Scanning the index, he found his subject and flipped through pages with a scholar's dexterity.

"Ah, yes, good!" He pursed his lips and tore off a piece of paper from a notebook. "I will write it down—unless you would like to read this yourself, also, but I think you will have difficulty, it is written in Italian."

If Martin was offended by the suggestion that his knowledge was gleaned from a paperback book of saints—good.
Gerald was insulted by his condescending attitude. But
seeing Martin's affront, the silly investment in his own
expertise, saddened Gerald. Martin's slovenly grooming
habits made a sort of poetic sense really, scholarly, myopic,
unconcerned with appearance, his sense of worth was book-
learned, he was a type. At one time, Gerald might have
enthusiastically noted the details of his appearance—the bad
shave, the dirty collar, the quick, excited sniffs of air as he
warmed to his subject—hoping to incorporate them into a
character, a bookworm, say, or a pedantic professor. But age
had given Gerald so many quirks of his own, he suspected he
could draw from his own repertoire without borrowing the
eccentricities of others.

"This, then, is the quote from Saint Augustine—let me
see—'*Tu me colge en ardore,*' which means—"

"Can I say it in Italian?" Gerald asked.

"Well . . . William has asked for several languages in the
final scene to give a Tower of Babel effect, but it still makes
more sense to let an Italian actor speak a line in Italian."

"The Italians are multilingual, most of them speak French
or Spanish. You've got German and English, Ariela speaks
Hebrew—I'd like to learn this line in Italian."

"As you wish."

Gerald replaced *The Penguin Book of Saints* on Martin's pile
of books.

"I don't think I need this. Not much character work I can
do in a day. Besides, in this play, I could probably send my costume on without me."

Martin stopped his shuffling and stared over his glasses, at Gerald.

"Yes, this type of work must sometimes be as frustrating for an actor as it is for a dramaturg." He lowered his voice. "I can't *wait* to leave."

"When is that?"

"After the opening." Martin leaned back in his chair and stared into space, a hazy smile playing at the corner of his mouth, as if he were already seated at a smoky little Salzburg café.

"Well, thank God you were here for us," Gerald said, thinking the empty phrase sounded like a backstage compliment for a bad actor.

"All right, people, listen up." Bonnie stood in the center of the space with her hands on her hips and a Balinese clicker in each hand.

"Bill's on his way over, and he wants to work on the new scene, so don't wander off."

Gerald read the words on the piece of paper Martin had given him. *"Signore, tu me colge en ardore."* He'd forgotten to get the translation.

"Enzo, what does this say?" he asked, handing him the slip of paper.

"It say, *'tu me colge in ardore.'* "

"No, I mean, in *English?*"

"Eh, *signore*—mister! You know, eh? *Ardore* mean . . ." Enzo wrapped his arms around himself and rolled his eyes skyward.

"Love? Mister, I'm in love?"

"No, no—*Mee-ster I-ee-ya yam in love*—very funny. Like

231

love, but more like church, love for . . ." Enzo pointed up. "*Dio*. " He brought his hands in a prayer position and, once again, rolled his eyes upward.

"Adore!"

"*Si!*"

"Mister, I adore you?"

"*Si!*"

Gerald found Enzo's translation questionable—was Saint Augustine gay?—but thanked him anyway.

"And by the way," he asked, "what saint are you?"

"Sebastian," Enzo said, with a broad smile. Gerald felt a slight pang of envy. A few wounds, an arrow or two, would immediately identify Enzo as Saint Sebastian, but how would anyone know he, Gerald, was supposed to be Saint Augustine?

He leaned close to Enzo. "Tonight, after rehearsal?" he whispered.

Enzo lowered his eyes like a child about to be punished.

"I-ya think, no, not tonight because Loo-ees, he come from Palermo."

"Lewis?"

"My friend."

"He's coming tonight?"

"No tonight, tomorrow, stay for the performance, but, eh, very difficult you, me."

Gerald didn't want to hear about Enzo's friend. He knew he was English, ran a dance company in Palermo, and wasn't having sex with Enzo. Gerald imagined him as older—probably his age—pretentious, especially about modern dance, and wildly jealous. He was powerful and manipulative in his narrow world, and that's what had attracted Enzo.

Gerald squeezed Enzo's arm and stepped away to join Letizia and Ernesto as they watched Vincenzo spin round like an ice skater. Until Bill arrived. Then he lost his balance, and his arms flailed wildly as he fought to come to a stop. The room was silent as Bill padded across the sand and sat next to Martin. He took one of Martin's cigarettes from its pack and held it, unlit, between his fingers.

"Let's see the spinning."

Gerald felt an icy wave of nausea. He was rarely asked to do anything "dancey." He edged himself to the back of the group. As the others began to turn, he held his palms together in front of him, focused on his thumbs and began. At first, he felt as if one foot were nailed in place as the other hopped around in a circle. Then he discovered that by imagining he was always stepping back, to look behind himself as it were, his feet followed a more natural pattern. But the movement was difficult to maintain, and after only a few rotations, he felt dizziness and a growing panic. He seemed only able to go faster, not slower, and felt that if he lost his balance, the blurred world beyond his two thumbs would crash along with him. When he tried a full stop, his feet continued to circle in a lurching Frankenstein gait and he fell.

Gerald was not the only amateur spinner. In fact, most of the other actors dissolved into lurching monsters after a few rotations.

"Terrible!" Bill shouted. "Why aren't they doing it, Bonnie? Everyone should have this by now."

"A lot of them *do* have it," Bonnie said frankly, "I think we're seeing a little performance anxiety. Can I try something?"

Gerald wondered if his courtyard talk with Bonnie had led

to her empowerment, and if it had, would he then be responsible for her inevitable humiliation? The other actors waited to
see Bill's reaction to this bold request from a woman he'd
recently reduced to tears, but Bill said nothing, and Bonnie
continued.

"Okay, people, you're turning too fucking fast, it's not a
race. I want you to try again. Not all at once, but one at a time.
Start when I say your name. I'll start with some of you who
have it down, so you others—watch."

Bill sat still, his expression neutral, the unlit cigarette dangling between his fingers.

"Ariela. Go!"

Ariela began spinning slowly and without fanfare. Her gaze
was calm. The slow pace gave her effortless control and made
it apparent why Bonnie admonished them about speed.

"Vincenzo, go!"

Vincenzo resembled a spinning matador. And though his
grace and posture were magnificent, a childish arrogance would
always preclude empathy between Vincenzo and an audience of
mere mortals.

"More interior! Stop projecting!" Bill shouted.

"Stop showing off!" Bonnie echoed.

Bill smiled. "Yes, stop showing off!"

Gerald expected to be the last one called. It took supreme
control, when he heard his name called just after Vincenzo's,
not to scream. It doesn't matter if I'm not perfect, he told himself, Saint Augustine probably couldn't spin.

"Gerald! Long neck!"

Bill's voice nearly threw him off balance. But sensing
Ariela, who continued her snail's pace rotation, he slowly began

to turn, kept his balance, and was grateful when another name was called.

On one side of Bill, Bonnie nodded or shook her head like a sidelined coach, on the other, Martin sucked nervously on an unfiltered cigarette. Nine o'clock, and Bill was still fine-tuning the procession of Saints in the final scene. Each time one of the saints raced, moved in slow motion, or fell into a wedding-march tempo, the whole line was sent back to begin again. As Bill often pointed out, walking was a difficult stage task to master. Especially, thought Gerald, after being on one's feet the better part of twelve hours and rehearsing without a break for the last two of those hours.

"Space between your fingers," Bill called out, "don't swing your arms. It's not a natural walk. The theater is not nature, it's artifice."

Gerald gritted his teeth at each new aphorism. Well, hardly new, he'd heard them all before.

Mima was just ahead of Gerald. Before she stepped onto the sand, she held up her palms to show the stigmata marks painted with red lipstick and whispered, "I'm going to try something."

Please don't, Gerald wanted to implore. When Bill saw, he'd humiliate her and send the procession back—he loathed initiative. But it was too late. Mima was already in her light and Gerald watched in horror as her hands floated skyward.

"Who's that one with her arms up?" Bill asked Bonnie.

"Mima," Bonnie replied.

"But who is she supposed to be?"

"She is Saint Perpetua, the third-century martyr," Martin

explained, "famous for her written record of visions prior to martyrdom."

"But how will anyone know she's Saint Per . . . what was the name again?"

"Per-pe-tu-a." Martin's tone was careful, modulated. "William, you asked for saints from various ages, and that is exactly what I have chosen. Perhaps you could have a note in the program—"

"Stop!" shouted Bill. The procession stopped. "If she was a queen she could wear a crown and you'd know—*that's* a queen."

"But she is not a queen, she is Saint Perpetua." Martin offered a thin-lipped smile at the absurdity of Bill's suggestion.

Mima, reimagining herself as a queen, dropped her stigmatized hands and raised her chin.

"And Vito—who is he supposed to be?"

"Saint Ignatius," Martin snapped.

With a sharp sniff, Bill stood and walked away from the table into the center of the space. One finger rested against his lips, and he stared down, motionless, silent, as if drawing inspiration from the red sand.

"He could be Magellan," Bill said, "and carry a globe. They should all be famous people in history. Someone could be the astronomer. What was his name?"

"Galileo," Zuzie offered, sweetly.

"Galileo should carry a telescope. Let's keep some of them saints and turn the rest into famous people in history."

"No! It is impossible to change so late!" Martin's voice was shrill with disbelief, as if he'd just been told the sea, not the sand, was red. "You cannot do this!"

Gerald drew circles in the sand with his toe, willing the dramaturg to silence. Argument was useless. Bill did whatever he wanted anyway, and a "no" only steeled his will.

"Besides," Martin unwisely continued, "each one of them has learned a line attributed to a specific saint." He stubbed his cigarette out with emphasis, as if this final argument would go unchallenged.

"Let them keep the lines," Bill said cheerfully.

"Famous persons in history are *not* saints!" When Martin's hand came down, the little tin ashtray jumped on the table. He, himself, appeared shocked by the dramatic gesture, and tried, once again, to modulate his voice, which came out strangulated. "I chose these saints precisely because written records of their words existed or because they, themselves, had left a written record. The line must go with the saint!"

Bill continued to stare down into the sand, saying nothing. The William Weiss pause. A shiver ran down Gerald's neck. The actors froze. Even Martin's look of pained incredulity sagged into a sort of glazed attention. When Bill finally spoke, it was in a voice so quiet, so natural, the focus of the room tightened, and Gerald felt himself lean into the words.

"In a Broadway play"—at the mention of "Broadway," Ian sniggered, and Bill glanced up sharply—"a woman tells a man, *don't—leave—me—I—love—you*. The man tells the woman, *I—love—you—too—but—I—have—to—go—you—know—I— have—to—go*. The man and woman embrace. Perhaps lights dim around them until they're left in a warm amber spot. Romantic music swells. The audience is *told*, 'this scene is tragic,' or 'this is romantic.' They're told what to feel. It's a sort of fascism." Bill glanced toward the door as if he suddenly remembered something, but his attention quickly returned to the circle of actors. He pushed his hands into his pockets. "I don't make Broadway plays. I wish I could."

Gerald yearned to communicate an "oh sure" roll of the eyes to Ariela, but she too remained focused on Bill.

"In my plays, dialogue is not connected to action or plot or character or anything else. It's a little like . . ."

"The skins of an onion," Gerald mouthed.

"The skins of an onion," Bill said. "The words are one layer, the music is one layer, the action is another, and so on. The audience is left to make their own associations." He looked at his watch. "I don't know, maybe I'm wrong, it's just another way of doing things."

"But this is absurd!" Martin's strident words, spoken from behind the table, shattered the mood of quiet intensity. "The play is called *Rivers, Saints, Space,* not *Rivers,* Famous Persons, *Space.*"

Bill did not turn to face the dramaturg, but his voice rose to an angry falsetto.

"I have today and tomorrow! *Two* days until we open! If you're unhappy with my method of working, don't come to rehearsal."

Martin, his expression grim, gathered his books and papers and quietly left the theater. The actors shifted uneasily, like horses after a clap of thunder.

"All right! Let's finish blocking the scene. Bonnie! Can you think of any more famous people in history? I mean, honestly— Saint Per . . . Per . . . what was it? Saint Pertuba? And send someone to stop Jean from making more saints costumes. Tell him I need to see him here."

"Oh, that'll be a nice messenger job for someone," Bonnie muttered as she passed Gerald. "Who don't we like?"

"Send Otto," whispered Gerald, who stood nearby.

"Why?"

"We don't like him."

Bonnie looked at Gerald.

"And Jean has a crush on him, so he'll come out alive," he added.

"Otto!" Bonnie shouted. "Come!"

Jean was not angry. He quietly accommodated Bill's changes, and both men behaved as if the afternoon's tantrum had never taken place.

"The saint costumes, they are only white," Jean explained, "I cut them from white felt, quite thick. I make a cape, say, and hold it over the shoulders with a little clasp. And this they would wear over white tights and leotards, or I wrap a little fabric around the body and with a few stitches—*basta!* Here, I show you. *Maria! Franco!* "

Most of the saint costumes were equally suitable for the newly assigned famous people. Perpetua's cape, for instance, with the addition of a rhinestone crown, could still be worn by Mima as Queen Elizabeth the First.

Enzo remained Saint Sebastian. Jean wrapped him in a felt loincloth, and as Gerald had foreseen, the feathered ends of arrows, affixed to his torso with wound-red adhesive tape, made him easily identifiable. Enzo clasped his hands around an arrow taped to his flat abdomen and rolled his eyes in a cartoonish grimace of death. As Gerald watched him mug for his friends, he saw another Enzo, one fully aware of his physical allure: the Enzo whose hands moved unselfconsciously over the bare sections of his torso and adjusted and readjusted the scanty felt loincloth.

"Gerald, will the pope come see my play?" Bill asked when Saint Augustine became Pope John.

"If he does, I'll shoot him," Gerald said.

"No!" Letizia cried.

Gerald's costume, a white felt cape and tall two-pointed miter, remained unchanged, and Gerald, in his own mind, remained Saint Augustine.

"I look like a condom," he said, gazing at himself in a full-length mirror.

When they had been fitted into whatever costume Jean could jerry-rig, the procession began again, and proceeded without interruption until the actors stood in a wide circle. Bill went to each and stood, silent, grave, a Zen painter meditating before the first brush stroke. Suddenly, his hands flew into a series of unrelated gestures. Two raised fingers moved back and forth to "erase" an eye, a hand played an imaginary piano, a fist was held between teeth. Bonnie caught the moves with a hand-held video recorder. After Bill had choreographed gestures for everyone, Bonnie played the video back in slow motion, and the actors gathered round to study the exact bend of a finger or the angle of a forearm to the torso.

Gerald's first two gestures looked something like a papal blessing followed by a baseball pitch. His final gesture, in which he extended his arms, palms facing out, and shook both hands, reminded him of Anna Magnani in *The Rose Tattoo* when she tried to silence the old women bringing news of her husband's death. "Don't say, don't say," she cried, holding them back with her shaking hands. The hand sequence was easy enough to learn, but became more difficult with the spinning.

At break the actors spent their precious free time rehearsing the moves, ignoring interruptions like the arrival of the technical crew. Men climbed onto light and sound scaffolding, moved the cherry picker onto the sand to check overhead rigging, and carried in mattresses, which they piled in the center of the space.

Throughout the rehearsal, Ian had been conspicuously absent. Gerald went out on the back patio and saw him being fitted into a harness by Jean and the two costume assistants. Gerald slipped back inside the theater without being noticed

"All right, everyone!" Bonnie called. "We're going to run through Saints. There'll be some surprises at the end but stay focused."

"What surprise?" Letizia asked.

"Audio for one. We're also going to try some lighting," Bonnie explained, "but I can't tell you any more, Bill just wants us to run the scene."

As they stood in a line waiting for a cue to begin the procession, the lights dimmed. A click from Bonnie signaled Vincenzo to take the first step upon the sand. The sound of wind stirred through the speakers. The light shifted from dark to dim, wind grew stronger, adding an eerie atmosphere to the slow procession. A gull cried out, then another, then more gulls, until their shrill clamoring suggested violence and became, Gerald thought, a little too reminiscent of Hitchcock's *The Birds*. But as the actors reached their places in the circle the wind began to die, the birdcalls receded, and they began to turn in place as the soft patter of recorded rain began to fall. As they spun, slowly adding hand gestures, the intensity of the rain increased, sending a hard rhythm through the loudspeakers. Overhead spots brightened into a circle around each spinning, gesticulating actor. The rainfall became torrential.

They had been instructed to begin speaking ten seconds into the spinning (another aural layer on the onion), but beneath the sound of downpour, the voices were barely audible. Gerald was having difficulty holding a focus point, turning, *and* making his hand movements—bless, pitch, *don't say, don't say*—and when he tried to speak, he couldn't.

"Signore . . . Signore . . ." he finally panted out. What followed? The piece of paper with the Italian quote was in his pocket, but without glasses, and while spinning, he'd never be able to read it.

"Lines!" Bill shouted. "I can't hear anyone! Project!"

Next to him, Mima, as Queen Elizabeth, recited Saint Perpetua's line with support and passion. "You-ah judge-ah us: God will-ah judge you!" Was she putting on the Italian accent? Gerald wondered. No, of course not, she *is* Italian, it just sounds like a bad accent.

"Signore . . . Signore, Signore, Signore," he chanted, as nerve-racking thunder underscored the torrent. "Can you hear what I say? I can't hear what I say. Signore . . . I adore you. I do, I do. Turn, turn, turn. Round and round I go. How long, oh Lord, how long. Wake up little Susie, wake up. God helps those who—"

The next crack of thunder startled him, and he began to lose his balance and slowed to steady himself. His gaze was drawn up to the open glass dome of the skylight. A pair of feet appeared, followed by a pair of legs, as Ian descended from fifty feet above them. Valentina gasped. The spinning stopped and the actors stared up at the floating figure.

"Spot," shouted Bill.

A spotlight illuminated Ian, a flying harness just visible beneath the gauzy see-through fabric in which he was swaddled. With arms stretched up, legs slightly bent, and feet pointed, he appeared to be caught in a balletic mid-leap. But he doesn't read hermaphrodite, Gerald thought.

Ian descended gracefully, and had almost reached the mattresses, when the fly wire jerked him to a stop, and he dangled several feet off the floor, flailing his arms like a drowning victim.

"NO!" shouted Bill, "NO! NO! NO!"

The work lights came on and the taped storm stopped abruptly.

"What is all that wind and rain? It sounds like a horror movie! Where was the spotlight for the hermaphrodite?"

"Bill, it's the first time they've run it with all the tech," Bonnie said, "it was bound to be a mess."

Bill looked at Ian, now playfully pushing himself off with his toes and swinging over the mattresses.

"Ian! What happened to the text?"

"What text?" Ian put his feet on the floor and pulled himself up to stand.

"He should be miked and he should have text. Martin, you'll have to write it, Dede hasn't sent hers. Martin!"

Bill looked around to the production table where the dramaturg had sat.

"He's gone, Bill," Annalisa said.

"Gone?"

"You told him he was no longer needed. He called a car to take him to the airport. I asked him to stay until the opening, but he refused."

"Is there a plane this late?" Bill asked.

"To Roma, *yes*. He will probably stay overnight and fly to Salzburg in the morning."

"We've got to get him back."

"I'm afraid it may be impossible," Annalisa warned.

"We might catch him at the airport! Daryl! Can you drive?"

Daryl, who had been sitting against the wall asleep during most of the rehearsal, looked up sheepishly.

"Aw, no, don't think so. Maybe if I had a map—in English."

"I can drive," Bonnie said.

"All right, let's go!"

"I will come with you," Annalisa said.

"Gerald!"

Gerald, thinking himself an invisible onlooker, was shocked to hear his name spoken.

"Yes?"

"Come!" Bill demanded. "Ariela! Come!"

They didn't hesitate to follow Bill, and Gerald felt a little swell of pride as he handed his bishop's miter to Mima, hurrying past Ian and through the circle of saints and people in history. Ariela joined him near the door. They exchanged a knowing look as they ran to catch up with Bill, Bonnie, and Annalisa.

CHAPTER FIFTEEN

W hat did I do?" Bill asked from the passenger seat of
Annalisa's car. Bonnie drove, and Gerald, Ariela, and
Annalisa were crammed in the back seat. "What did I do?"

"Well, you changed Saint Perturba to Queen Elizabeth and
Saint Ignatius to Magellan, and then when Martin got pissed
you said maybe he shouldn't be at rehearsal," Bonnie
explained.

"I did not!"

"I am afraid you did, Bill," Annalisa said.

"Martin and I are very different. He uses too many words
for my taste, but I never told him to *leave*. Did I? Bonnie can
you drive any faster?"

"Not without getting stopped for speeding."

"Ariela! What did I say?"

Ariela was saved from answering when Bill spotted a sign
for the *Aeroporto*. "Bonnie! Faster!"

Ariela, sitting between Gerald and Annalisa, leaned forward. She disliked casual physical contact. Gerald gently pulled
her back and whispered, "Make *luf* to me!," in a silly German
accent. She looked annoyed, but remained where she was,
wedged between him and Annalisa.

Gerald liked Ariela's shoulder pressed against his. Her warmth was comforting. How natural it would be, he thought, to slip my arm affectionately through hers, but she'd probably pull away. Well, friends were what they were, and if you wanted to have any, you had to accept their oddities. The car raced past dark silhouettes of pines and olive trees, past the ugly ghosts of stucco homes built along the highway. Gerald leaned his head against the seat back and let the evening air flood across his sore eyelids like cool water. He was glad to have been summoned by Bill. Glad to get away from Bellina. It was funny how once you got involved in a place, you forgot there were *other* places. How familiar everything had become: the Palazzo dell'Arte, the Sociale, the town square—even Enzo. The claustrophobia of the last weeks flew out the window, absorbed into the dark, passing landscape. Bonnie, as capable behind the wheel as she was in rehearsal, kept the little car going at a steady clip. Bill had asked him to come, *Gerald* was one of the chosen—but he dared not think what this jaunt would cost in terms of lost sleep.

"What do we do if he's already gone?" Bill asked.

"I don't know, Bill," Annalisa said, "perhaps we must let him be gone."

Bill didn't wait to park when they arrived at the airport, but commanded Bonnie to stop and leapt from the car.

"Annalisa, Ariela, Gerald. Come!

The Palermo airport was surprisingly crowded for the time of night. It was tourist season, Annalisa explained, and a Friday, when many natives left the island for more exciting ports. Italian security men stood in front of the turnstile leading to the gates, checking the tickets of departing passengers.

"Should we all go different ways?" Bill asked.

"There are not so many ways to go," Annalisa replied. "If he is still on this side, he is buying a ticket or in the coffee bar or perhaps in the toilet, but I think he must be on the other side."

"And what if he's on the other side?" Bill asked.

"Then he waits for his plane or he has already departed. Either way, the *polizia* will not let us through without a ticket."

"Come!" commanded Bill, walking up to one of the men. "Officer, we need to find a friend before he gets on the plane, it's very important." The stern expression of the policeman did not change. "Explain to him, Annalisa."

"As I told you, Bill," Annalisa explained, after a brief conversation with the guard. "We cannot pass through unless we have a ticket."

"Well, let's buy a ticket to somewhere near. Can we return it later?"

"That is not necessary. There is a public address system. We can go to *Informazioni* and have them call for Martin over a . . . a—"

"Loudspeaker," Gerald offered.

Bonnie ran up, out of breath, and looking like a Miami tourist in her Bermuda shorts, baseball cap and a local version of a Hawaiian shirt.

"I had to park miles away. Where are all these people going?"

"Bonnie, wait here," Bill commanded. "If Martin tries to go through the gates, stop him! We'll call him over the loudspeaker."

"Is he still here?"

"Stay by the gates!"

Annalisa, Ariela, and Gerald ran to keep up with Bill. Suddenly he halted—"Where am I going, Annalisa?"—then started off again in the direction she indicated.

They passed by the little kiosk where Gerald had bought aspirins. Wasn't that years ago? At that early point in his journey, he hadn't even seen the Sociale and still imagined a whitewashed room overlooking the sea.

Judging by her precise pronunciations and vocabulary, the young woman behind the information desk was proud of her English. She dutifully wrote out Martin's name, calling out each letter.

"M-ah, as-ah een moose, A-ah, as-ah een angel, R-ah, as-ah een rat . . ."

"Tell her it doesn't matter *how* she spells it, we have to stop him before he gets on a plane," Bill said.

"You have just told her," Annalisa said quietly, "as you hear, she speaks English."

"Miss, it's an emergency, Mr. Lustinger must come to the information desk, immediately."

"I cannot give the alarmist effect, sir. Eef-ah your friend has not departed previously, he wheel-ah alert when I call his name and-ah, eef he follows my instructions, he-ah wheel be forthcoming."

"But if he's about to board the plane, he might *not* come—especially if he doesn't know it's an emergency."

"Is it an emergency?" The young woman addressed her comment to Annalisa who answered her in Italian.

"Did you tell her, Annalisa? I have an opening tomor—"

"Bill! I explained that Martin has left his medicines behind and that without them he is in grave danger." Annalisa gave Bill a warning glance.

"Medicines?"

Gerald grabbed Bill's arm, but the young woman seemed not to have heard and had already begun to speak into a microphone so large it appeared to be a relic from the early days of radio.

"*Attenzione!* " She spoke too close to the mike and the word reverberated loud and unintelligible through the terminal. She moved a few inches away. "*Passeggero Martin Lustinger, per favore—*"

"He doesn't speak Italian!"

"Be patient, Bill," pleaded Annalisa, "she will repeat the message in English."

Bill yanked the microphone from the girl's hand, but the cord was short, forcing him to lean awkwardly over the counter.

"Martin! Martin!" His amplified voice had the effect of thunderclaps. "What did I do? I'm sorry! They can all be saints!"

Bill's booming voice was interrupted by a screech of ear-splitting static. Travelers stopped and covered their ears or looked up, as if an hysterical god had spoken from the heavens.

"Martin! Martin! Come to the information desk! The play will not go on without you. Martin! Come back! We love you!"

The young woman tried in vain to retrieve her microphone. Now she looked as if she might cry as she waved her arms frantically to summon security.

"Bill!" Annalisa said, pulling him up by the shoulders. Alerted to the source of the god-voice by the running *poliziotti*, people stared in alarm. Gerald was frightened. Weren't Sicilian policemen ultrasensitive to assassinations and bomb threats? They might all be shot.

"Does anyone see him?" Bill asked, ignoring the commotion coming his way.

Four *poliziotti* surrounded them. Annalisa, with her tattoos and piercings, appeared the most suspect, but she could speak Italian.

Gerald's heart beat against his chest. As a future anecdote, this evening had enough drama to warrant telling for several decades. But he didn't have decades. Bill was crazy. What if they were taken to jail, where the bathroom was a metal toilet in the middle of the cell and the bed was a bench? By tomorrow, the others might be exhausted, but he'd be a minute from dead. His mouth was dry and he'd broken out in a sweat. I haven't the strength for impossible situations anymore, he thought. His side itched—were the bites coming back? He wanted to scratch, but the *poliziotti* might think he was reaching for a weapon and shoot him dead.

"Bill! I found him!"

Bonnie's arm was locked through Martin's as if she'd dragged him back against his will. Released, he quickly pulled a cigarette from his pack, lit it, and took a long drag. His hands were shaking. The policemen stiffened, hands at their holsters, as Bill broke through the circle to embrace the dramaturg.

"Martin, good to see you," Bill said cheerfully, as if he'd run into an old friend. "Thank God you're still here. You had us worried. Let's have a drink." Bill turned back to Annalisa. "Annalisa, ask the policemen if we can buy them a drink—or dinner. Is it late?"

"I cannot have a drink," Martin snapped, "I am going to

Rome where I must find a hotel room for the night, in high tourist season and without a reservation."

"Don't go to Rome," Bill said. "Or go tomorrow after the opening. I need your help."

Martin sniffed at the air and looked away, but his self-assured manner was unconvincing, and after a bit more bargaining and a few more apologies, he agreed to return.

In the end, the *poliziotti* were quite civil. No one was jailed, and Annalisa even talked them out of a fine by convincing them of Bill's eminence as a great American director. "*Ciao, Signore, Regista,*" one policeman said as he left. Bettina, the young woman behind the information desk, was not so easily placated. But in the end, she admitted a great love for the "theatrical arts" and accepted complimentary tickets for her, her mother, her two brothers, her fiancé, his parents, and her best friend Emmanuelle.

When Martin joined them in the back seat, Gerald lost his window position. Ariela had to sit on his lap, though she leaned as far forward as possible, painfully supporting herself with her elbows on the driver and passenger seats. "I'm all right," she assured everyone.

Gerald checked his watch. They'd never get back to Bellina before two and tomorrow there was rehearsal all day and an opening. Why had it been so important that he be a part of this entourage? The guru calls your name—*Gerald! Come!* —and you follow, but had Gerald's summons been an apology of sorts—for not casting him as the hermaphrodite? Sometimes, Gerald believed Bill saw everything, and that nothing he did was without a purpose. Like the five A.M. call inviting him to do the play. He knew Gerald was ill, so he called him back—like Lazarus—from the dead.

Gerald's legs were falling asleep under Ariela's weight. He fought an urge to open his knees quickly and let her fall.

Martin leaned forward to discuss Ian's final text with Bill.

"Mm, mm," Bill hummed, punctuating the dramaturg's enthusiastic rant.

Gerald replayed the airport scene, the incredible moment when, grabbing the microphone from the girl, Bill pleaded, *Martin, come back! We love you!* What an idiot Bill is. We could have been arrested. Or shot. He never thinks, he just acts.

"Do you mind if I smoke?" Martin asked, lighting a cigarette. He rolled down the window.

Beneath the sound of wind and engine, Gerald heard a whisper, "Gerald, come back! We love you!" A moment later, he was asleep.

CHAPTER SIXTEEN

Gerald lay in fetal position on a bare plastic mattress cradling a tangle of damp sheets. As the door opened, light from the nurse's station streamed into the room. He held up his forearm—the one without the IV—to shield his eyes. An unfamiliar doctor, towering above his bed, shifted from one foot to another.

Rivulets of sweat pooled upon the plastic mattress cover beneath his naked body. *What have they done with my gown?* he wondered, trying to twist onto his back to see the doctor. But he couldn't move, as though he'd been tied down, and he shut his eyes to wait for the cool touch of a stethoscope or a sudden, violent blow.

"Jrr-al, get up! Rehearse!"

Rehearsal?

Like the dry ice "fog" that vaporizes in a graveyard scene to reveal painted tombstones on canvas flats, the ominous mood of the hospital room vanished at the mention of rehearsal and he was on his mattress in the Sociale staring up at Timothy.

"Where's my watch?" Gerald asked.

As he patted the floor for his watch, his hand brushed

Timothy's sandled foot, which drew back like a frightened animal.

"Umm, nine thirty-three."

"You're joking?"

"No, Jrr-al. No joke."

"Okay, Timothy. You told me. Thanks."

Timothy's heavy-footed trot, as he left the room, sounded like a cut from a sound-effects record: *person leaving a room.*

Last night, when he was half-asleep, Bill called his name. "Sshh," whispered Annalisa, "he's asleep." "Ariela, is Gerald okay?" Bill asked. "He's okay," Ariela replied. This morning the inquiry both flattered and alarmed Gerald. Bill was concerned, but what about him was worrisome? That he'd fallen asleep? That his behavior was strange?

Ariela's figure appeared in the sunlit rectangle of the door. "Gerald! Come on! Everybody is leaving. Hurry up. I'll wait for you out here."

In front of the toilet, Gerald fumbled for the fly in his boxer shorts and found he'd put them on the wrong way, with the opening in back. Dementia? He giggled at his own dramatic diagnosis. Light through the pebbled glass shone on yellowed tiles edged in black mold. They had not been cleaned since they arrived and the strong smell of piss sent a little shiver through Gerald, reminding him of an incontinent hospital roommate, a man who seemed to have no family or friends but was visited by Filipino nuns, who never spoke, never offered the man comfort, only sat and prayed with a rosary. When they finally took the man off to a Catholic hospice, Gerald felt a guilty relief because he had the room to himself. And wasn't the man's doctor a tall African-American like the one he'd imagined Timothy to be?

Outside the bathroom window, Zuzie and Otto spoke in Gerrman. Gerald aimed just above water level to silence the endless stream of urine, but redirected a final splash into the center of the bowl. After brushing his teeth, he pulled on yesterday's clothes. For an alarming moment, he couldn't find his knapsack, then remembered he'd left it in the theater. He didn't have dementia.

Ariela was not outside. Had she left in the van because he'd taken too long? Had they driven off without him? Panic curdled Gerald's stomach as he ran across the Sociale courtyard and through the gate. The van was still parked in front. The actors sat dumbly inside, while Daryl leaned his head against the steering wheel. They were waiting for him.

Otto and Zuzie didn't move to make room for Gerald, who had to climb over their knees to wedge himself against a window that didn't open. The actors rode to the theater in silence, staring ahead like soldiers on their way to battle. Gerald found the silence strange. Was everyone hungover? Then he remembered, tonight was opening night, the actors knew not to squander their energy.

Gerald took deep breaths. His heart still raced. He wanted to speak to Ariela, but she was two rows ahead in the front seat. When Daryl changed gears, she lurched forward stiffly like a mannequin. Gerald glanced down to check the time. *My watch!* He clutched his wrist, as if stanching a wound. His day depended on watch watching: How long till lunch? dinner? bathroom break? And there was no clock in the third-floor library. What about tonight? In the last hour before a play opened, he always checked his watch continually.

"Is there a dilemma?" Zuzie asked.

Gerald's need for a comforting word momentarily displaced his dislike for the woman.

"I've left my watch back at the motel."

"And now it is too late to retrieve it. What a shame for you," she said, with a sympathetic grimace.

Gerald stared out the dirty glass window for the rest of the journey. When the van pulled into the palazzo's gravel parking lot, Daryl opened his door and threw up. The others muttered sounds of disgust as they gathered their things.

Why was everyone carrying so much? Gerald wondered. Even Ariela had a garment bag folded over her arm. Shit! Clothes for the opening-night party. He'd forgotten those, too.

The passengers in the middle seat disembarked through the sliding side door, but in the back, Zuzie and Otto remained seated, blocking Gerald's way, while Zuzie frantically thrust her hand between the seats. Otto spoke to her in German, and she rudely shushed him, before turning to Gerald with a nervous smile.

"My sunglasses—they are prescriptive and rather expensive."

"What a shame for you," Gerald said, touching his shirt pocket to make sure he hadn't forgotten his own.

A moan, like a choral lament in a Greek tragedy, came from the side of the van. Gerald pressed his face to the window. Daryl, on hands and knees, arched like a cat as he dry-heaved, his head falling low and his mouth gaping open as if he intended to feed on the gravel.

"The man disgusts me," Zuzie announced, searching the littered floor with her hand.

"Someone should shoot him to put an end to his misery," Otto said.

"Excuse me," Gerald muttered, as he squeezed past Otto and Zuzie.

"Please! You may step on my glasses," Zuzie cried.

"Be careful," Otto said.

Gerald hopped out of the van and went round to the driver's side. Daryl had stood up and was wiping his mouth on his forearm.

"You gonna be okay?" Gerald asked. "Go back to the Sociale, get some sleep."

"Nah, Bill'd kill me," Daryl mumbled.

"You're no help to him sick. Come back after lunch."

"Don't say lunch!" Daryl pressed his hand over his mouth. When the spasm relaxed, he fell back against the driver's seat, swung his legs into the van, and started the motor. Gerald knocked on the window, and Daryl rolled it down.

"Can I ask you a favor? When you come back, will you bring me some stuff I left in our room? A sports coat and pants hanging in the wardrobe, makeup in a cookie can in my suit-case—it's the white one—my watch by the bed, and oh, my blue robe—rolled up in the suitcase."

Daryl's face, a pair of crimson eyes set in a bowl of oatmeal, looked blank.

"Here, I'll write it all down." Gerald pulled a small note-book from his back pocket. "And I know this isn't a good time to hear a lecture," Gerald said, ripping a page from the note-book and handing it to Daryl, "but you have to end the sui-cide mission."

"Yeah, thanks."

Daryl pressed on the accelerator, sending a cloud of dust and gravel behind him.

"Fucking alcoholist!" Otto shouted at the departing van. Zuzie's desolate expression confirmed the glasses had not been found.

Gerald dreaded walking even the short distance to the canteen with the hideous couple, but they appeared to share his reluctance and started off without a backward glance.

The morning heat augured an intolerably hot afternoon. Gerald stared at the ground. It wasn't covered with gravel, but shells: thousands of bleached, broken shells. What a sad end for a shell, he thought, walking slowly toward the palazzo. He didn't want to join the others at the canteen yet, but a pain, like a small, insistent voice, hovered above his left temple. And he needed to silence it with caffeine, before its whisper grew loud, into a sharp, demanding litany of *I am, I am, I am.*

Gerald was not surprised to see the scenic shop open as he passed. Bill's demands for last-minute changes required the tech and design crews to work around the clock. But when he looked in, he saw only Lars, leaning over a table saw, his hands straddling the blade. Behind him, on rows of wide planks, baby heads the size of medicine balls stared serenely. Their precocious smiles sent shivers down Gerald's back.

For the last week, sometimes twice a day, Lars had appeared at rehearsal, hanging by the entrance of the theater until his nervous glances drew Bill's attention. "Do you wish to use the babies' heads now?" he'd asked Bill. "Not yet, Lars," Bill said. After a few days of similar interruptions, Bill ignored him. Yesterday, Lars had stood and stared in silence for what seemed eternity, before lowering his head and slinking out.

"Morning," Gerald mumbled, without stopping. Lars

might be depressed and need a sympathetic ear, but Gerald needed coffee.

Gerald was standing on the patio with his second espresso when the Italians, looking fresh and stylish, arrived. How is it, he wondered, that people wise enough to value good food and long naps still bother to iron their jeans?

Gerald was disdainful of any preoccupation with clothes. While he was still in his twenties, the *New York Times* had asked him to appear in a fashion spread profiling young actors in the city. "I refuse to promote clothes neither I nor any of my friends can afford," he told his agent. When the article finally appeared, with flattering portraits of his peers looking smug and successful in their expensive outfits, he'd been unable to leave his apartment for a week. But the jealousy only strengthened his resolve not to bend to the dictates of fashion, and he clung to a wrinkled, secondhand style.

Lately, Gerald wondered if wearing a decent suit to an interview or audition in those early days might have improved his chances in the competitive showbiz marketplace. Now he had no reason to spend money on clothes. He'd packed an ancient three-season cashmere blazer inherited from a friend, to wear for the opening-night party—though a Sicilian summer was not one of its three seasons. Enzo sauntered toward him in snug dress slacks and an avocado-green silk shirt.

"You look like a runway model," Gerald said, but immediately worried Enzo might think models shallow and the comment insulting.

Enzo was not insulted. He assumed the exaggerated pout of a model and executed an elaborate traipse and turn down the patio.

"I-ee would like to do runway," Enzo admitted, "but you must go to Milan for this."

"Well, you should," Gerald said, "someday. Are you getting coffee? I'll walk to the theater with you."

As they walked across the courtyard, Enzo unzipped the garment bag. "You like this coat? I'm not sure it go."

The gray-green coat in the bag complemented the green silk shirt perfectly, as Enzo must have known. Had Lewis picked it out?

"*Bello*," Gerald said.

Enzo studied the coat seriously. "I-ee-ya hope so." He zipped up the bag. "I-ee-ya very nervous for tonight."

Because of the opening or the arrival of a cuckolded lover? Gerald wondered.

He noticed Enzo looking at his T-shirt. "I'm going to change later."

Many of the actors were already in the theater, changing or warming up. Gerald excused himself from Enzo, took a mat from the barrel and moved to an isolated corner. The coffee hadn't helped, he still didn't feel well, and he unrolled the mat and lay down with his eyes closed trying to breathe away the tightness in his chest. He'd suffered through many openings and knew the ritual. As curtain time drew near, panic, like labor pains, occurred more frequently and with greater intensity. The mind juggled costume changes, prop placements, blocking, and lines. Just when Gerald thought he had everything down, an entrance cue might elude him, and like a man who must check and recheck an address, he'd reach for the script he'd just put down, note the cue and sigh because he *knew* he knew it before he looked.

When his memory bowed under the burden of nerves and self-doubt, Gerald made lists. A preshow checklist in one pocket, the blocking for each scene in another, a list of scenes taped on a backstage wall, costume changes on a dressing room mirror, and of course, glasses, kept always at hand, to read the lists. After the lists were in place, he needed to find a few moments before the show to sit calmly, close his eyes, and move through the play, step by mental step.

An arriving audience produced another increase in panic and triggered Gerald's most self-defeating philosophy. Performing in front of a live audience was self-inflicted torture. Why am I doing this? he asked himself—before answering himself with a quote from Ecclesiasticus, "Vanity, vanity, all is vanity." He had a recording of it by James Mason and recalled the words in the actor's weary inflection.

When Gerald finally stopped mouthing lines and Bible sayings, stopped going over blocking, he reached a state of calm in which he could tell himself, I'm a professional, I've done all I can do, now I'm ready.

But today there were hours of worry before that moment came, if it came at all. He was healthy when he last performed in a play. Was professionalism any match for fatigue, headache, and nausea? He shivered. The theater felt icy. He cradled his forehead in his palm and felt the heat rise from his skin. Had he *willed* a fever? Bill's amplified voice lifted him to his feet.

"Let's start where we left off yesterday." The actors looked at each other, hoping one of them would move into some recognizable position in the playing area. "Bonnie! Tell them where to go!"

Bill worked slowly and meticulously throughout the

morning, as if the opening were still several weeks away. A lunch break was finally called around three. The dressing rooms were ready to be occupied. Some of the actors headed to the back patio to secure a spot in front of a mirror, others rushed off to the canteen, opting for a place in the food line. Though Gerald had no appetite, he dragged himself to the canteen and got in line behind Bonnie.

"Bonnie, what kind of break do you think we'll get before the show?" he asked.

"Oh, I'd say . . ." She wrinkled her nose and gazed skyward, feigning deep concentration. "*None!*"

Gerald took his tray out to the patio, where Ariela sat at an empty table without an umbrella.

"Why don't you get something to eat before everyone else gets here?" Gerald asked, squinting down at her.

She always waited until the others had gotten food before going into the canteen, and today he found her self-control infuriating.

"I'm okay. Are *you* okay, Gerald?"

"What's that supposed to mean?" he snapped.

"You look a little pale."

"I *am* a little pale. I don't go into the sun. If I go into the sun, I bubble up like elephant man."

Ariela shaded her eyes to look up.

"Do you want to sit with me, elephant man?"

"Gerald, my man, you eating with us?" Holgar arrived at the table, his plate piled high with food.

"Too much sun, see you later," Gerald said, wrapping his sandwich of ham, mozzarella, and tomato in a napkin.

He longed to sit in some shady spot and close his eyes. By

this time of day, the theater cast a shadow across the courtyard, so he went back, placed his knapsack on the pebbled ground, lowered himself down and leaned against the still-warm marble façade.

Zuzie and Otto were just coming out, and didn't see him as they stopped mid-courtyard for a long kiss. Otto let his hand fall to Zuzie's bottom making her laugh and wriggle from his embrace as she continued across the courtyard. Class slut, thought Gerald, I'm jealous.

Ian came out.

"Did you see the dressing rooms?"

"No."

"They're shitty."

"What do you mean?"

"They're just . . . tables. Outside. With a bunch of sheets separating the women's side. I hope it doesn't rain. You okay?" Ian asked

Gerald wanted to be alone. His face and neck prickled, and he felt he might cry if Ian stayed another minute.

"Just a headache. You better get in the lunch line. Food is going fast."

"Do I look stupid as the hermaphrodite?" Ian asked.

"No, not stupid, not at all—erotic. And not much like a hermaphrodite."

"Erotic? Really? Cool!" Ian stared across the courtyard as if he were getting his bearings. "Take care."

Gerald unwrapped the sandwich and tried to bring himself to take a bite, but the doughy baguette was daunting. As he lifted the top slice of bread to peel a slice of mozzarella from its bed of lettuce, he thought of Damon, who used to hold a sandwich in one hand, lift the bread slice as if he were lifting the top of a powder compact, then pretend to powder his nose. When he snapped the compact-sandwich lid shut, he'd pretend a puff of powder had blown onto his shirt and he'd try to brush the loose powder away, only to discover his necklace was missing, which made him clutch his throat and scream, *My pearls! My pearls!* It was a silly routine, highly polished, and Gerald always laughed.

Gerald shook his head. Poor Damon. Poor everyone he knew who died so young: tricks, roommates, friends. Sometimes he'd recall one after another, guys who'd been so much a part of those early, sexy years in New York, until he'd cocooned himself in the past and peopled his present with the dead. Looking down at the wilted lettuce in his sandwich, Gerald wondered why anyone bothered to eat at all, *ever*, and he got up to throw the thing away.

Gerald's eyes took a moment to adjust to the dark interior of the theater. He walked around the perimeter of the red sand, out to the back patio to see the "shitty" dressing rooms. Four picnic tables, in two pairs set end to end, had been placed on either side of a line of ordinary clothing racks draped with sheets. One sheet, blown off its rack, lay on the ground.

Actors had claimed most of the spaces by placement of towels, tubes and jars of makeup, powders, hairbrushes, and hand mirrors. Gerald spotted an uncluttered rectangle on the men's side, a corner place, the very spot he'd have chosen if he'd had first pick. The thin, floral-patterned tea towel he'd nicked from the costume shop looked cheesy next to his neighbor's white terry-cloth towel. Who was sitting next to him? Dob kit items—razor, brush, comb, toothbrush, Q-tips—were lined up with military precision, while a big windup alarm clock stood sentinel top center. Timothy. The only other person he knew with that kind of mania for order, who would place objects with such fanatical care, was Bill.

Gerald reached into his bag, and remembered Daryl had not yet appeared at the theater so his makeup was still down the hill. He'd have to borrow some later, if Daryl didn't show up. Modern plays rarely required makeup—a cheap cover-up stick for blemishes and an eyebrow pencil were sufficient—but Bill's actors used a signature stark white base to pick up light. Even bare arms and hands were covered in white grease stick, then set with powder. Facial features were shaded or outlined in charcoal black and hair was slicked flat to the skull with heavy gel. The look was stark, dramatic, and dehumanizing.

Gerald lit a cigarette. Was I in love with Damon? He stared into the mirror and watched himself smoke.

Chapter Seventeen

"William, you know the audience will begin to arrive soon." Fernando, dressed in an expensive summer suit, smiled nervously. "We do present a show at eight, you know."

"So they tell me," Bill muttered, without glancing back at the producer.

Bill was putting the finishing touches on the Saints scene by giving additional hand gestures to the frustrated actors. Behind him, the crew was dismantling the production tables. Two sun-browned locals, rakes in hand, waited to smooth the sand. Lars appeared in the doorway behind them.

"All right, once more—and not so stylized. Don't move in slow motion. Remember the space behind your head," Bill warned the actors. "*Be here!*"

This last command was followed by a flurry of chatter among the Sicilian actors as they searched for a reasonable translation. "Where to be?" Valentina asked in a frantic whisper. "Where is here?"

Bill noticed Lars, who stared at him mournfully.

"My God! The baby! I forgot about the babies! Everyone go to the studio and get a baby head. Lars, show them what to do," Bill said.

Lars was out of the theater and back at the shop before the actors. He carefully took the heads off the planks and handed one to each actor. When the cast reassembled in the theater, Bill began to block the final tableau of the play.

"*Crawl* across the space—and make sure you hold the baby heads on straight."

Though they easily fit over the actors' heads, it was impossible to hold the big heads in place without using both hands, so crawling, as Bill envisioned, was not an option.

"Hold the heads on, but walk on your knees like people making a pilgrimage."

"But my eyeholes are too high. I can't see," Zuzie said.

"You don't need to see," Bill said, "start from where you enter and count knee-steps until you get to the middle."

Ordinarily, there would have been much silliness and play with the heads, which could look quite comical, depending on what foolery the bodies beneath might concoct. But the actors were nervous, and not in the mood for play. They needed time before the audience arrived to wash, gather their things, get into makeup, and generally collect themselves for the performance. Bill was oblivious to all such needs.

"No! Stop sagging in the torso—the audience doesn't need to know the heads are heavy—let's start again!"

Gerald thought he might faint. His knees hurt, and his arms ached from holding the clay head. He moaned softly to himself inside the stifling plaster. He desperately needed aspirins and ten minutes in the library with his eyes closed. So typical of Bill, this insensitivity toward anyone's needs but his own. I loathe him, Gerald thought.

"Round the arms!"

Gerald, deprived of the disapproving facial expressions at which he was an expert, felt compelled to speak.

"WHAT?" he shouted under the head. "I CAN'T HEAR A WORD YOU SAY."

He pulled the baby head off his own. His voice had echoed inside the plaster head, but he was unsure if he'd actually been heard outside. Daryl slunk into the theater, unseen by Bill. He was carrying a shopping bag.

My clothes and makeup from the Sociale, my robe. Gerald felt his stomach unknot as Bill turned back toward the actors.

"Okay, this isn't working. Actors! At the bow, run on, bow, run off, run on again, bow, and run off. For the third and final bow, run on with your baby head and place it in the sand, and let the audience see the faces staring at them as they leave the theater," Bill said.

After they'd rehearsed it, Zuzie knelt in front of one of the heads.

"It's like the babies are asking, *What? What does it all mean?*" she said.

"Oh God, I hope not," Bill said. He started to leave, but stopped and turned back to the actors. "Don't say what it is—ask, 'What is it?'"

"What he said," Valentina whispered, "what is it?"

"All right, you've got a half hour before half hour," Bonnie called. There was an excited commotion among the actors as they returned the heads to the back patio and raced to gather belongings.

Gerald was relieved. Most of Bill's shows rehearsed right up until the show, the cast barely had enough time to pee. But a half hour before half hour! Bonnie might just as well have announced a vacation in the Bahamas. He'd be able to take a nap of sorts, or maybe meditate and—he lowered his nose discreetly toward his armpit—wash himself at the basin in the library bathroom. As Gerald left the theater, the two Sicilians began to smooth the sand into conforming waves.

Vito and Vincenzo were arguing in the courtyard. At least Gerald assumed they were arguing. The Italians spoke with an aggressive animation that often *appeared* argumentative. Vito held out a folded section of an Italian newspaper and jabbed his finger into a gaudy color picture of a soccer player who hung horizontally in space, the blur of a ball flying off one balletically pointed foot. He held the front section of the paper under his arm and the headline caught Gerald's eye. *Cura Miracolosa.* Miracle cure—for what? he wondered.

"Vito, can I see your paper?" Gerald asked.

Vito handed it to him without interrupting his conversation with Vincenzo. Gerald pulled out his glasses and tried to manage the first paragraph of the article. "AIDS" The acronym stood out among the Italian words. Farther down he noticed the word "protease." Could that be? The class of drugs he was (or wasn't) taking in the trial study were called "protease inhibitors." He handed back the paper and hurried across the courtyard into the front building and up the two flights of stairs to the library.

The room still held the day's warmth, and a calm silence cloaked it in eeriness. Objects—desk, globe, bookcases, fainting couch—seemed unrooted, as if a thin layer of air suspended them an inch or two above the oceanic oriental carpet. Gerald fell upon the couch.

Miracle Cure! How often had he heard that in the last few years? He and his friends had injected, swallowed, or shoved miracle cures up their asses for a decade. The best "cures," like bitter melon or the Israeli egg lipid treatment did nothing, the worst, like AZT, killed people. If there were really a cure for AIDS, wouldn't we know? Even here in Sicily? Wouldn't the news dominate television stations everywhere? Wouldn't there be public announcements, screaming in the streets? Wouldn't Bill cancel the show or make an announcement so the audience could take a moment of silence to mourn the untimely deaths?

Those pills, maybe they did a little *something*, prolonged or shortened *something*—but in that case wouldn't he at least have heard rumors? Wouldn't the drug company have canceled the placebo branch of the study before now and given the drug to everyone? The sensational headline triggered stupid hope.

Two years ago, Gerald gave an over-the-phone interview for one of those "How I Still Hope" pieces, to an in-house AIDS magazine. The female interviewer, who sounded like she was about twelve years old, asked predictable questions: *What alternative therapies do you use? Is anger a good medicine? How do you pray?* But a last question, asked almost as an after-thought, floored Gerald.

"How different would your life be," asked the little-girl voice, "if they discovered a cure for AIDS tomorrow?"

Gerald couldn't answer. Literally. He tried, not even sure what he might say, but his throat closed, a sob welled up through his chest, and he had to hold the phone away. After the years of hospital visits, dead friends, and his own death-row expectations, he had not stopped to imagine a life without a daily fare of sickness and death.

The air in the library smelled of carpet fibers warmed by the sun, old books and lemon furniture polish. Gerald needn't worry about getting caught by the awful housekeeper, she must have left by now. The building was silent. He closed his eyes and drifted off to sleep.

Gerald had no idea how long he'd slept when he jumped off the couch with a sickening jolt. I'm on, he thought, I've missed my entrance! But when he went to the window he saw a handful of early audience members in the courtyard below. He must have only drifted for a minute or so, but when he woke . . . Now, getting up so quickly, he felt dizzy standing at the window. Annalisa said the opening-night audience included many wealthy contributors to the Festival dell'Arte, and he imagined tumbling through the glass and landing at the expensive foot of an Italian princess. He took a step back and hurried out of the library. He'd started down the wide stairway from the second to the main floor, when he heard someone coming up, and quietly retraced his steps.

"Gerald!"

Bill's voice surprised him, and he clutched his heart like an opera singer.

"Oh, hi . . ." he said, doing his best to recover.

"Where are you going?"

"Oh, I just came from . . . there's a library on the third floor. And a bathroom. I was going to wash my face, but I fell asleep. Is it late?"

Under the baby head, Gerald had rehearsed a harsh lecture for Bill—*How dare you treat us, treat anybody, like cattle*—but face-to-face with this up-close-and-personal Bill, his anger thawed like ice cream in a microwave.

"Come, you can wash in my room," Bill said, walking past him, up the stairs.

Bill's suite was dark. The windows, which looked over the courtyard, were still shuttered. He switched on a table lamp, and the soft light revealed what might have been the generic carpeted comfort of a good hotel in St. Louis or Chicago. But something was different about this hotel room. The walls showed bright rectangles where Bill had removed the paintings, and every flat surface was covered with objects of all sizes: baskets, bowls, pottery, a strange beaded hat, a kitsch portrait of a fascist party VIP, tiles from a Roman bath, an ancient headrest in bronze. Each object was arranged, along with its neighbors, into a gridlike order reminding Gerald of Timothy's arrangement of his toiletries on the dressing room table.

"I found this bowl outside Palermo," Bill was saying. "Second century B.C.—beautiful, no? Two thousand lira."

Bill was often late for rehearsals because he was still "shopping." He loved to show his acquisitions and bragged shamelessly about his bargaining powers.

"I said, 'How much will you take for the hat on your head?'"

Gerald, lost in the cool carpeted atmosphere of the room, heard Bill's voice as background sound to the hypnotic hum of the air conditioner. This was the first air-conditioned space he'd been in since he'd arrived in Sicily, and a deep sense of luxury made him want to giggle.

As Bill continued to show off recent purchases, cradling a charred urn like a newborn, holding an index finger aloft to display an ancient ring of soft, yellow gold, Gerald felt a growing wave of panic. Bill was quite capable of giving the history and price of everything in the room, leaving Gerald no time for a bath.

"I'm a little worried about time," Gerald said as Bill was explaining why there were more Greek artifacts in Sicily than in Greece. He stared curiously at Gerald, as if he couldn't remember inviting him into the room.

"And this is a Roman comb made of shell," he continued, "a thousand lira."

At first, Gerald was unable to relax given the oddity of his situation. Here he was in William Weiss's bathtub shortly before he performed in William Weiss's play. The circumstance seemed at once privileged and terrifying. But gradually the heat of the water, the sweet scent of the salts Bill had so generously sprinkled into the tub, and the polished tile surfaces turned opaque with steam pulled him into sensory comfort and calmed his mind. Gerald herded a thousand bubbles across the water's surface in the crook of his arm until they bunched round his throat like a fox fur. His concerns grew blissfully shallow. Which was shampoo and which conditioner? He held a bottle at arm's length and squinted, trying to bring the tiny print into focus. He needn't rush, his makeup took ten minutes, but then he hadn't used stage makeup for a couple of years. He got out of the bath, patted the steamy, scented moisture from his body, and went to the mirrored cabinet above the sink to explore more bathroom products—moisturizer, hair gel, deodorant—and helped himself to everything. Everything except the expensive cologne. Bill's scent was so distinctive, so *him*, that it came with a responsibility Gerald did not feel up to. He found a bottle of Tylenol 3—Tylenol with codeine—but his hand froze mid-reach. This might be stealing.

"Can I take a couple of your aspirin, Bill?"

"Of course."

He shook three onto his palm. Bill came in wearing a towel and carrying a phone.

"Don't look at me, I'm fat," Bill said, leaning over to turn on the water.

Before Gerald left the bathroom, he glanced back at Bill preparing his bath. There was something comforting about seeing this everyday Bill. But wasn't the everyday side always there? With Bill there was little distinction between public and private persona. He was the god who scratches his ass in front of the reverent, and it was for this reason that he was such an entertaining subject of gossip. He got too drunk at "serious" fundraising dinners, he yawned and complained ceaselessly about jet lag, he lost his credit cards, passport, airline tickets, on a bimonthly basis, he shared at length with cab drivers, delivery people, waitresses—"Driver, why am I so tired?" "Waitress, please don't let me eat that pie, I'm too *fat!*" "Miss, you should be a *movie star!*"—and he got himself into astounding situations, like the hunt for Martin at the Palermo airport. Gerald knew all about Bill's daily habits—maybe everyone did, since Bill hid so little. And though Bill's idiosyncrasies were a subject of gossip, they never dimmed the respect inspired by his enormous presence and his singular artistic vision. Bill was as charismatic in a towel and flip-flops as he was in his uniform black suit.

The air-conditioned bedroom now felt chilly. Gerald had only his dirty rehearsal clothes to put back on, but studying himself in the full-length mirror on the closet door, he looked fresher, even in a soiled T-shirt. He looked at the three pills he still held in his hand. I shouldn't take them before the play, he thought. He touched his temple to feel the slow rhythmic beat of his pulse, then threw the pills in his mouth and washed them down with a glass of water beside the bed. But the thicker-than-water sensation told him, before taste or smell, that the liquid was vodka not water. Pills and liquor, not a good mix. But it was a large gulp not a bottle and Tylenol 3s were kids' stuff.

"Thanks, Bill," Gerald called through the closed bathroom door.

"*Merde*," Bill shouted back.

Bill had opened the shutters in the sitting room. On his way out, Gerald walked over and looked down into the courtyard below. Valentina, Eunice, Vito, Letizia, and Vincenzo stood around an old man sitting in a chair placed on the cobblestones. The old man wore a white linen suit, which appeared too big for him, and an incongruously youthful baseball cap. Gerald couldn't see his face, but his chicken-thin neck and slumped posture suggested fragility or illness.

The actors appeared shyly flirtatious around him, like adolescent girls hovering around the handsome faculty chaperone at a school dance. Letizia, who usually wore sexuality like an everyday housedress, held her hands folded in front of her and smiled primly. Vincenzo, feet together, stood a respectful few feet away as he nodded vigorously to something the man said. Who rated such deferential treatment? Whose father or grandfather?

Enzo came around the theater with a glass, hurrying over the cobblestones, but careful not to spill any. He presented the glass to the man and looked at his watch. After the old man had taken a few, slow sips, the glass was taken away, and Enzo and Vito helped him to stand. Valentina and Letizia kissed him on either cheek. Then they left Enzo and the old man standing in the courtyard and went into the theater. Enzo put his arm through the man's and with small steps began to turn him in the direction of the canteen. When they faced the front building where Gerald watched from the second-story window, Enzo went behind the man to get the chair. It wouldn't fold properly, and as Enzo struggled, the old man removed his baseball hat and looked up.

Gerald didn't have time to move away from the window, but the man seemed to look straight through him rather than see him. His hair was—no, not white—bleached blond, and crew-cut short. His eyes appeared enormous in his skull-like face. But it was not quite an old man's face. Illness made it difficult to tell his age, but Gerald guessed he was no more than fifty, and perhaps as young as forty. His eyes lowered slowly from Gerald's window as Enzo took his arm again and, holding the folded chair under the other arm, guided him slowly and with great sensitivity out of the courtyard toward the canteen.

Lewis, Enzo's lover. That's why the others showed such reverence, because Lewis was their teacher and a respected choreographer—though Gerald could not imagine he was still able to work. Why didn't Enzo tell me? Gerald wondered. He must know about me, too. He's a professional widow, who mates only with the dying. He turned from the window, and quietly let himself out of Bill's suite.

Outside, the deceptively bright sky suggested endless day, but the descending sun had taken with it the suffocating afternoon heat and the air was cooler. A ghostly moon hovered in the still blue expanse above the domed roof of the theater and in the nearby orchards frantic choruses of birds warned of evening's approach.

More theatergoers had arrived in the courtyard. Some sat at the edge of the dry fountain. Two men and a woman, all dressed in black, all in dark glasses, like mourners at a society funeral, leaned forward to protect their clothing as they sucked on syrupy ices bought from a vendor. Instinctively, Gerald lowered his head. Like a bride before the wedding, he was superstitious about being seen before the show, as he hurried around the side of the theater to the dressing area.

Everyone except Enzo was on the back patio. Gerald pictured him hovering over his lover, asking if he needed to go to the toilet, fetching him tea or a gelato. Would he worry about the impossibly frail man making his way back to the theater alone? Or did they both pretend Lewis was not really so ill?

Sheets had been battened to the clothing racks to reestablish a division between the men's and women's sides, but the racks didn't quite meet. Letizia, in lacy push-up bra and minuscule underpants, stood near the partition. When she glanced up and saw Gerald watching, she assumed an "Eve banished from the garden pose," modestly covering her breasts and crotch, but with a coquettish grin and a wink. Like most dancers, Letizia was unencumbered by physical modesty. She devoted countless hours to staying limber and toned. Her body was her tool, and a beautiful one, so why hide it?

Gerald took stock of the men. Fabio wore a very short terry-cloth robe that would have had him hooted out of an American dressing room, but didn't seem to cause undo attention here. Ian was in his uniform tank top and camouflage shorts. The alpha males, Vito, Vincenzo, and Holgar, were shirtless. Though not a macho type, Giovanni was also shirtless. His newly shaved back, shoulders, and chest made him look like a grub worm. Even Herr Otto defied his Soviet-influenced priggishness by removing his shirt to expose a V of pink sunburn pointing down a belly of Bavarian white. His large nipples reminded Gerald of ripe Sicilian grapes—grapes that would soon wither on the vine. For uptight straight men like Otto, nipples were as useless as gallbladders.

Gerald sat down at his place along the makeup table. Next to him, Timothy was already dressed for Hell of a Party, in a black choir robe over a harness to which his black, fallen-angel wings would be attached. He stared at himself in the mirror, apparently unaware of Gerald's presence.

The first thing Gerald took from the bag Daryl had brought was his blue silk kimono, bundled up tightly and bound with its own sash. He undid the sash and let the robe unfurl to reveal the red, gold, and orange dragon stitched on the back. He put the kimono on and hid his arms and hands in the deep folds of the wide sleeves, while he explored a ripped seam with his finger.

The kimono had been his backstage robe in every professional job for twenty-five years—since college. The blue was no longer electric, the golden threads, which had made the crimson dragon shimmer, had faded to a dull yellow, and the collar was permanently stained with makeup. He'd almost left it at home, but at the last moment, too superstitious to do a show without his lucky robe, he'd rolled it into a ball and stuffed it into his suitcase.

"Very nice, this coat—*bello*," Letizia said, as she walked

past and stroked the back of the kimono, setting off sparks of sensation along his spine.

"*Grazie*," he replied.

He and a schoolmate were tripping on LSD when he discovered the kimono in an antique clothing store in his college town. Its exotic flamboyance might have appealed to his heightened senses in any case, but the robe had also been emblematic of the twin oceans of joy and relief he felt as a newly out gay man. He bought it, wore it from the shop, and once outside, ran down a campus hill, holding his arms out to let the wind catch in the long sleeves. After some harsh teasing the next day, Gerald buried the Japanese robe at the bottom of his school trunk and didn't unearth it until he got his first professional acting job in New York. He'd worn it backstage in every show since.

Gerald removed his sports coat from the bag and hung it over the back of his chair. He took out the makeup and his watch. He didn't want to look at the watch just yet, not until he was made-up and in costume, *then* he could begin to worry about the minutes. He unscrewed the lid on his jar of water-based, hypoallergenic clown white and brought the jar to his nose. It had the pleasant, slightly perfumed scent of art gum erasers.

A table away, Vincenzo and Vito burst into laughter. Valentina shouted something in Italian from the women's side, which made them laugh harder. Vito got up and ran around the sheeted partition prompting stagy screams and more laughter. Holgar, not wanting to be left out of the fun, followed Vincenzo. More screams.

Gerald wanted to stand on the table and scream for quiet.

He felt hollow and shaky—probably from not eating—and was shivering slightly. Just let me get through the show, he begged, to no one in particular. He tapped Timothy on the shoulder. Timothy, who wore no makeup in the show, held a grease stick poised above his forehead, an inch from his third eye.

"Timothy, has half hour been called?" Gerald asked. He knew Timothy could read his lips in the mirror.

"Uh, no, Gerald, no. It's, uh, twenty-six minutes after seven."

Gerald pulled his watch from the bag and turned to Timothy.

"How did you know that?"

"Wha?"

"How did you know it's exactly seven twenty-six? You didn't look at your watch."

Timothy pressed the stick against his forehead and held it there like a unicorn's horn.

"I, uh . . ." He lowered the stick, leaving a full moon on his ebony forehead. "Don't know, don't know, don't know."

Timothy always grew anxious when quizzed about his numerical abilities. He could name the day on which a person was born seconds after being given a birth date, but if asked *how* he did it, his brain short-circuited. (The result, perhaps, of too many adults and teachers trying to find the key to that unusual mind). Gerald felt clumsy and insensitive.

"Sorry, Timothy. Sorry."

Holgar burst through the clothing rack, ripping the sheet that separated the men's and women's dressing areas, and stomped back to his place with a silly grin.

"*Idiot!* shouted Eunice. "*Asshole!*" called Mima. But they were laughing. Letizia, still in bra and panties, pulled the sheet off the other rack, wound it round her head, leaving a long train, and began to dance about in a dramatic, Theda Bara fashion. Timothy bounced up and down in his seat, clapping his hands.

Electric lamps clamped onto the makeup mirrors pulsed in evening light. Gerald closed his eyes and saw zigzag lines rising through the blackness. It's heat radiating from my brain, he thought. The lines and the darkness began to fade until, suddenly, he was back in his apartment with the blinds closed. The white-noise machine on the bedside table hummed dully. The place was a wreck. He hadn't had the energy to do laundry. His only set of sheets smelled musty. He prided himself on not needing things, a philosophy that served a poor actor well, but lately, in the shrunken world of the sick, he'd felt deprived of those comforts other people took for granted, like extra sheets, cable television, and snacks on hand—especially the sheets since he spent so much time in bed. I should call Barbara and ask her to buy me a cheap set on her way over today, he thought.

Barbara was the only person in the world he'd give permission to drop by without calling, though she wasn't especially helpful, or even very considerate—after a cursory inquiry about his health, her own dramas usually occupied the remainder of their visit—but she broke the long boredom and loneliness of the afternoon with tragic tales of faithless boyfriends and law office intrigues. Her self-involvement didn't really require a reaction, and these days, Gerald was too tired to react. What time is it? he wondered. Where was she? Maybe she'd forgotten. The bell rang.

"Barbara?" he called out. "Is that you? Barbara?"

"Half hour!" Bonnie shouted, still swinging a little silver bell like an old-fashioned schoolmarm. "Gi' me your valuables."

Gerald's head dropped into his hands.

"You okay, buddy?"

Bonnie stood over him. Gerald sensed others watching, though when he looked up, the actors seemed involved in putting on makeup.

"I think I was hallucinating."

Gerald smiled.

"Lucky you," Bonnie said, "but you look real pale. You may not *need* any clown white tonight—got any valuables?"

Gerald reached in his back pocket and gave her his wallet.

"Yell if you need anything." She squeezed his shoulder.

"Want a bottle of water, Tim?" Gerald asked when Bonnie was gone.

Timothy already had a bottle in front of him, but said yes. Gerald went to the cases stacked along the wall.

"Seven thirty-three, Gerald," Timothy announced when Gerald returned with two waters. "Get ready."

Gerald had trouble keeping makeup on his damp forehead. He was still powdering down when Bonnie returned to give the fifteen-minute call. "Thanks," he said and put down the powder brush. Enough. He looked in the mirror. His handsome face surprised him. The makeup gave his skin an even tone, and shading on the sides of his nose, at his temples, and under his eyebrows threw his features into sharp relief. His gelled hair emphasized his gauntness, but the makeup was so stylized that the effect appeared dramatic rather than unhealthy. But how accurate was his perception? Enzo ran onto the patio, breathless.

"I-ee-ya yam very late, yes? My friend—he is here—at the canteen."

He sat on the other side of the table from Gerald, but only his eyes were visible above the mirror.

"Is he staying tonight?" Gerald asked.

"No, he is . . . not so well. He must . . . back to Palermo. I-ee take. Come back tomorrow."

"Sorry he's not well, Enzo."

"*Si*. Me also, I-ee-ya yam sorry."

Gerald imagined a rueful smile on Enzo's half-hidden face.

"I saw you both from the window," he said. Enzo's eyes looked up to meet Gerald's. "He's very elegant."

"*Si*. He was—*is*—a very beautiful man."

"I can tell."

"He be okay, I-ee-ya hope, to see the play."

"I was watching you from Bill's suite."

Bill's suite! Why had he added that when Enzo hadn't asked? Because he still hoped his close association with the director made him more attractive to Enzo? *Vanity, vanity . . .*

"Fifteen minutes!" Bonnie yelled. Gerald drew a deep breath and exhaled slowly to meet the wave of panic sweeping over him. Bonnie glanced over at him. "But we'll probably hold a few minutes." She turned and went back into the theater.

As Enzo concentrated on his makeup, his dark eyebrows rose up his forehead like sparring caterpillars.

Gerald took out his notebook of lists and went to the prop table. His martini glass for the Hell of a Party scene was set, so was his mask for Warriors, with the awful grimacing mouth cut into it. Where was his stick! He spotted the bamboo sticks leaning against the wall and sighed with relief. White gloves for Bed. Did Bed come after Cupid and Psyche? He checked his list of scenes. All his costumes were on the rack. The wardrobe ladies had written a version of his name, "Jerol," on white tags and sewn a tag in each piece of clothing. He remembered he had to set his baby head before he went on as Saint Augustine. And he'd need to place the costume near the side entrance. He got up and removed the white felt cloak and matching bishop's hat from the rack, turned the corner of the building and heard, from the courtyard, a voice giving what sounded like a lecture. He went to the edge and peeked around the building and saw Fernando Arcuri on the steps of the theater addressing the audience.

"And in the best of all worlds, the William Weiss premiere of *Rivers, Saints, Space* would begin on time. As I say, I must apologize for this temporary delay. We are experiencing some technical . . . challenges."

The audience nodded politely.

"I promise you, the doors will open in a very short time. Thank you for your patience." The producer turned and went into the theater.

When Gerald returned to the back patio, the actors were gathered around Bonnie. Bill stood behind her wearing a black suit and a glum expression. Fernando arrived, fresh from giving his little speech, and smiled as if he still had to charm a paying audience. Annalisa played nervously with her rings. Bonnie glanced at Gerald when he joined the actors but continued speaking.

"So, we're waiting for another generator to arrive from Palermo. If it doesn't get here soon, we will have to start the show and do the best we can. If lights begin to flicker, just keep going."

"But the lights were working this afternoon, no?" Vito asked.

"Apparently, the power weakens in the evening, because we share the current with the town. And we do *have* lights, they just begin to go on and off when the power fades," Bonnie explained.

Fernando stepped forward. "This is our problem, not yours. We have already arranged for the extra generator and we simply ask for your patience. Just relax and we will soon bring you more information." He extended his hand toward Bill, who stood with his arms folded. "Do you wish to add something, Signor Director?"

"Why wasn't the extra generator ordered from the beginning?" Bill asked. "Why wasn't this solved weeks ago?"

"As I explained, the problem did not appear until this afternoon. The electrical current in Sicily is very unpredictable."

"Let's cancel and open tomorrow night."

Fernando's smile faded. "Bill, tonight is the opening. There are important people who have come a long distance."

"Well, it's important for them to be able to *see* the play!"

"And they will. Let us all hope the generator arrives within the next half hour."

"This play will not be performed in disco lights!" Bill turned and went into the theater.

Fernando, left alone with the actors, smiled broadly. "As you can see we all are suffering a little from opening-night nerves. I think if we all remain calm and just . . . remain calm. Annalisa!" They hurried off around the side of the theater.

"All right, people," Bonnie said, "stay in makeup, but you don't have to stay in full costume. I'll warn you when we're close to places."

CHAPTER EIGHTEEN

The mood was somber. A large audience chatted and laughed in the courtyard on the other side of the theater. Actors kept themselves in a suspended state of tension, waiting to find out if the show would be canceled. Mosquitoes arrived with dusk and little slaps and curses punctuated the soundscape. With the play's delay, each performer fought to sustain the physical and mental concentration needed to get through the evening. Valentina sat on a packing crate chain-smoking, Mima shot angry glances into her mirror, and Ernesto begged for cigarettes with unquenched avarice.

"Where's the fucking stage manager?" Ian addressed no one in particular. "When we gonna start the fucking play?"

Gerald sat at the makeup table with his eyes shut. An inner voice predicted memory failure and public humiliation. Usually, the awful self-doubt before a show was finite and could be measured by the minute hand of a watch. Now, with the announcement of a delay, his nerves were a net, wide and taut, snagging unsettling questions: *What's my first cue? Did I set my scepter? Where do I enter in scene three? Do I need the bathroom again?* Only an intimate familiarity with his terror kept him from drowning in it.

The nauseating whine of a mosquito momentarily distracted him. He swatted at his ear and pulled his feet up on the chair, tucking them under the hem of his kimono. He hid his arms and hands in the deep folds of the sleeves and, with his finger, pulled a few more stitches loose from the ripped seam. He was chilly and pulled the kimono around him like a skin. An orange saved from lunch glowed on the makeup table. Imagining the explosion of sweet juices upon his tongue, he snatched it up, plunged his thumb into the navel, and tearing off a strip of orange peel, sent a shower of citrus sparks into the air. The orange was rather bitter, but he ate each section until the whole was gone, then slyly brought his fingers to his nose to inhale the sharp, fresh scent.

In the mirror, Gerald noticed Timothy standing behind him.

"What happen, Jrr-al?" Timothy asked.

"The lights aren't working, we have to wait for a generator."

"Oh, no. Oh, no. Oh, no. How long, Jrr-al?"

Timothy, alarmed by any deviation in schedule, rocked back and forth on his feet, but Gerald felt anxious himself and too impatient to reassure him.

"Ask Ariela, she knows."

Timothy hurried off to the women's side of the dressing area. Gerald noticed his makeup streaking, he might have to reapply it. He took a bottle of water and drank it until it was empty, then saw Mima standing at the edge of the patio, smoking a cigarette. She'd soaped out her eyebrows and redrawn them in charcoal an inch above, which gave her a permanently startled look. Beneath the raised brows, her eyes were ringed in purple and brown, her cheekbones sharpened with purple shading, and her mouth was painted a deep red outlined in black. Her hennaed hair was pulled back from her face. The whole effect was of a tribal mask used to frighten evil spirits. As Gerald approached, she handed him her tobacco.

"What do you think? Will we have an opening, or will the audience get tired and go home?" She inhaled on the cigarette and blew smoke through her nose.

"Mima, I've never been in a William Weiss premiere that opened on time. His audience expects to wait, they love it." Gerald licked the edge of the cigarette paper and rolled it carefully between his fingers.

"Look how beautiful you roll your cigarette," Mima said.

"I learned in college."

The match glowed in the dusk. The actors heard a soft tinkling of bells, punctuated by the insistent crys of goats, and looked up the hill in anticipation. The old herder appeared on the path twenty feet above. He stopped. Behind him, the goats appeared, walking slowly along the path like old women trudging home from market. They stopped and nosed the dry ground for some bit of stray vegetation. The herder squatted on his haunches and looked down at the actors.

"He like your titties," Vincenzo said to Valentina, who was shimmying out of her goddess costume.

"Yes, and maybe you like some of his goats, eh Vincenzo?" she said, wriggling out of the last few feet of fabric.

The actors laughed. The old man grinned as if he understood the joke. He got up and, without even a glance back to check his herd, started off along the path. The goats cried out their approvals and followed. Gerald and Mima watched as the flock disappeared around the side of the mountain.

"Despite the craziness here, there have been many beautiful

moments," Mima said. She turned to look at Gerald. "And how are you, my friend?"

That question again.

"Okay. I took some codeine pills from Bill. I feel a little gaga, but my headache's gone. I had a slight fever, but I think that's gone, too. But this morning I had this weird hallucination . . ."

Once Gerald began to share his anxiety, he was unable to stop. Suffering in silence was a lonely business. He recalled the strange morning dream, the afternoon fantasy, headaches, nausea, loss of appetite. Finally, he sputtered out to Mima what he'd meant to tell Enzo.

"See, I was sick last year—over a month in the hospital— nearly died from pneumonia—*Ouch!*" He threw the butt of the rolled cigarette to the ground and studied his thumb and fore-finger for a burn. Mima was quiet. Gerald, who'd felt unbur-dened for a moment, now felt a little ashamed. She's trying to remember if she ever drank out of my glass, he thought, frowning at his thumb.

"My friend," Mima said.

He looked up.

"I think you are very, very brave."

A conversational style that suggested everything was up for interpretation had been so integral to conversation between Gerald and his New York friends that now, he sometimes had difficulty taking anything he or anyone else said at face value. However, beneath Mima's painted mask, her expression lacked all irony, and unable to bear her sympathetic gaze, Gerald embraced her. Both actors were careful to keep their heads well to the side in order to protect their makeup.

"Thank you," Gerald said.

"If there is anything . . ."

"No, no. Don't worry, I'm okay. I just need to sit," he said, and went back to his place at the makeup table.

"Nice kimono," Ariela said, leaning across the makeup table. "You need to touch up the white on your forehead."

"Does my makeup look awful?"

There was excitement nearby. Eunice had overheard an argument between Fernando and Bill, and she was telling the others.

"Mad as a wet hen," she said, describing one of the men. Between the rush of words and Vito's simultaneous translation into Italian, Gerald caught only the high points of Eunice's tale. "'Not until the generator arrives!' 'We open now!' 'Over my dead body!' And for a minute, I thought he'd get his bloody wish," she concluded.

"How long before the fucking generator comes?" Otto demanded.

"The transport was arranged through the electrician's union," Vito explained, "many people must be involved and this causes delays."

"Now you sound like Fernando, darling. So I guess no one wants to hear the rest of my story?" Eunice pressed her lips into a little-girl pout.

"Tell! Tell!" the actors insisted.

"Oh, all right then. When Bill said. 'The play will open over my dead body,' Fernando flew into a rage. 'It's my bloody money at stake,' he said—well, he didn't say 'bloody'—then Bill said 'My audience will wait!' and Fernando shouted 'You are fooling yourself with this bullshit!' He told Bill that one of the richest women in Palermo—oh, what's her name, Vito? You can't build anything in Sicily without her father's permission, you know who I mean—anyway, he said this rich bitch couldn't wait any longer and left in a big huff."

"What did Bill say then?" Letizia asked.

"Said the show was going up in ten minutes, didn't he. And that was five minutes ago."

Bonnie appeared across the patio. She didn't have to call for attention. The actors immediately ran to her and began to ask: What happened? What about the generator? Will we open? Gerald and Ariela joined the crowd.

"The generator has not arrived," Bonnie said, "but we're starting anyway. The only scene where we use a full board in the first act is Hell of a Party. That's where the lights may go haywire. But by intermission, the generator should be here and we'll have full lights for the rest of the show. The call is five minutes."

"*Five minutes,*" Eunice moaned, "that's bloody quick."

Gerald snatched up his sponge and quickly repaired his forehead. He removed the kimono and (vaguely pretending to dab at his lip) kissed the fabric before placing it over the back of the chair. The actors in the Prologue crowded around the clothing rack looking for heavy felt coats and broad-brimmed black hats with their names. Gerald could not read the nametags and ran back to the makeup table for his glasses. When he did find his coat, he also discovered the seamstresses had forgotten to stitch the hem, which was still held by straight pins. Luckily, the men didn't move much on their mountains.

The felt coat itched his skin. He tugged at his tights until the waistband reached chest level. At least some of his torso would be protected from the rough fabric. He lined up the

Velcro strips in front and closed the coat, then found his wide-brimmed hat. Bonnie appeared on the patio.

"Places," she called, as Jean came running into the dressing area holding a razor blade in his hand.

"Wait! Wait!"

Jean grabbed Gerald's right arm and began to slice through the stitching that connected the sleeve to the shoulder. His breath smelled like stale red wine. He yanked the sleeve off Gerald's arm.

"There," he said, surveying Gerald in the one-armed coat, "better."

"Places for the Prologue," Bonnie shouted as Jean desleeved the other Prologue actors.

"*Merde! Merde!*" Zuzie called, blowing little kisses about.

Gerald desperately wished to avoid the preshow ritual of well-wishing: *break a leg, merde,* or *ptooey-ptooey,* the German version, air-spat on either side of the head. He yearned for a moment of quiet concentration to calm his nerves. Hurrying around a cluster of hugging actors, he stepped out of his flip-flops at the door of the theater. The soles of his feet had become sensitive, and the irregular stones of the patio floor threatened his balance.

"*Ptooey-ptooey,*" someone spat from behind.

"I hate that one," he said, carefully turning to face Ariela.

"I know," she said, "well, good luck then."

"*Never* say 'good luck,' it's bad luck!" Gerald used the moment of mock indignation to duck into the theater. Immediately, an afterimage of the makeup lights danced in front of his eyes before evaporating into the darkened theater. The bags, clothes, water bottles, espresso cups, that had littered the edge of the big room had disappeared, the space was pristine. During the last week, extra scaffolding had been erected around the perimeter of the space for follow-spot operators, musicians, and sound and lighting technicians. Now the structures disappeared into a darkness peppered with starpoints of blue-gelled work lights. Preset lights were up. Below, an amber wash picked up minute reflections in the red sand, giving it the appearance of finely ground glass. Within this stadium-sized area of sand stood seven Styrofoam mountains, painted in craggy relief, each about as tall as Bill.

As Gerald crossed to his mountain (the second from the left, between Vito and Vincenzo), he lifted the hem of his long coat. The soft sand was forgiving to the sensitive undersides of his feet. He was the first actor in place. He carefully lowered himself onto the slanted seat carved into the side of his mountain. The Styrofoam was hard against his ever-diminishing bottom, and the slant caused his body to pitch forward, cantilevering over his knees so that an ache in his lower spine began almost immediately. An overhead spot fixed him in a bright circle of light. He focused his eyes upon an exit sign and held his pose, letting the warm rays of light shore his posture. He angled his head to catch the overhead brilliance, but felt no warmth on his face, which was hidden in shadow cast by the wide brim of the hat.

"I'm not lit," Gerald called up into the dark perimeter of the theater where he imagined the lighting technician perched. "I mean my face."

There was no answer.

Eunice arrived and was sitting two mountains down. Her spot had also come up, and her face too was shadowed.

"You know, our faces aren't lit under these fucking hats," Gerald said.

"I know," she called back pleasantly. "We had this problem in the tech yesterday and they promised Bill they'd find a way to light us from below."

"From below?"

Just then a man ran across the sand with a box and stooped down a few feet in front of Gerald. He took a small lighting instrument out of the box, scooped away some sand to reveal an electrical cord buried underneath, attached the lamp, then signaled to the board operator. Gerald flinched when the light hit his eyes.

"*Scusi,*" said the electrician, adjusting the glare.

There was something wrong with the man's face. The right half of his mouth pulled up into a smile, but the left half remained immobile, and his left eye was lifeless. Gerald focused on the good eye and genial side of the man's mouth, but it was the dead eye that drew him in.

"Okay?" the man asked.

"*Perfetto, Valerio,*" Gerald said. "Welcome back."

"Valerio?" the man asked with a crooked smile. His eyes were suddenly normal.

"Oh! I thought you were someone else," Gerald said.

The man moved on with his box of lights. Other actors had arrived and were getting in place, adjusting themselves on their mountains. Bonnie came in, her sneakers crunching on the sand as she plodded across the playing space. Metal pipes squeaked under her weight as she climbed a scaffold to her stage manager's lair. Gerald shivered. Safety railing now lined every scaffold, but the memory of Valerio's broken head lying on a pillow of blood was revivified after seeing him in the face of the man with the crooked smile.

"Warning: sound, cue two, and lights, cue one." Bonnie spoke calmly into the headset. "Sound and lights, go."

The amplified chord of a solo violin soared out through suspended speakers. Gerald's eyes snapped open. He tilted his head slightly to avoid the direct light of the spot. The Styrofoam rock was hard, the big felt coat hot, and he was ready. Only the audience was missing.

"Annalisa, house is open. Annalisa? Put on your headset. Annalisa?" Bonnie's voice remained calm, but was loud enough to be heard over the violin.

Gerald adjusted his bottom against the Styrofoam seat, arched his spine a little, and glanced to either side. The other actors also used the delay to adjust their rigid positions. They slumped, leaned back, shook an arm, extended a leg. Vincenzo stood up and stretched.

"Vincenzo!" Bonnie hissed. "Get in place! House is open!"

A soft rectangle of evening light shone into the theater as the big double doors swung open. The actors froze. The audience, pleased to be let in at last, chatted happily. There were no ushers, no numbered seats to match their ticket stubs, but once inside, the sustained chord warned them to silence. Well-dressed men and women circled the sandy area, clinging to the shadows under the scaffolding. Shy and tentative, like sheep waiting for a shepherd's command, they stared out over the sea of red sand at the odd black figures in big hats perched on mountains. When the violin dropped into a minor key, the figures began to move, slowly, one finger at a time, as if the note had awakened them from a cryogenic state.

Gerald channel surfed through his imagination as he executed the sparse choreography, plucking keys on an imaginary piano, air-writing a secret alphabet, casting a spell, or dropping an arm at the whim of a sadistic puppeteer. Of course, the audience couldn't identify these split-second scenarios, but that didn't matter. "Let them make their own connections," Bill always admonished, "don't tell them what to feel."

Audience members drew closer. Soon, one or two brave souls in the crowd stepped out from the dark perimeter, onto the sand. Some opened campstools provided by the theater and sat down to observe. Others followed, giggling and whispering as they tried to navigate the artificial beach in dress shoes. Women removed heels. A young couple gazed up like tourists in a Renaissance cathedral into the vast, domed ceiling hung with lighting instruments. A sudden change in hue—from amber to violet—felt as if a cloud had passed in front of the sun and the room grew cooler, darker, while the mountains glowed brighter.

Gerald registered the blurred shapes of people. He checked his tendency to *act*, keeping his movements steady and precise. The glare from the lamp buried in the sand made his eyes water and his nose run. Soon, tears coursed down his cheeks. The violin morphed into a steady, jarring chord, and the movements of the actors picked up in tempo. Like a Buckingham Palace guard, Gerald's eyes remained fixed on one point, though he yearned to cast a quick sidelong glance to check the other actors.

A second violin resolved the discordant note of the first, and the violet wash faded to black, leaving only the men on their mountains illuminated in bright hard-edged circles of light: the Prologue was coming to an end. The audience barely noticed the overhead spots begin to dim, but the actors, cued by the light change, began to slow their mysterious signing. The violinists' bows froze in unison, plunging the scene into an abrupt silence, and in that silence, the overhead spots went out leaving the cathedral space dark except for seven faces, eerily lit from below.

Audience members gasped. When a dim changeover light appeared, they began to applaud. Not polite or confused applause, but hearty clapping.

Gerald felt neither headache nor fever. He kept his posture erect as he headed toward the exit. When Eunice whispered his name he understood his error even before she'd hissed, "Wrong way!"

Without missing a step he made a graceful U-turn and followed her out.

"Where were you going, love, for an espresso?" she asked him when they'd arrived safely back in the dressing area.

"I don't know, I was—"

"Not to worry," Eunice assured him, "everyone's a bit confused tonight."

CHAPTER NINETEEN

Once the play began, it moved forward like a great, unstoppable machine. Bonnie called lighting and sound cues, stagehands made set pieces appear and disappear as if by magic, and efficient costume ladies stripped and redressed actors in an eyeblink. By the second scene, most of the audience had removed their shoes and followed the action, literally, chasing across the sand barefoot, folding stools in hand, to witness a new scene in a new location. Only Enzo's Lewis, wide-eyed and gaunt under his red baseball cap, sat in a real chair at the edge of the sand. Occasionally he raised an opera glass, although the effort seemed to tire him, and the glass quickly fell back to his lap.

On the back patio, actors coming off stage brushed the sand from their feet and stepped into thongs as they whispered enthusiastically about the responsive audience.

"The lady in the pink Fortuny thing, she eat me with her eyes," Vincenzo exclaimed.

"I hear one *bravissimo* and a whistle, and is only the third scene!" said Giovanni.

"*Shhh*, there's a play going on!" an assistant stage manager hissed.

The actors were quiet for a moment, but the chatter resumed as they retouched a smudged cheek, rolled a cigarette, or stared unashamedly at their mirrored reflections.

Gerald pulled the sash tight around his blue kimono. He'd promised Ariela he'd try to watch a bit of the Cupid and Psyche scene. She and Holgar were costumed in next to nothing and Holgar's physical perfection made even the lovely Ariela doubt herself. "Just tell me if I look fat next to him," she'd begged. Gerald slipped into the theater unseen to watch from beneath the scaffolding, but the audience circled around the actors and blocked his view. With effort, he hoisted himself up upon a metal crossbar for better vantage.

Holgar and Ariela danced around a pedestal upon which a vertical glass tube was suspended over a Bunsen burner. As the flame was drawn up into the tube, a steady hypnotic tone, like the sound of a moist finger circling crystal, cut into the air. Holgar towered atop six-inch platform shoes worn in ancient Greek drama. A swathe of fabric covered his loins and bisected his muscular dancer's bottom in back like a sumo wrestler's diaper. Ariela wore a strapless dress of shimmering, translucent toile with a satin bodice shaped into two stiff triangles that curved around each breast like a lighting sconce.

Of course, she looked beautiful, Gerald could tell her so. But he wondered if the display of fresh flesh didn't clash a bit with the artistic merits of the piece. Although he couldn't actually discern greedy eyes and lips kept moist by darting tongues, Gerald suspected audience members were not just entranced by the postmodern interpretation of a Greek myth. But, did it matter? The singing glass tube was simple and odd, the changing lights painterly, the scene incomprehensible but arresting, and Ariela and Holgar were gorgeous—who wouldn't stare at them?

"Pervert!" hissed Vito.

Gerald, nearly losing his balance, reached out to steady himself on the pipe. Vito and Letezia giggled behind him. They were dressed head to toe in black as Zeus and Aphrodite, ready to climb to their places on the scaffold. When the spotlights hit them, near the end of the scene, their disembodied heads would seem to float in the darkness. Gerald let himself down off the bar.

"See you in Hell of a Party," he whispered, hurrying off to get into costume.

On the back patio, Gerald searched through the clothing rack for the tuxedo with "Jerol" written on a white sewn-in label. The older costume lady rushed over and easily found his tux. He tried to take the pants from her, but she pushed his arms away and gathered the legs in her hands, then squatted at his feet holding the trousers for him to step into. Her brusque efficiency made him feel small and helpless, like an invalid being dressed by his nurse for a walk round the garden. She even buttoned his trousers and zipped him up, then put her finger under the waistband and pulled it from his waist. "Eat!" she commanded. After attaching his suspenders and helping him into his jacket, she spun him round under the rough strokes of a clothing brush, effectively erasing the intimacies of their dressing ritual.

The entire cast performed in Hell of a Party. An aluminum settee, giraffe-high chairs, and Noguchiesque sculptures suggesting potted palms were placed upon the sand to define a ballroom. The partygoers spoke simultaneously in low voices, not for coherency, but to supply an aural layer of "party chatter" to the scene. Occasionally, a scream or laugh was choreographed into the chatter and when the odd bomb blast reverberated through the speakers, they fell in unison to the ground, then slowly rose to begin the scene anew. In the background, a piano tinkled an almost recognizable tune.

The actors kept track of the stage business around them. Ginger pivoted to Otto, cuing Zuzie to throw her drink in Holgar's face, Timothy to sing, Letizia's scream, Gerald's laugh, and climaxing with Enzo's leap upon the table to deliver his "I-ee-ya yam" line. One missed cue could throw the whole party off.

Gerald, pinching a martini glass by its delicate stem and careful not to let his pinky drift out, held mock conversation with Valentina, who wore a violet beaded gown and a headdress with a single plume. He recited the cadent poems he'd memorized in high school and still knew—"Out of the night that covers me/Black as a pit from pole to pole"—while she recited Italian nursery rhymes and stared into Gerald's eyes with an unsettling ferocity, unnatural for stage, camera, or life. Under her dark brown irises Gerald could see quarter-moons of white. Sanpaku, he thought, the upward roll of the eyes toward death. He remembered the term from *You Are All Sanpaku*, a book written in the seventies showing the phenomenon in photos of Marilyn Monroe and John Kennedy, taken shortly before their untimely ends. He longed to look away but was fascinated at the same time. Then the lights went out.

After the intensity of the stage lighting, the shock of total darkness silenced both actors and spectators. For a moment, Gerald thought there'd been a cuing mistake. But the exit lights were also off and the taped piano music silent: the power failure was complete. The attention he'd focused on his acting partner leaked into the darkness like air from a punctured tube. To regain his bearings, he mapped an aural landscape. Valentina swallowed, a swivel chair creaked on the scaffolding, a spot operator shifted his weight upon a board, and Bonnie, deprived of a sound system, whispered frantically to the board operator through cupped hands. As his eyes adjusted he realized the room was not completely black. A dim moonlit lozenge floated upon the sand beneath the pale circle of the skylight and gradually he discerned the silhouettes of the audience around the perimeter of the playing area. A play without a stage, bombs, Timothy—perhaps they thought the extended blackout was all part of this strange, beautiful presentation.

The lights came back with an ominous electronic buzz, and in the sudden brightness, Gerald strangled an impulse to shield his eyes. They began to flicker on and off catching the look of confusion and fear on Valentina's face in strobe effect. Actors stood still as statues, afraid to smile or blink. Finally, Eunice—or was it Vito?—began to speak, and others joined in to revive the party chat.

Ginger turned to Otto. Gerald's laugh cue was approaching, and he was nervous. He searched for a funny memory, but was distracted by the unchoreographed pulsing of lights and piano, and the edge of choral hysteria rising in the party chatter. The frantic mumbling reminded him of a childhood visit to a turkey farm where a farmhand demonstrated how turkeys, when spoken to enthusiastically, gobble back with the same level of enthusiasm, like a responsive crowd at a political rally. He concentrated on Valentina, who had regained her composure and once again eyeballed him like a heroine on a Spanish soap opera. Her full painted lips chewed out nonsensical Italian beneath the arching feather of her headdress. Gerald could even imagine a turkey wattle quivering beneath her chin. He began to laugh when the lights went out again, and the tinkling piano music stopped—a laugh, happy for release, echoing in the dark theater. The darkness quelled his inhibitions, and he varied the laugh, letting it wane into giggles and then, as if the joke had tickled him anew, build back into hilarity. His silliness infected the audience and they began to laugh along with him—softly at first, then more freely, as if everyone were in on the same joke. When the lights flashed on, Enzo jumped on the table and shouted with maniacal passion, *"I-ee-ya YAM!"*

Now, the actors chatted hysterically through the nerve-racking dim and flicker of lights, and the smiling audience seemed to think that the electric failures were part of the show. At last, the scene ended, the audience applauded, and as Gerald followed the others out of the theater onto the back patio, he noticed Bill among the crowd, arms folded, staring (at him?) with a look of cold disdain.

At intermission, Gerald sat at the makeup table with his head lowered, too embarrassed to face his fellow actors. "There are no stars in my shows," Bill often reminded his company, "just do the work." Bill hated my laugh, Gerald thought. "But what could I do?" he imagined telling Bill. "The lights went out—I didn't know when to stop laughing, what would you have done?" Building his defense, he warmed to a discomforting anger. All these years of anticipating Bill's moods, attending his needs like a courtesan, when nothing ever pleased the director. Nothing *he* did, anyway.

He looked up with a start, thinking he'd sat too long, that the intermission must be over and he'd missed the call for places. But the rest of the company was still on the patio. Ariela giggled at something Giovanni was saying, Enzo was locked in a wide-eyed conversation with Letizia, Eunice licked the gummed edge of a rolled cigarette. Gerald looked at his watch. His sense of time was still off, only a few minutes had passed. Maybe he'd misperceived his performance, too, maybe Bill wasn't mad, maybe Gerald had saved, not ruined, the scene.

Bill came around the side of the theater and Gerald smiled, but the director passed by without a word, directly to Bonnie on the other side of the patio.

An engine rumbled, and an ancient flatbed truck appeared and began to maneuver itself up to the edge of the back patio, then with a metallic hiccup, stopped. The generator had arrived.

"People, the cables need to run through the doors into the theater, so move some of these makeup tables and pick up your stuff," Bonnie shouted

Already numb from the evening's variables, the actors were not unduly bothered by this disruption mid-opening, but Gerald's hands shook as he picked up his powder brush, a hand mirror, and his makeup and dropped the items into his knapsack. He glanced over at Bill who now stood alone. Gerald placed the knapsack full of toiletries on a chair and hurried behind one end of the table.

"No, no, I will move this, Jer-ol—you rest," Giovanni said, moving in to replace him.

"Rest? What are you talking about?" Gerald said, in a firm voice, gripping the table and bumping Giovanni out of the way.

"Slow down," he hissed at Vincenzo, who supported the table at the other end. When they'd moved it out of the path of the truck, Gerald felt a silly sense of accomplishment, as if he'd passed some difficult ordeal. He wanted to do more. The driver, a fat man in a gray undershirt, who looked as if he'd been cast as *trucker*, sat in the cab waiting for people to clear.

"Watch out, Letizia. Eunice! *Attenzione!*" Gerald warned.

He stood in front ready to guide the driver a little to the left or right, or to indicate between his hands the inches from wall to fender. He marveled at himself calling out instructions. "Bring it left! Bring it left!" This was the sort of activity, along with barn building and putting himself in front of hard speeding balls, he never imagined doing. Squinting into the headlights, he raised his hand to motion the driver forward.

The gears ground into first, but the truck had barely moved when the clutch pedal hit the floor with an audible thud and the driver braked. Luckily, he'd seen Gerald fall into a dead heap on the patio floor.

"Don't move yet, love." Eunice's voice offered a coziness he felt he must rebel against, though he wasn't sure why, but it was the sympathetic faces peering down that embarrassed him into real action.

"I'm okay," he mumbled, trying to get up. He couldn't. A hand lifted his head and placed a towel beneath. Its smell of cold cream, of the theater, encouraged him to rouse himself, and with a bit more effort and the support of several hands, he stood.

"I'm *okay*," Gerald insisted.

"Sit him," Holgar insisted, as he and Giovanni led Gerald out of the headlight beams into a chair vacated by the young costume assistant. The gathered crowd parted when Bill approached. He looked down at Gerald.

"What happened?" he asked.

"I'd already started the laugh when the lights went out, I couldn't just stop with nothing else going on—"

"Did you faint?"

"I guess," Gerald said, "I stood up too fast." The excuse sounded false, like a movie heroine saying she was dizzy, when what she really has is a brain tumor.

"Can you finish the show?" Bill asked, over the disquieting pant of the idling truck.

"Of course I can," Gerald said, smiling as if Bill's question amused him. "It's not anything serious."

"We should at least let someone else carry the altar on in Wide Earth," Bonnie piped in.

Gerald laughed. He wanted to kill her. "Barbara, I feel fine. The altar is nothing, and I'm only in Saints at the end of the act—I can handle that."

"Barbara?" Bonnie said.

Bill looked at the truck. "Bonnie, how long will it take to connect the generator?" he asked.

While they spoke, Gerald quietly returned to his table, which had now been placed back in its original spot. He marveled at how quickly he'd been forgotten. Bill's concern had lasted what, thirty seconds? Timothy edged into the chair next to him.

"Hi, Timothy, are you okay?" Gerald wanted to be on the interrogating end of the stupid question.

"Yes, Jrr-al."

He was grateful for Timothy's pat answer.

While the crew hung a masking of black fabric in front of the door, which now had to be kept open to accommodate the cables, Bonnie announced a rule of silence backstage during the second act. "And the makeup lights have to be left off, so any last-minute primping should be done now, before places."

Gerald looked in the mirror and saw abraded flesh, like a friction burn, on his right cheek and temple. He didn't remember hitting the ground. Tomorrow, he'd have a scab. He patted white base onto the scraped skin. How could Bonnie not think he was well enough to carry the alter, when he'd just carried a table? And why did she have to say so in front of Bill?

The dryness in his mouth reminded him of the medication buried at the bottom of the laundry bag. He lowered his eyes to the table, so he wouldn't have to look at himself. "Miracle Cure." What an awful word, "miracle."

"Places," Bonnie announced, "places for act two."

Saints didn't come on until the end of act two. Timothy's solo and Wide Earth came before, so Gerald had about half an hour. When he returned from the bathroom, the patio was almost empty. Most of the company had gone into the theater to watch Timothy's scene in which he was dressed as a monkey and performed a comical—or shocking, depending on whom you asked—little jig. Mima sat in front of the mirror at her makeup table with her eyes closed.

Gerald had barely sat down when Annalisa came round the side of the building and stopped behind him, placing a hand on his shoulder. She looked at him in the mirror.

"Gerald," she said, quietly.

"I'm fine," he answered quickly.

"Bill has asked me to speak with you. We want you to go

back to the motel and rest. For tonight only. Bill is—we all are—very worried about you."

"But I'm fine," Gerald insisted.

"When you are fine, you do not pass out. And Gerald, you are looking a little pale, a little tired."

"I'm wearing white makeup."

"Yes, but—"

"And who would do my part?" He knew the answer as soon as he'd asked the question, no one would need to.

"For tonight there will be no pope. Tomorrow, if you are feeling better, you will come back into the show."

"I'm fine now," Gerald said.

Annalisa looked at her watch. "Just for tonight. Daryl is going to take you back in the van. You must change out of your costume. I'm sorry, Gerald, Bill has insisted."

She left him and went back into the theater. Gerald was energyless and empty, unable even to get out of costume. Somehow, being asked not to do the show, not to perform on opening night, defined his illness more than being in the hospital, more than waiting to die in a seedy New York apartment.

Only a blue-gelled lamp kept on for the costume ladies illuminated the patio. They checked Ian's harness as he stood, his arms stretched out in crucifix pose. He looked at the ground when Gerald looked over. Had Ian heard his exchange with Annalisa? Did everyone in the company know he'd been told to go back to the motel? But when the costume ladies finished, Ian came over.

"How do you get up on the roof?" Gerald asked, anxious to divert another well-meant inquiry into the state of his health.

309

"There's like a ladder up the other side of the building."

"Is it scary?"

"Not going up. It's scary coming down hanging from a chain off that winch thing."

"I bet."

"And the harness cuts into my balls—I probably will be a fuckin' hermaphrodite by the time we leave."

"That's a eunuch."

"Yeah, yeah," Ian said. He looked down at his feet. "You scared the shit out of everyone." Gerald was silent. "I mean the fainting thing."

"Oh, you know, anything for attention." Ian looked at him. "Bill wants me to go back to the Sociale and rest."

"Just for tonight though, right?"

"Why does everyone keep saying that? Just for tonight? Tonight is opening night and they won't let me finish the show."

Ian looked at the ground. "Fuck. Must be tough. Sorry."

"I'm not going, Daryl." Gerald wore the blue kimono over his tuxedo trousers.

"Bill told me to take you back to the Sociale," Daryl repeated.

"Yeah, well, he changed his mind."

"Look, get dressed, I have to get the van keys from the production office. Meet me there in five minutes."

Gerald sat down. The lights were off, but his white makeup, as if charged under the stage lights, retained a pale glow. He flattened some unruly hairs that had escaped the gel.

"C'mon, man, I have to take your place to help move the altar in Wide Earth. I'll never get back unless we get a move on."

"Okay, okay," Gerald said, without moving from the chair.

"Sorry, Ger. Just get some rest. You'll be back in the show tomorrow."

"Don't call me 'Ger.'"

"Meet me by the production office." Daryl stopped at the edge of the patio. "You told me to get some rest, remember? That was great advice." He disappeared around the side of the theater.

Across the patio, Mima leaned back in her chair with a wash-cloth across her eyes.

"Mima, my St. Augustine line—*Signore, tu me colge en adore*—do you know what it means in English?"

She answered without removing the washcloth. "He ask God to take him when he—*en adore*—I don't know how to say this: when he has a fever, like a religious fever."

"Oh, okay. Thanks."

Near the changing tent, both costume ladies sat with their hands resting in their laps. Though their sitting positions were sim-ilar, the young girl sat on the edge of her chair, eyes fixed upon the curtained entrance to the theater in case an actor needing a quick change emerged. The older woman sat stone-still, weighted, as if the heaviness of evening air pushed her down. Nothing about her suggested the fierce efficiency Gerald had witnessed earlier.

How hard it is to do nothing, he thought. Actors rarely managed to convey that kind of simple inactivity onstage, characters were usually portrayed full of active intent. And yet, in real life, people often did nothing, even when they were doing something. Gerald had formed this idea during his con-valescence, as he lay in bed watching a televised production of *As You Like It*. The actor playing the great Shakespearean mal-content Jacques spat the "All the world's a stage" speech

311

through clenched teeth, "railing" against Fortune. It sounded so wrong that Gerald dragged himself out of bed and recited the speech, which he knew by heart, into the bathroom mirror. The muscles in his face were slack from months of inactivity, and he'd spoken so little, just forming words was an effort. His Jacques was beyond anger. So what if life ended "Sans teeth, sans eyes, sans taste, sans everything," he'd already given up.

Gerald looked up at the little fingernail paring of a moon. He opened his knapsack, dumped the contents on the table, then put a bottle of water in the sack and walked across the patio toward the hill. No one saw him except the young costume girl who stood up, thinking he might need her help. Gerald shook his head. He must look odd, he realized, in ghostly makeup, a kimono, and carrying a knapsack on his back as he headed up into the dark wooded area beyond the patio. Would the girl not point in the direction of his escape when Daryl came looking for him? He hurried up the embankment toward the wide ridge where the herder and his goats had appeared earlier.

The climb was not as physically demanding as he'd imagined, but he had to tread carefully in the cheap sandals, and just before the ridge, where the hill grew steep, he slipped and fell forward onto the dry ground, landing on his already scraped knees and hands.

When he reached the path, Gerald looked back down at the patio. The costume girl watched from below, and he hurried along the curved path until he was out of her sightline. The path continued to curve and climb between a scattering of trees. Insects whirred and crackled like a high-voltage line. From this far side of the hill, he could see an ugly stucco

building below, standing not ten yards from the highway. Perhaps the goat herder had been moved there from his woodsy
cottage, another victim of urbanization. Filmy clouds obscured
the moon and stars. Gerald turned off the worn path, onto the
rocky and uneven land that led up to the crest of the hill. He
felt for the ground through his thongs before putting his full
weight into the next step. After several minutes of careful stepping, he reached a grassless, treeless stone plateau that would,
he thought, look like a friar's tonsure if viewed from above. The
remains of a campfire blackened the stone surface. One
boulder, as tall as Gerald, looked as if it could be pried from its
spot with a plank and rolled all the way down the hill to crash
onto the highway below. Gerald took the bottle of water from
his knapsack and sat with his back against the big rock. He
pulled the knapsack under his bottom, but it offered little
padding. He folded it into a pillow and curled up on the
ground. The silk robe offered surprising warmth, but his body
could not find much comfort in the contour of this stone bed.
He stood and began to circle the boulder. After a few circles,
he was able to continue without looking forward, keeping his
eyes on the thickening clouds above and the barely visible glow
of a moon. It had not rained in all the weeks he'd been in Sicily.
Now, it looked as if the sky might open on opening night. He
became disoriented when he closed his eyes and had to let his
fingers trail along the surface of rock as he circled. He hummed
"The Hall of the Mountain King" from *Peer Gynt*, circling
faster as the tempo picked up. The automatic movement was
consoling. He'd rather run around this rock until he dropped
dead than be sent home on opening night. They'd find his
body tomorrow: *like an animal, he went into the woods to die.*

Serve Bill right. His decision wasn't based on concern for Gerald, Bill was simply drawing another ring of chaos around his play, *the sand, the lights, now Gerald—it's a diSASter.*

Gerald stopped abruptly, opened his eyes and leaned back against the rock. The clouds spun, the earth spun.

"*Signore,*" he prayed aloud, "*tu me colge en adore:* take me while I am in ecstasy."

Still dizzy, Gerald grabbed his knapsack and started down the hill, groping his way from tree to tree for support until he reached the path. Drops of water hit his face. Faintly, under the rumble of thunder, he heard the beats of a kettle drum that signaled the end of Wide Earth. He could still make his entrance for Saints. His sash was missing, and as he ran down the path, his robe flew behind him like a cape.

KEITH MCDERMOTT is a novelist, director, and actor. His writing has appeared in *Fresh Men: New Voices in Gay Fiction*, *Men on Men 7*, *Boys Like Us*, and *Loss within Loss*, as well as in *Out* and the *James White Review*. As an actor, Keith has worked on, off, and off-off Broadway, making his Broadway debut opposite Richard Burton in *Equus*. He has worked with director Robert Wilson in America, Europe, Russia, and Japan. He lives in New York City.

CPSIA information can be obtained
at www.ICGtesting.com
Printed in the USA
LVOW07s0819070717
540442LV00001B/3/P